Praise for I[...]

'A truly remarkable ride [...] with one of the forem[...] fully written but with th[...] only a master can produce. Secrets and subterfuge abound. Five stars!'
Imran Mahmood

'*In the Shadows of Love* is a book that will transport you into a world hidden behind a veil of tradition and social norms. Remarkably beautiful but haunting and thrilling in equal measure, Khan's writing is assured, accomplished and compulsive. I loved it.'
Helen Fields

'Another beautiful book from Awais Khan, one of my favourites. Set in Lahore, Pakistan, a city full of extremes, of violent gangs and incredible wealth, we follow Mona and Bilal as they navigate family secrets and forgiveness. Stunning.'
Louise Swanson

'*In the Shadows of Love* is a real page-turner, full of drama and intrigue. A fascinating insight into high society in Lahore. I couldn't put it down.'
Lisa Timoney

'A captivating and compelling journey through contemporary Lahore, Awais Khan masterfully combines depictions of glamour and wealth with a darker, troubling web of secrets. *In the Shadows of Love* is a thrilling story of the lengths people will go to hide from the secrets that

threaten to destroy them, as well as a powerful exploration of the devastating effects of sexism.'
Lucy Ashe

'A terrific read that kept me gripped all day and a fascinating glimpse into both the glamour and the sometimes suffocating social codes of high society Pakistan.'
Frances Quinn

'A dark drama showing the raw reality of Pakistani high society, beautifully written, with a clever twist in the tale. You're going to love it.'
Michael Wood

'I loved *In the Company of Strangers* and this stunning sequel measures up in spades. A phenomenal follow-up by Awais Khan and a triumphant return to the glittering world of Pakistani high society.'
A.A. Chaudhuri

'An unflinching portrayal of the contradictions in high-society Pakistan where even the most privileged are entrapped by convention and fear of scandal and the threat of kidnapping looms as the dispossessed take their revenge.'
Eve Smith

'I was completely invested in the couple at the heart of this story and their complicated mid-life marriage. Khan combines a heart-warming family tale, set in Lahore high society with the pace and suspense of a thriller. An emotional and poignant read, but also so suspenseful that it kept me gripped with twists that I never saw coming. Highly recommended!'
Aliya Ali-Afzal

'*In the Shadows of Love* is a searing indictment of Pakistani high society that nonetheless gives us reason to be optimistic. I thoroughly enjoyed this masterpiece by one of Pakistan's best writers.'
Alan Gorevan

'*In the Shadows of Love* is a compulsive, immersive read, filled with captivating characters and a plot that builds to a pounding, heart-in-your-mouth conclusion. Bravo to brilliant Awais Khan!'
Alex Hay

'A compelling, addictive page-turner that is exquisitely written and yet unflinching in its portrayal of abuse and threat. Beautiful, breath-taking and bold.'
Danielle Ramsay

'Just as profound as his previous ones, centred on love and threat in modern-day Pakistan. The shackles its high society puts on its women are even more confining than the kidnappers that roam the streets.'
Heleen Kist

'I loved the insight into upper class Lahore society. It's superbly written and immensely enjoyable. It tackles some hard subjects. I raced through it. What a triumph!'
Catherine Balvage Yardley

In the Shadows of Love

Awais Khan was born in Lahore, Pakistan. He is a graduate of The University of Western Ontario and Durham University and studied Creative Writing at Faber Academy. In his free time, he likes to read all types of fiction, especially historical fiction and psychological thrillers.

Also by Awais Khan

In The Company of Strangers
In the Shadows of Love

AWAIS KHAN
IN THE SHADOWS OF LOVE

hera

First published in the United Kingdom in 2024 by

Hera Books
Unit 9 (Canelo), 5th Floor
Cargo Works, 1-2 Hatfields
London SE1 9PG
United Kingdom

Copyright © Awais Khan 2024

The moral right of Awais Khan to be identified as the creator of this work has been asserted in accordance with the Copyright, Designs and Patents Act, 1988.

All rights reserved. No part of this publication may be reproduced or transmitted in any form or by any means, electronic or mechanical, including photocopy, recording, or any information storage and retrieval system, without permission in writing from the publisher.

A CIP catalogue record for this book is available from the British Library.

Print ISBN 978 1 80436 810 7
Ebook ISBN 978 1 80436 811 4

This book is a work of fiction. Names, characters, businesses, organizations, places and events are either the product of the author's imagination or are used fictitiously. Any resemblance to actual persons, living or dead, events or locales is entirely coincidental.

Look for more great books at www.herabooks.com

Printed and bound in Great Britain by Clays Ltd, Elcograf S.p.A.

For my parents

The greatest glory in living lies not in never falling, but in rising every time we fall.

–Nelson Mandela

To love someone who doesn't love you is like shaking a tree to make the dew drops fall.

–African Proverb

Chapter 1

Bilal

Lahore, Pakistan – Then

It's not mine.
It's not mine.
It's not mine.

That was all he could think of on the way to the hospital. There was an important meeting taking place when the call arrived, but he'd abandoned everything and rushed to his car. Although he'd been through this experience twice before in his life, this time it felt strange… maybe because this one wasn't his.

Bilal shook his head as he stepped inside the massive air-conditioned lobby of the private hospital, his leather shoes squeaking against the polished marble floor. The call had come from his mother, who, despite her advanced age and health issues, had still been robust enough to drive Mona to the hospital.

'Not a driver in sight when you need them,' she'd panted over the phone as she drove. 'I'm eighty-four years old, *kanjaro*! I am not built for this sort of drudgery.' Before he could say anything, she'd continued, 'No, there was no time to call anyone else. Unless you want her to give birth at home, because the baby is coming. Oh, it's coming all right.'

A scream from Mona indicated that his mother hadn't been lying.

Thoughts of Ali rushed into his head before he could stop them, and, for a moment, the world around him spun. He could see his wife with him clear as day, the result of which he was going to meet momentarily. Shaking his head again, more vigorously this time, he pushed the thought from his mind. This was not who he was any more. He had left that person behind when he'd begged Mona for forgiveness. It didn't do to ponder on the past. Even his own mother marvelled at the fact that he'd been forgiven after the way he'd treated Mona – his wife of several decades, the mother of his children.

You are pathetic, Bilal.

He brushed the tear from his cheek, blinking rapidly. If anyone saw him right now, a grown man in his fifties crying, they would never respect him again.

The hospital teemed with people, plenty of whom recognised him from the countless times he'd been here with his mother. A few male nurses gave him a salute while one of the female nurses he used to flirt with in the past reddened under his gaze.

He wasn't *that* kind of man any more either. He ignored her.

His feet took him away from the cardiology wing to the very unfamiliar labour rooms where Mona would be giving birth. To make a point, perhaps, even the walls of this wing were painted a soothing baby pink. Just for a moment, he considered turning back and running home. Did he have the strength to see his wife give birth to another man's child? But then, he caught a glimpse of his elderly mother outside the entrance to the labour rooms, walking stick in hand and her back erect, as if poised to rush in at the merest hint of trouble. The metal stool she sat on didn't look comfortable.

Bilal drew himself up.

'Late for the birth of your own child,' his mother remarked, tapping her cane on the floor, making him wince. 'And then they ask what the trouble is with having kids in one's forties, or in your case' – she peered at him – 'fifties.'

'Thanks, Amma,' he replied drily, although his heart was pounding in his throat. 'You should go back home. At your age, you shouldn't be doing these things.'

His mother let out a savage laugh. 'Don't you tell me what to do. If it wasn't for me, we'd be pulling out the baby at home, and that's not a pleasant task, let me tell you that. Besides, your entire staff at the house is bloody useless. The army of maids you employ were shaking with fear at the prospect of driving a car. My own driver – that traitor Bashir – is on leave, of course... probably busy putting another baby in his wife's belly as we speak.' She scowled. 'I tell you, these servants—'

'Where was Mona's driver?'

'Pissing in the mountains.' His mother threw up her hands. 'How the hell would I know?'

'Amma, please! At least, lower your voice.'

'I haven't reached the age of eighty-four only to be told by men to lower my voice. I will say whatever I want. I've been sitting here like a faithful guard dog for ages for *your* wife. Have you noticed how everything in this hospital stinks, including the staff?' She wrinkled her nose. '*Especially* the staff!' Adjusting her dupatta over her expansive frame, Nighat narrowed her eyes. 'Now, what's the matter with you? You're looking ill. Do you need a doctor too? I swear, if I have to wheel you somewhere,

I will pass out right here. *Khuda ke liye*, it's just a baby. Relax, will you? Millions are born every day, and if there's one thing Pakistanis excel at, it's having babies. Lots of them.'

How could he tell her that it wasn't just any baby. It was *his* baby. How could he ever pretend to love a child who would be living proof of his wife's infidelity? A bead of sweat ran down his temple. On the flip side, it wasn't as if he'd been faithful to Mona, and looking at his mother, he knew exactly what she'd say if she knew the truth.

She'd side with Mona.

Sometimes, he wondered if she did know.

'You know, I do worry about the two of you,' she began, the creases on her forehead deepening. 'After what happened between Mona and that boy…'

So, she did know.

For a moment, his heart seemed to have stopped. 'You know about that?'

Nighat laughed. 'Don't be ridiculous. Of course I know. Your wife was the epitome of unhappiness before and then all of a sudden, when that boy came into her life, she just bloomed like a flower. Do you think I'm a fool? She mourned that boy for months. I've been around long enough to know true love. You have too. Despite your considerable flaws, I know you love her.'

'She doesn't love him any more,' Bilal whispered.

'Of course she doesn't. He's dead.' But then, her gaze softened. 'Treat her well, Bilal. She's like delicate china right now. Women feel much more deeply than men. One misstep and she could leave you forever, and I wouldn't blame her, if I'm being honest.'

'What if I can't love it?'

'It?'

'The baby,' he whispered.

His mother straightened herself on the metal stool. 'Why don't you go inside and find out?' She pointed towards the double doors. 'You'll find the baby in one of the rooms inside.'

All he could do was stare at her. '*Tauba*, Amma! She's had the baby already, and you didn't even tell me?' His vision blurred, the ground beneath him tilting. 'Were you planning on sitting on this news forever?'

Nighat shrugged. 'You didn't ask. Now go inside and meet your baby while I find out what they've done with that blasted private room. Another moment on this stool and I'll either relieve my bowels right here, or they'll have to remove me on a stretcher. Or both. I tell you, the day our hospitals stop treating people like cattle, not only will I dance, but…'

Bilal wasn't listening. The doors loomed large and forbidding in front of him, but before he could push through, his mother grabbed his hand.

'Do well by this one,' she said. 'I know you were too busy and distracted to care for the previous two, but God is giving you another chance.' The sternness on her face broke for the first time, revealing the love Bilal knew she held for him. 'I don't want to see you fall to pieces again. I can't. I won't survive it. You're my only son, after all.'

'I may be your only son, but you've got Qudsia too.'

'She hates me.'

Bilal bent down to plant a big kiss on his mother's forehead. 'Nobody can ever hate you, Amma. Least of all your own children.'

That got a chuckle out of her. 'Stop buttering me. It's not my heart you need to win. I'm your mother.'

Bilal smiled at her. 'I love you. You know that, right?'

'And I will love and scold you from beyond my grave too, mark my words. Now go!'

Taking a deep breath, he pushed past the double doors, pausing in the doorway long enough for one of the doors to whack him on the ass. Ignoring the pain, he walked down the corridor, squinting in the fluorescent lighting, the smell of antiseptic mixed with something else thick in his nostrils. It took a moment for him to notice what it was.

Blood.

Bringing life into the world was a strange business. As soon as he opened the door to the section containing the nursery and adjoining rooms, the duty nurse looked up from her desk, her face breaking into a smile. 'Mr Bilal Ahmed? Your wife already described you to us and said that you would be coming to see the baby.' Walking up to him, she continued, 'Congratulations. You're the father of a healthy boy. He weighs nine pounds and has ten fingers and ten toes.'

Bilal looked at her blankly, his teeth chattering.

Instead of frowning, the nurse smiled again. 'The jitters never really go away, do they? Even when you're having a child at this – ahem – age.'

Under any other circumstances, he would have given her a piece of his mind, but right now, all he could do was nod. He took in the sight of expensive paintings in the reception area, the walls painted a delicate dove grey to exude peace and calm. Unfortunately, they did nothing for him.

As if taking pity on him, the nurse took a hold of his elbow. 'Let me take you to him.'

Bilal closed his eyes, allowing himself to be steered towards his fate. His mother would be so ashamed of him if she could see him right now. Thankfully, she was probably resting in the room now. His heart began pounding again as they came to an abrupt halt.

'Here we are, sir.' Anyone in her position would have laughed seeing a man in his fifties so nervous, but the nurse was remarkably calm as she said, 'Now, now, sir, I assure you he's a beautiful baby boy. You may open your eyes.'

And without warning, Bilal did.

The first thing he saw was piercing blue eyes, the kind that arrest your attention. The baby was watching him, his tiny fist in his mouth. Questions would be raised about those eyes. Nobody in their family had ever had blue eyes. It was obvious where the baby got them from, but Bilal found that he couldn't take his own eyes off him.

'I told you he was a pretty baby,' the nurse whispered. 'Newborns generally aren't. And those eyes. This little man will captivate hearts wherever he goes. You and your wife are very lucky.'

Beside the cot, Mona was asleep on the bed, her face radiating both exhaustion and relief. He bit into his fist to stop himself from crying. He could see bits of his wife in the baby, especially the way he blinked his eyes and frowned. Although the eyes were blue, the shape of them was unmistakeably Mona's. Something in him erupted as he thought back to all those times when he had raised his hand against her, all those times when he hadn't been man enough to admit that he was wrong, that he had never lifted a finger to help with the children. His crimes were endless, and yet she had chosen to stay with him. He blinked back tears, aware of the fact that the nurse was hovering nearby.

Bilal reached out to touch the tiny hand, an involuntary sigh escaping him as he felt the velvety skin. He'd forgotten what it was like to be around babies. Beside him, his wife was awake now, and watching him intently. The peace she'd been radiating was gone, replaced by nervousness as her gaze swivelled between him and the baby. With a jolt, Bilal realised that she was afraid. He gave her a tentative smile as he turned his attention back towards the baby, allowing those large ocean-blue irises to draw him in. The baby gurgled, enclosing Bilal's finger in his tiny fist, and without warning, he laughed.

Mona reached out to take his other hand and squeezed it, the fear gone from her face as she relaxed and let her head fall back on the pillow.

And that's when he knew. He would do his best by this child. He would be the father he hadn't been for Farhan and Aimen. This, right here, was his last chance at redemption. As his thumb grazed the baby's soft skin, he knew that he would love this boy till his last breath.

Chapter 2

Mona

Lahore, Pakistan – Present Day

Mona groaned as the alarm woke her up. Her finger swiped at the phone to hit snooze, just so she could get a few more minutes of precious sleep. Beside her, Bilal hadn't stirred. With the pills he took to sleep every night, it would take an earthquake to wake him.

Probably for the best, she thought to herself. It was way too early in the morning for them to lock horns. She snuggled against him under the duvet, the sheets smelling faintly of lavender, but sleep didn't return. Her neck hurt from sleeping in a weird position, and there was already a dull ache building up in her forehead.

She needed coffee or it would only get worse.

All of a sudden, she thrust the duvet off, the heat becoming intolerable. Her face was aflame and there was a dampness on her nightclothes as her body broke into a sweat. She didn't need a doctor to tell her what was going on. Without warning, she turned on the fan and air conditioner, sighing deeply as the rush of cool air dried off her sweat.

'Have you lost your mind?' Bilal said, his voice muffled as he pulled the duvet to cover his face. 'It's the middle of December, for crying out loud. Are you planning on killing me?'

'Sure, make it about yourself,' she murmured. 'I am just having a hot flush. I'll turn it off in a moment.'

'Wasn't your last period a while ago?' He whispered the word, like it was something sinful. 'How come you're still having hot flushes?'

'They're irregular now, tapering off maybe. Menopause isn't an exact science, Bilal.'

The duvet came off his face, his salt-and-pepper hair tousled from sleep, but his eyes sharp and playful. 'Unless this is your body's way of telling you that you need something.' Smirking now, he added, 'You need only say the word, you know.'

'Oh God, Bilal. You're in your sixties with a heart condition to boot. Isn't it time you grew up? I am not in the mood.'

Bilal frowned. 'What heart condition? I'm in peak health. Just because I've had a few hiccups along the way doesn't mean I'm at death's door. And besides, I was only trying to lighten things up. What's wrong with having a torrid morning together?'

Mona sighed, pushing herself out of bed. 'What's wrong is that I have a grumpy twelve-year-old to drop off at school and then a full day ahead. Why don't you spend some time with your dear sister? She might even tell you a bit about the side effects of menopause.'

'Must you say the word?'

'Oh, for God's sake. It's the twenty-first century, and I would like to think that men in Pakistan are now enlightened enough to not cringe at the mention of menopause.' She looked away from the full-length mirror in their room, as had been her habit for a few years now. No point in getting depressed first thing in the morning.

Bilal groaned and collapsed back in bed. 'I'm going to sleep a bit more before I get up for work. You'd think our son would have the sense to return back home to help his ageing father in the family business.'

Mona paused on her way to the bathroom. 'Weren't you just saying that you're in peak health and can have all the sex in the world? Besides, why must our son return from a good life in London to this – this country?'

'When you're this combative, it means you need your morning coffee. Go!' With that, Bilal pulled the duvet back over his face.

It took her a good thirty minutes in the bathroom, and once she was showered and dressed, she felt better. There was nothing to be done about the lines around her eyes and mouth. She still used some of the best anti-ageing creams money could buy, and sometimes hated herself for it, but she also relied on the contouring skills she'd learned in a make-up class to bring some shape to her face. Buttoning her shalwar above her navel, she was able to hide the weight she'd started gaining, and her shawl did the rest. By the time she emerged from the bathroom, she felt like a new person.

There were no snores, which meant Bilal was awake, and sure enough, as she opened the door to leave, he said, 'Listen...'

'Yes?' She knew what was coming, but she wanted him to say the words.

'Sorry about earlier. Breakfast in an hour? Just you and me?'

A small smile crept up her lips. That was more like it. 'Sure.'

'Have you got everything you need?'

'Yes.'

'Your lunchbox?'

'Yes.'

'Your gym bag?'

'Yes.'

'It's bad manners to look away when someone is talking to you, Arslan.' Mona reached out and turned her twelve-year-old son's sullen face towards her. 'I'm your mother, and I love you. I will always love you, but you can make life easier for me by being nice.' Her heart missed a beat as she felt the fine hair on his chin. Her baby was growing up. 'I want you to be a good boy, okay?'

Arslan rolled those beautiful blue eyes that everyone fell in love with. 'Okay, Mum!'

'Don't call me Mum, Arslan. You're not a Westerner. Call me Ammi like I've taught you.'

'Dad doesn't mind when I call him Dad. Just grow up, *Mum*.' Arslan turned away and walked towards the school building, leaving her standing alone.

'It's because your father loves you more than anyone in the world,' she murmured to herself. It was silly of her, but at that moment she couldn't stop the tears from gathering in her eyes. If Bilal were here, he'd blame this on her hormones too. Sometimes, she couldn't help but feel jealous of the love Arslan had for Bilal. The way they would always hang out together, go to cricket matches and shopping trips. Her usually cold and unforgiving husband had even accompanied Arslan to play dates when he was younger. He had never been like that with the older children. As a matter of fact, she couldn't remember a time when Bilal had done anything with Farhan and Aimen, always preferring to keep them at arm's length, leaving them perpetually thirsty for some affection. The responsibility had fallen on Mona to raise them well. But Arslan… it was as if Bilal lived for the boy. She could never have imagined him to fall in love with a child that wasn't even—

Don't go there, she thought, clamping the wayward idea before it could take further root. No, Arslan was Bilal's son. That was the only life he had ever known, and she wouldn't let anyone take that from him.

She looked around, grateful that the place was relatively empty, with only a few women fussing over their children – thankfully, ones she didn't know. She hated making small talk with these women who were decades her junior, and who spent most of their time judging her, as if she'd committed a crime by having a child after forty.

'Mona, is that you?'

Mona groaned inwardly as she came face to face with Humaira, one of the school mums and the star of Lahori society at the moment. For some reason, she insisted on being friends with Mona. Not one to be left behind, Humaira was already dressed and decked in diamonds. Mona smiled. 'I was just leaving, but nice to see you.'

'I say, I do admire you for doing the school run at this age. If I was in my fifties, all I would do is rest. But look at you, all dressed up for the day already.'

'Being over fifty doesn't mean you're dead, Humaira. As a matter of fact, I'll be going straight to work from here.'

Humaira's forehead creased. 'Work? But you're so rich! Why do you even need to lift a finger? Hamid, bless him, employs an army of servants to look after my every need, so I can put all my energy into looking smart and sexy for him.' She pulled off her Louis Vuitton shawl to show how the black top and skinny jeans hugged her toned body. 'A body like this doesn't come easy, especially not after having two kids.' She nodded, looking pointedly towards Mona's midriff. 'Instead of the school run, someone ought to be doing a gym run.' She laughed at her own joke.

Mona felt the blood rushing to her face. 'I think I'm fine with the way I look, thanks.'

'Fifty is the new thirty, Mona. Have you even seen what some of the women your age look like? Drop-dead gorgeous, the lot of them. Those Beverly Hills surgeons must be working overtime. Besides, if you can have kids this late, then you sure as hell can work out in the gym. Your oldest child, how old is he now?'

Humaira was so unspeakably rude. Mona looked around for an escape, but she knew she had to indulge her. Humaira was the queen bee of Lahori society, coming from old money and being married into old money too. Any PR person worth their salt knew better than to antagonise Humaira Hamid. 'Farhan will be thirty-two next month,' Mona replied, her voice tight.

Humaira whistled. 'Mashallah! The oldest thirty-two, and the youngest twelve. Looks like you and your husband get plenty of action, if you know what I mean.' She winked, leaning forward. 'If the factory is still running, I would recommend birth control pills at this point. As pretty as your blue-eyed boy is, I don't suppose you want another one? You'll be seventy by the time *that one* graduates from high school.'

Mona's eyes widened, and for a moment, she was lost for words.

Humaira continued smirking. 'Of course, you mustn't mind any of what I say. I'm always getting in trouble for my big mouth, but I will see you at the next get-together, I'm sure. I can't wait to discuss what's happened with Kulsoom.'

That was a name Mona hadn't heard in a while. 'Kulsoom? You mean my friend, Kulsoom Ayaz? What about her?'

The tip of Humaira's pink tongue was poised between blood-red lips. 'Don't tell me you don't know the gossip, Mona. I thought you were friends with Kulsoom.'

Mona didn't want to tell her that she hadn't heard from Kulsoom in over a year. Perhaps it was because she'd grown closer to Meera over the years, but she hadn't quite bothered to reach out to Kulsoom when she'd disappeared. She made a show of checking her watch. 'I actually need to leave. I'm getting late for work. What is it you wanted to tell me about Kulsoom?'

Humaira's eyes gleamed. 'Good things happen to those who wait. See you soon.'

With a small wave that showed her Cartier watch and diamond bracelet to full effect, Humaira left.

All through the return journey home, Mona couldn't shake off what Humaira had said. She'd always been mean and ageist, but what was it she knew about Kulsoom? A sense of guilt engulfed her as she realised that she hadn't been a good friend to Kulsoom, and had paid no attention when she began excusing herself from their meetings, spending more and more time in the gym.

'Oh, she's just trying to lose weight because her husband has been eyeing younger women,' Shabeena had said. 'Pay no attention to Kulsoom. She never really was the brightest bulb.'

'Humaira probably put her up to it,' Alia had added. 'She's on a mission to send every woman in the city to the gym. I swear she must have a stake in these gyms, because I see no other reason for this.'

Women like Humaira were bullies, and it seemed to be her singular purpose to shame people for their weight and age.

Mona's phone pinged with a message from Meera.

> SOS. Come straight to the office after dropping Arslan.

Mona sighed, wrapping her shawl tightly around her shoulders. 'Head for Garden Town instead of home,' she instructed the driver. 'We're going to the head office.'

Despite the heating in the car, it was frigid. It always was at this time of the year, and especially in the mornings. The day would warm up eventually, but Mona had learned to leave nothing to chance and now travelled with an extra shawl in her bag, just in case. If Humaira was here right now, she'd make a snide remark about Mona's age.

'Fuck you, Humaira,' she whispered, surprising herself. She couldn't remember the last time she'd even thought of this expletive, let alone used it.

Another reason for her annoyance was these early summons to Meera's office. Ever since starting part-time work at her modelling agency, managing PR, Mona had been assailed with work. It seemed like Meera's star was constantly on the rise, and as such, there was always lots to do. Little by little, the part-time gig had turned into full-time work. It also meant that she wouldn't be able to have breakfast with Bilal. Whipping out her phone, she left him a quick voice note, but to her disappointment, he saw her message instantly and rang her.

Heart in throat, she held the phone to her ear. 'I am so sorry, but I have to get to work. Something has come up.'

'Weren't you supposed to be working part-time? And why do you even want to work? You get more than enough from me.'

'Bilal, we've been through this.'

For a moment, he said nothing, his steady breathing the only evidence that he was still on the line. 'I swear, if I didn't know better, I'd say you do this on purpose. We were supposed to have breakfast together.'

These theatrics might have scared her once, but not any more. 'You can have breakfast with your sister. She's the one poisoning you against me all the time, anyway, so why deprive her of the opportunity?'

'Don't start, Mona.'

'You don't start!' Mona's voice rose, and the phone in her palm grew clammy. 'I apologised about breakfast. What more do you want from me? I am fifty-three years old, Bilal. I am not a child any more.'

'Hold your horses, woman. Can't I even complain about missing you? I miss you, that's all.' And then, as Mona knew he would, he asked, 'Did you make sure Arslan went into class safely?'

His concern always made her smile. 'Yes, Bilal Sahab. Your grumpy son is safely in school and learning new ways to disrespect his mother.'

'Cut him some slack, will you? The boy is growing up.' He sighed. 'Right, Qudsia's just come in. I'll catch you later tonight?'

'You bet.'

'I love you,' he whispered before ending the call.

She shook her head, her mouth curving into a rueful smile as they made their way through the palatial bungalows of Defence, the most happening part of the city. All the schools that mattered were now in this part of town, and although it took ages to get here, she and Bilal had felt that it was a necessary sacrifice to make for Arslan's education. For a while, she lost herself in the magic of the city, as the clean and impeccably planned streets of posh Lahore gave way to the slums around the railway lines, a stark reminder of the poverty that divided the two posh areas of Gulberg and Defence. Mona watched the plastic bags flying in the air, ultimately snagging on the barbed wire around the railway lines. Heaps of rubbish littered the area, with buffaloes and wild dogs feasting on whatever scraps they could find. It turned her stomach to imagine that the very same buffaloes went on to get milked after eating this garbage and they, in turn, consumed that milk.

She thought of asking Bashir why he'd taken this road instead of the flyover that rose over the slums, but her eye caught a young girl standing on the side of the street, her eyes lined with kaajal as she shivered in the cold, and she was instantly reminded of her own childhood when her parents didn't have enough money to heat the house. She produced a thousand-rupee note from her purse for her.

As always, Lahore was a city of contrasts, never failing to remind her that where there was money, there was also penury. One only had to know where to look. She was sure that people like Humaira didn't even deign to do that, finding it preferable to scroll through their phones instead. She wasn't even sure Bilal noticed the poverty that surrounded them. Even after all these years, her husband was still an enigma for her. His anger ebbed and flowed, but she had to admit that over the years, Bilal had mellowed. He wasn't the same man who would occasionally raise his hand against her. Mona wasn't entirely sure that she would ever be able to forgive him for the way he had treated her, but lately, she'd come to realise that she cared for him. And she worried for him.

All the time.

His health was deteriorating, but he was as stubborn as a mule and refused to acknowledge it. His own mother had died from heart disease, but Bilal didn't seem to care.

Mona was so lost in her own thoughts that she didn't realise that the driver had turned on to Gurumangat Road.

That was where—

'What on earth are you taking this road for?' she said, suddenly breathless. 'Bashir, I have told you a million times not to take this road.'

'There was a diversion, Bibi ji,' Bashir replied, scratching his beard. 'We'll be out of here in no time.'

'But…'

Mona paused. If she said any more, it would only make Bashir suspicious, and having worked for her mother-in-law for decades, Bashir was an old hand at society gossip. Besides, all of this had happened years ago. For someone who had been incredibly close to her at one point, someone she had thought of running away with, someone she had thought she could never stop loving, it surprised her that she hadn't thought of him in months.

'Ali,' she murmured.

There, she'd said his name. Despite everything, it still sent a shiver through her. They passed the graveyard, a sprawling space with towering trees and ornate graves, protected by a metal fence painted white. Even in death, nobody was ever really safe in Pakistan. Mona averted her gaze, focusing instead on the stalls selling barbecue meat. She couldn't bear to look at his grave, even though she saw him every day in his son's eyes.

Chapter 3

Bilal

The dining room was quiet except for the clink of their cutlery as Bilal dug into his omelette with gusto. No matter how much salt he sprinkled on it, it tasted bland to him. As he picked up the salt shaker again, his sister cleared her throat. Bilal paused, holding the shaker mid-air. 'Yes, Qudsia? Is there anything you want to say?'

'There's no need to take your anger out on the food, that's all I am saying.'

Bilal put down the shaker. 'I am not angry.'

Qudsia's lips twitched as she fixed the dupatta on her head. 'If you say so, although it isn't the omelette's fault that your wife isn't here to have breakfast with you.'

'She's busy with work.'

'Work.' She spat out the word like it was abuse. 'A wife's primary responsibility should be towards her husband. You are a billionaire, Bilal. Mona doesn't need the pittance she earns from working with that – that horrible woman. It's beyond me how you even allow your wife to be in the presence of that *gushti*, Meera. She should be at home, looking after you and the house. It's not my responsibility.'

Bilal speared a piece of omelette with his fork and put it in his mouth. This time, all he could taste was the salt. His eyes watered as he swallowed it. 'Mona is a good wife... most of the time. And, if you hadn't realised, we live in the twenty-first century, Qudsia. I can't stop her from being friends with Meera.'

Qudsia paused between mouthfuls of yogurt. 'That's the kind of filth Western media peddles all the time, making it easy for women to shirk their duties. I tell you, our amma was always hell-bent on pushing me to start working, but I knew better. You're making a mistake.'

'You do know that our amma, may God bless her soul, was one of the most progressive women of her age?'

'Our amma was a fool.'

Bilal closed his eyes for a moment. He could feel sweat breaking across his forehead and trickling down his back. 'She did what was right for her children,' he managed to say. 'She raised us well.'

Qudsia sneered. 'Maybe she did her best for you, but she never really made life easier for me. Always meddling in my married life, asking stupid questions, pushing me to be independent. What kind of mother does that?'

'The kind that cares, Qudsia.'

'If she cared so much, she wouldn't have thrown me at the first person who asked for my hand and sent me away to live in Dera Ismail Khan. Do you have any idea how claustrophobic that town is? To go from living in Lahore to that God-awful shithole.'

'It was Abbu who married you off. That was the one decision our amma had nothing to do with.'

Qudsia roughly wiped away a tear from her cheek. 'Then, she should have stopped him.'

And there it was – the reason Qudsia resented their mother. She put up a good impression of being the devoted housewife, but Bilal knew that Qudsia had expected more from life. Born and brought up in Lahore, it mustn't have been easy for her to adjust to life in Dera Ismail Khan, a town where houses had walls so high that they blocked out everything... sometimes even the sun.

'I loved my husband,' she continued, 'but that city – oh, Bilal, that city killed me. How was I ever supposed to be independent in a place where you can't even remove your burqa? A place where wearing lipstick and make-up outside meant that people treated you like a prostitute?'

For a moment, he felt sorry for his sister, who had been forced to come and stay with them because her husband had gambled away their wealth, and then conveniently died... his sister who had suffered so much after her only child passed away in childhood.

However, his sympathy for her was short-lived as she drew up in her chair and said, 'As difficult as Dera Ismail Khan was, I always realised that my rightful place was beside my husband. Not like Mona, who isn't even home most of the time. Only God knows where she is. If there's one thing I made sure of, it was that I was with my husband the entire time he was home.'

'Smothered him to death,' Bilal mumbled to himself.

Qudsia narrowed her eyes. 'What did you say?'

Bilal shrugged. 'Nothing at all.'

'I honestly think you need to put a leash on that woman. It is not right for your sister to be looking after you. It's your wife's duty. It's not like she's ill or something. Ripe as a fig, I'd say, after having a baby in her forties. *Her* son.'

Bilal's gaze drew level with his sister's. 'He's my son too, Qudsia. Your nephew.'

She laughed, holding up the edge of her dupatta to her mouth. 'Excuse my language, but I am not suggesting that she went off with someone else and had Arslan, dear brother. He is my nephew and I love him. I'm just saying that she shouldn't have saddled you with this burden at this age. We are supposed to have babies in our teens and twenties. Nobody has kids in their forties or fifties.'

'Arslan is not a burden,' Bilal whispered. 'He is my son.' Sweat was streaming down his face now, staining his collar. Why was it so warm in the room all of a sudden? 'Who the hell has turned up the heating in this room?'

'He is having an adverse effect on your health. Look at yourself. You are well past sixty now, for God's sake. You shouldn't be running around after kids at your age. I worry for you, that's all. If that woman had been clever enough to use some sort of contra—'

'Qudsia, shut up!' Blood rushed in his ears as he watched his sister's mouth form a perfect O. Taking a deep breath, he added, 'I'm sorry, sister, but I'm just not feeling very well today. Please excuse me.'

It was the truth. He did feel a bit unwell. His heartbeat was erratic, and his shirt was soaked. His hand shook as he reached for a glass of water.

Qudsia, however, rose from her seat, pushing away her plate of half-eaten food. 'If I wasn't absolutely desperate, I wouldn't stay here a moment longer. You disappoint me, Bilal. You used to be a man. What happened to you?'

I saw sense, he thought.

Before he could answer, however, one of the maids, Shugufta, scurried into the dining room. 'Shall I clear away your plate, Bibi?' she asked Qudsia, her voice breathless with fear. If there was one thing his sister had inherited from their mother, it was her short temper.

Qudsia huffed. 'Yes, and while you're at it, go and pack my bags as well, why don't you? It doesn't seem like anyone needs me here.'

Shugufta bobbed her head. 'Shall I pack your bags first, then, Bibi? I do all the packing around here. I can have your room cleared and packed in an instant.'

Qudsia all but exploded. 'No, you idiot! It was just a figure of speech. Must I be surrounded by imbeciles? Clear away the plate only.'

'*Ji*, Bibi.'

Bilal couldn't help it. He broke out laughing as his sister stormed off with her nose in the air.

Passing a tearful Shugufta on his way out of the dining room, he gave her a reassuring smile. 'Don't mind my sister. You're the best employee in this house.'

Chapter 4

Mona

'Yes, that's what I would call a sexy walk,' Meera crooned. 'Oh yeah, work those hips. Don't sway them like a girl, Zarrar! Just, you know, be a man who is in touch with his feminine side.' She clapped her hands together as the poor model did the thousandth variation of the same walk. 'Oh, you've finally got it, I think. Well done.'

Mona shook her head as she watched a red-faced Zarrar leave the room. 'Must you treat him like this? A man in touch with his feminine side! You do know how most men in Pakistan would react to something like this?'

Meera blew a kiss in her direction. 'And that's why I love you. You don't sugar-coat stuff. But if I didn't run a tight ship, I wouldn't be where I am today. It wouldn't kill Zarrar to behave like a proper model. There is nothing more boring than a talentless, entitled brat. Professionalism died a thousand deaths before it reached Pakistan, I often feel.' Spreading her arms, indicating her giant office, she added, 'Besides, this is my way of getting back to these men for treating us like crap for decades.'

'Poor Zarrar wouldn't hurt a fly.'

Meera arched an eyebrow. 'Poor Zarrar isn't as innocent as he looks. He has been sleeping with me. The man is a marvel in bed.'

Mona clapped her hands to her mouth. 'Meera, you didn't.'

Meera smirked. 'I sure did.'

'But it's unethical. You employ him.'

'He's freelance, and if you must know, he asked me out on a date first. Contrary to popular opinion, I am not a cougar. And his father is loaded, so rest assured, I am not exploiting him. What we have is a mutual admiration of each other... and our bodies.' Meera leaned forward in her chair, reaching out for a cracker in a tray on her desk. 'Please tell me you're getting some action yourself? The way you're blushing like a schoolgirl, I am not very sure of it.'

Mona waved her pen at Meera. 'If I remember correctly, you called me here to help out with Lahore Fashion Week, not answer questions about my personal life.' She snorted. 'And if you must know, I am fifty-three. Sex is the last thing on my mind these days. I'm too old for all that stuff.'

Meera raised an eyebrow. 'We're the same age.'

'You look about thirty.'

Judging by the small smile on Meera's face, Mona knew she'd struck gold. Her friend was many things, but modest wasn't one of them. Blowing on her nails, Meera said, 'God bless that doctor up in Beverly Hills. He told me I was his muse, so I let him work his magic on me.'

'His magic seems to have trickled down from your face to your chest too. I don't remember them being so big.'

Meera put a hand on her chest in mock horror. 'How dare you! They're all mine. Bought and paid for.' A mischievous smile appeared on her face. 'Madam Mona, are you tempted to get a boob job?'

Mona shuddered. 'No thanks. A fifty-something woman with implants? Society alone will tear me to bits, and Humaira will feast on the bones.'

'To hell with Humaira. I'd like to see how she looks when she's in her fifties.'

'Not to mention my sister-in-law, Qudsia, who lives with us. She might just die of a heart attack at the sight.'

Meera rolled her eyes. 'Oh, please! She envies you for having a natural life. I ask you, what's wrong with women in their fifties having sex? We have desires just like everyone else. If men can have babies till they drop dead, why can't we enjoy ourselves too?'

Mona sighed. As usual, Meera had nailed it. Society's obsession with suppressing women never really ended, not even after death. Mona still remembered how people had congregated at her dead mother-in-law's prayer meet six years ago only to gossip about her life, not pray for her soul. Despite her many flaws, Mona had admired Nighat for being the only voice of reason in that twisted household. It had pained her to see her mother-in-law's character being torn apart.

Meera had a faraway look in her eyes. 'Oh, being in love is the most wonderful thing ever, isn't it, Mona? I think I might be in love with Zarrar.'

Mona laughed before realising that her friend was serious. 'Are you kidding me? He's half your age. It cannot last, Meera. Surely, you can see it too.'

Meera rolled a paperweight on the table and met Mona's gaze. 'If I remember correctly, you fell in love with someone fifteen years your junior. Or have you forgotten about him?'

Mona looked away, gazing out of the window at a smoggy Lahore. 'Fourteen, and I can't believe you just said that, Meera. Why bring him up?'

'Because I wanted you to remember what it feels like to be in love. You shouldn't have to settle for less.'

Watching the spires of the mosques outside, Mona whispered, 'Did you know I passed his grave today? And now, you've brought him up again. Why did you do that, Meera? Isn't it enough that I've gone through that pain once? Must you remind me of what I've lost again and again?'

Although she wanted to, she didn't pull away when Meera reached for her hand across the table. 'I only meant that you knew true love, Mona. It would be foolish to say that you didn't love Ali.'

'I love Bilal,' she whispered. 'I don't love Ali. I hardly ever think of him nowadays. He has become a distant memory, and if someone doesn't remind me, I can sometimes pretend as if he never existed.'

'And Arslan? I don't know about you, but I think he looks remarkably like Ali. I'm not sure where he got those eyes from, but that nose is so much like—'

'He does look like Ali,' Mona admitted, 'but he's still Bilal's son. Ali was never a part of Arslan's life and never will be. Not after what happened.'

Her voice broke as she looked away, thinking about all that could have been if Ali hadn't gone down the wrong path and died. With Ali, it would have been a life far removed from luxury, but she knew that they could have been happy. Despite everything, something told her that they'd have been happy.

And now, she would never know.

Meera clicked her tongue. 'Oh, my poor Mona. Don't you see, though? You care for Bilal, but can you say for sure that you love him? When was the last time you two had sex?'

This time, Mona pulled her hand away, banishing thoughts of Ali out of her mind. It was foolish to reflect on something that never had a real chance of happening. Ali was her past, but Bilal was her past, present and future. 'Sex has little to do with love, especially at our age,' she said drily. 'Besides, I worry for Bilal all the time. I don't think he's well.'

Meera's eyes softened. 'I know, my friend. I just meant' – she shook her head – 'I don't know what I meant. Just ignore me. You're right. This thing with Zarrar is fleeting, and I mustn't let it get to me.' She rubbed her palms together. 'Let's discuss the Lahore Fashion Week, then, shall we? It's happening in a few days. and I need you to reach out to all the bigwigs to reconfirm their attendance. We don't want the front row seats empty...'

As they dove back into work, Mona felt some of the tension dissipate from her shoulders, allowing her to relax. Work was what she was good at, and it made her happy. However, as exciting as everything was at the moment with the fashion week upon them, she couldn't help but think about what Meera had said.

Did she really love Bilal?

It turned out that she had little time to ponder over that question because, when she got back home, her daughter, Aimen, was waiting for her.

Almost thirty now, Aimen was in her prime. Her high cheekbones, so much like her grandmother's, redeemed the plainer features she had inherited from Mona. Still, looking at her, Mona felt a flash of pride. She had made this beautiful human.

Smelling of the latest Balenciaga fragrance, Aimen gave Mona a big hug. 'Ammi, I have been waiting for you for ages. You are always late.'

'Beta, you know work can be stressful sometimes. We are preparing for the fashion week, so things are a bit—'

'Yes, we know perfectly well how busy you are, Mona. You are hardly ever at home,' Qudsia said, looking up from her mobile phone. 'Isn't it wonderful that you have a free housekeeper at home to do everything for you?'

Sitting opposite Qudsia, Bilal was busy on his laptop. 'Please don't start again, Qudsia. You know how grateful we are for your presence here and the lengths to which you go to keep this house running. You're my sister, not the housekeeper.'

Qudsia's cheeks turned pink with victory. 'Well, thank you, Bilal. I am glad that at least someone appreciates me.'

'We all appreciate you, Phupo,' Aimen said, skipping off to sit next to her aunt. 'We also love you, you know.'

Mona collapsed on the sofa, unable to look at Qudsia's smug face any more. 'I'm so tired.'

Bilal raised his eyebrows, but said nothing, typing away on his laptop.

'You're tired, and I am so bored,' Aimen said, pouting. 'There's nothing to do all day at home. How much time can one even spend with friends?'

'You could start working, Aimen,' Mona began, but Qudsia laughed.

'Yes, you could work like a commoner, Aimen. It's not like you've married into one of the most powerful families in Lahore. But sure, go and toil in an office for a pittance.'

Aimen laughed with her aunt. 'You're right, Phupo. I don't think Zahid would ever allow me to work unless it was for his company.'

'Then work for his company,' Mona shot back. 'You are a healthy thirty-year-old woman. You shouldn't be idle.'

'Come on, Mona,' Bilal began. 'Go easy on your daughter. Working in an office is not the answer to everything.'

'We sent her to one of the best universities in Canada, Bilal. What good is that education, then?'

Bilal snorted. 'Don't be silly. We only sent her to Canada for the optics, so that she'd get a better *rishta*. And she did. People in Pakistan want educated and well-mannered girls these days, but only for show. They don't expect them to work. Surely, you don't need me to tell you that.'

'It's also thanks to you, Mona, that your son is toiling in a dead-end job in London,' Qudsia said, wrapping her hijab around her head to stop it from slipping off. 'He ought to be in Lahore, helping out his father in the family business. Instead, he's there working his ass off for some random *goras*. Do you have any idea how much these white people hate us?'

'Pray tell where you've met these white people that hate us, Qudsia?' Mona murmured. 'In Dera Ismail Khan?'

Qudsia went rigid, her face darkening into an ugly scowl, but before she could respond, Arslan bounded into the living room, mobile phone in hand.

'Here comes my darling Beta,' Bilal said, pushing aside his laptop and patting the seat next to his. 'Tell me all about your day. Did you have fun? Did you have enough to eat?'

Turning to Mona, he added, 'Isn't he losing weight? He looks skinny.'

'He's growing up, Bilal. Of course, he will be all sharp angles.' Qudsia sat with her arms crossed, but it seemed that she'd temporarily set her rage aside. 'You need to stop doting on him. Let him become a man.'

'Isn't he too young for a mobile phone?' Aimen added.

'God knows the kind of sins he is seeing,' Qudsia added. 'It is not healthy. In my time, boys were allowed to run free and get filthy. In Dera, we never cared about our boys falling in ditches or getting a scratch or two.'

Neither Bilal nor Arslan, however, were listening. Arslan was whispering something in his father's ear, causing Bilal's eyes to crinkle up with amusement.

'Arslan and I have just decided that in a couple of months, we'll go on a trip together. Just father and son.'

Mona leaned forward in her seat. 'Am I allowed to join you two?'

'No!' they replied in unison.

Far from it hurting her, Mona felt joy spread through her as she watched her husband with his arm around their son, his phone and laptop forgotten. When it came to Arslan, nothing else mattered for Bilal. Not even his older children.

Over Arslan's shoulder, Bilal gave her a wink, to which she smiled back. In the past, he wouldn't have cared enough for her feelings to check on her. He had changed so much over the years, and it all brought such joy to her.

But can you say for sure that you love him?

Meera's question swirled in her head. Did she really love the silver-haired man sitting in front of her with his belly starting to poke out of his shirt, the buttons straining to hold it in place? Did she love the curve of that hard jaw that had now begun to soften and somehow gel into his neck? Did she love those big hands that had regularly struck her years ago, the very hands he had wrapped around her neck to squeeze the life out of her?

The answer was that she didn't know. She didn't know if she was capable of loving with reckless abandon again. That part of her had died with Ali. What she felt for Bilal was more than love. It was need. Life just wouldn't make sense without him and all the hardships that came with being his wife. Without Bilal, she was lost. Perhaps that was love too… a more different and enduring kind of love. A love that could last.

Her eyes welled up as she sat watching her perfect family, Bilal and Arslan still whispering, while Qudsia ran her fingers through Aimen's hair before planting a kiss on her forehead. For all her flaws, Qudsia loved Farhan and Aimen with the fierceness of a lioness. Her love for Arslan, though, varied – something Mona had never understood. On Arslan's eleventh birthday, she'd remarked, 'The boy really is a gift from heaven because nobody on our side of the family has ever had blue eyes.'

The remark had chilled her then, and it chilled her to this day. Maybe deep down, Qudsia knew…

That was preposterous. Nobody knew except for Bilal and Meera, and it wasn't like they would tell anyone. However, she had to admit that it wasn't unheard of for secrets to get out in Lahore. In fact, that's exactly what Lahori society thrived on: trading secrets and trying to bring each other down. Could anyone have found out? During the height of her relationship with Ali, although she had taken care not to be seen, it didn't matter to her as much as it should have. She had envisioned her future with Ali, and it was only a matter of time before everyone found out. What Mona hadn't foreseen was Ali's death. And now, the thought of anyone finding out about it terrified her. No, she was sure that her family was safe – intact. At that moment, everything was perfect, and she wished that she could capture that moment forever and hold it in her heart. The only person missing here was Farhan, her firstborn, but she reassured herself with the fact that he was happy in London.

And as if to spoil that moment, her phone pinged. Mona sighed, thinking it was Meera again, but the text was from a withheld number. Without her reading glasses, she couldn't read the text, but she knew that a lot of rich people liked to withhold their numbers. Over the years, it had become a status symbol of sorts, and it helped them avoid spam calls. This was probably one of them confirming their attendance for the fashion week. A part of her wanted to leave it till tomorrow as she desperately wanted to go upstairs and unwind after the tiring day she'd had, but she also knew that rest wouldn't come until she'd finished every last task for the day. Pulling out her reading glasses from her bag, she put them on, double-clicking on her phone's screen to illuminate it.

> I know your secret.

She froze. Blinking once as the message registered, she read it again, trying to scroll down to see if there was more.

There wasn't. This was it.

> I know your secret.

The sleep that had been enticing her seemed like ages ago, and when she looked up, there was a haze around her, as if she was being weighed down... drowning. Her gaze settled on Arslan, and her stomach dropped. Was this the secret they meant? She shook her head. It couldn't be – nobody knew. And nobody had known about her relationship with Ali either.

'Mona, are you listening to me?' Bilal asked. His head tilted to the left. 'Are you feeling all right? You're white as a ghost.'

Mona put a hand on her chest to calm her pounding heart. 'I'm okay, why? What were you saying?'

Bilal was still frowning. 'Are you sure you're okay? Is it something you've seen on the phone?'

Qudsia sat up. 'Oh, please don't tell me there's been another bomb blast in my beloved Dera Ismail Khan. These terrorists will not rest until they've flattened my poor city.'

Mona shook her head. 'It's nothing to do with my phone at all, and there's no news of Dera either. I guess I'm' – she struggled to find the right words – 'I guess I am just tired and need to head to bed.'

Aimen rose with her, stretching her arms. 'I'll head back too. Zahid will be waiting for me.'

'Beta, when will you plan a baby?' Qudsia asked. 'It's been two years since your wedding. People are beginning to talk. Just the other day, I was at a *milad*, and Humaira was asking me if I had any good news to share.'

Mona's face whipped up, suddenly alert, the text message forgotten for a moment. 'What did you say to Humaira? How is it any of her business when Aimen has a child?'

From the hint of a smile on her face, Qudsia was obviously enjoying the reaction from Mona. 'Contrary to popular opinion, Mona, I love my brother's children more than you think. I told Humaira that our Aimen was a progressive young woman and will have a baby when she's figured out a career for herself.'

'But I don't have a career,' Aimen said. 'I've just been unable to conceive. We've been trying, as you know.'

Qudsia batted a hand in her direction. 'Yes, but Humaira doesn't need to know that. Besides, given how fertile your mother is, I doubt you should have any trouble conceiving. You're just not doing it right.'

Aimen's lip twitched. 'And how does one *do it right*, Phupo? Last I checked, there was just one way to get pregnant.' She laughed. 'And I've done that more times than I can remember.'

Qudsia blushed. 'None of this language in front of your father. We'll talk later.'

As Aimen came to hug Mona, she whispered, 'I never thought I'd live to see the day when I get sex advice from Phupo. And that taunt about your fertility was uncalled for.'

Mona closed her eyes, and threw her arms around Aimen, taking in the familiar scent of her perfume. 'Thank you,' she murmured. 'And I am sorry for pestering you about starting work.'

'You're my mother. You're the only one who can pester me.'

Choking back a sob, Mona excused herself, rushing upstairs.

As she bounded up the stairs, she could hear Bilal say to his sister, 'Why must you always insult her, Qudsia? Can't we all be friends?'

'No, we cannot.'

It was faint, but Mona managed to hear Qudsia's reply before she was out of earshot.

What did I ever do to you, Qudsia, she thought, shutting herself in her bedroom and pulling out her phone again. There hadn't been any more messages.

In the past, Mona would have drowned out her anxiety with a stiff drink, but she'd given up on drinking when she had been pregnant with Arslan and had never resumed. The way her hands were trembling now, she yearned to reach into Bilal's secret cabinet and pull out a bottle of Pinot Grigio, but instead, she settled for water. Crashing in bed, fully clothed, she scrutinised the message again, but there were only so many times she could reread a simple sentence.

There was a storm brewing outside, and as a crack of lightning illuminated the lawn outside her window, for a brief moment, Mona found herself wondering whether her carefully constructed life was about to come crashing down. Things in Lahore had changed over the past decade. Today, social media ruled everything, and reputations were ruined in mere hours. She had seen first-hand how people like Humaira used their vast network of contacts to tear anyone who would defy them to shreds. Women had always been an easy target, but now, with social platforms like Twitter and Instagram, not to mention the hideous act of taking screenshots of WhatsApp conversations, the stakes were higher than ever. Like most people, Mona had taken to clearing her chats regularly. Humaira wanted to be the queen bee of Lahori society, and Mona knew that she wouldn't hesitate in taking her down, partly because Bilal's wealth had always irked her. It irked most people.

True to spirit, she brought up the anonymous text message again and clicked on delete.

There – out of sight, out of mind.

In Lahore, you couldn't trust anyone any more, least of all the ones closest to you. That's why Mona had grown distant from everyone, except Meera. Even Shabeena and Alia, who used to be her best friends, had taken a back seat.

She groaned into her pillow as she realised that, tomorrow, both of them were coming for tea, and she'd have to be on her best behaviour. They really couldn't be coming at a worse time, but before she could overthink it, the door opened, and Bilal crept in.

She pretended to be asleep, but Bilal knew her breathing patterns. 'Are you awake?' he asked.

Mona sighed and turned around. 'I am now.'

He climbed into bed and pressed himself against her. 'I'm sorry about Qudsia. You know she doesn't mean it.'

'Sure,' Mona replied, turning her head away so that Bilal wouldn't see she'd been crying. Qudsia's taunts were the least of her troubles.

'Are you going to tell me what's bothering you, then?'

How does he always know? A part of her felt elated that her husband noticed so much about her, the part that wasn't panicking about the message. She reached for his hand and squeezed it. 'I am fine.'

'If it's anything to do with money, you know you can always use our joint account.'

She wished it *was* something to do with money. At least it would be easier to deal with. When she didn't say anything, Bilal nuzzled his face into her neck. 'Is it to do with that holiday I am taking with Arslan? You know that was just a joke. We wouldn't go anywhere without you.'

Despite the chaos inside her, something about Bilal's weight against her back calmed her. His hand was warm in her own and a frisson of desire swept through her. 'Of course not,' she said. 'I love the relationship you have with him. I know how much you love your son.'

'I love you more than anything,' Bilal continued as he nibbled at her earlobe. 'Just saying... without you, there would be no Arslan. There wouldn't be anything, really, Mona.' Holding her chin, he turned her face towards him. 'It took me many years to realise this, but I finally have. My life begins and ends with you.'

'You're so dramatic!' she cried, but she was smiling.

'It's true. Sometimes, it scares me how much I depend on you. How much I love you.'

As she returned his embrace and allowed him to plant kisses on her neck, the realisation hit her that she didn't need to question her love for Bilal. Her love for him was as constant as her breathing. It was in every fibre of her being. Being with Bilal made sense.

'I love you too,' she murmured in his hair. As Bilal roughly pulled her towards him, she put a hand against his chest. 'Can we just cuddle tonight, though?' The text message still weighed heavily on her mind, and she didn't think she could go through the motions of intimacy right now.

Although his eyes were steeped in desire, his breathing ragged, he smiled and buried his head in her neck. 'Of course. Let's just talk.'

Pushing any further thoughts of secrets and lies out of her mind, she let Bilal lead the conversation on how difficult things were at the office.

It felt normal. It felt like home.

'The fashion week is all anyone can talk about,' Alia gushed the next day as they sat in Mona's drawing room for tea and snacks. 'I was at a wedding last night, and so many women there asked me for front row seats to the Haque show.' Smacking her lips together after applying a fresh coat of lipstick, she added, 'I didn't have the heart to tell those ladies that if I haven't been invited myself, how on earth could I get them invitations?'

Mona tried not to massage her temples. Her head thudded with a migraine that she seemed to have woken up with. Despite having knocked back two paracetamols, her head was still swimming. Sometime in the night, the thunder outside had made her sit up straight from fright. After that, it wasn't easy to fall back asleep, especially since thoughts of that text message wouldn't leave her alone.

> I know your secret.

For the thousandth time, she wondered who could have sent her such a cryptic message. There hadn't been anything else this morning, but she couldn't dislodge the rock of dread that had settled in her stomach.

Alia snapped her fingers. 'Earth to Mona. I just asked why you hadn't invited us to the fashion week.'

Blinking away thoughts of the text message, Mona smiled. 'Of course you're invited, Alia. That goes without saying. Sorry, I'm not feeling like myself today.'

'Meera is working you too hard, and, at your age, you ought to be resting, not working.'

'Don't be silly, Alia,' Shabeena cried out. 'Mona is still young, and women in general are good at multitasking, especially Pakistani women, given all we have to juggle.' Turning to Mona, she said, 'Although I have to say that we haven't had those embossed invitation cards for the fashion week that everyone else got.' Her scarf slid down for a brief moment to reveal grey roots. 'It is off-putting, to say the least.'

Alia screeched with laughter. 'With that hair colour, you'd be lucky to be invited to a *milad* let alone a fashion show.'

Shabeena whipped the scarf back in place. 'I am sixty years old. Stop being so ageist. I am allowed to have grey hair.'

'Not in Lahore, you aren't.'

'Okay, fine! I forgot to book an appointment with the salon. I was a bit preoccupied, but at least I am not desperate enough to resort to going under the knife like *some* people.'

Alia touched her own face, her razor-sharp red nails glinting in the light. 'Welcome to the twenty-first century, darling. Unlike you, I've got my husband wrapped around my little finger.'

Shabeena's eyes widened. 'That was a low blow and you know it. Besides, marriage is not all about intimacy. We're way past that stage. My husband and I are companions now. Best friends.'

'Exactly! He's cast you in the friend zone because he's busy giving it to his secretary.' Alia laughed at her own joke.

Shabeena pursed her lips. 'You're only embarrassing yourself. Such vulgar language is more suited to the whores of Heera Mandi.'

'Now who's the one resorting to vulgar language? And what's wrong with being like the whores of Heera Mandi? They're bold and financially independent, which is more than I can say about a lot of women in our society. By the way, most of the Heera Mandi lot have moved to the posh housing societies now. Who knows, maybe you've got one as your neighbour?'

Shabeena threw up her hands. '*Astagfirullah!* I could never have a prostitute as a neighbour.'

Alia smirked. 'But how would you know, my dear? That's the golden question.'

In an instant, Mona was transported to the past, when their friend, Kulsoom, used to intervene in these squabbles – a kind and occasionally reasonable voice, unlike the two women in front of her. 'I miss Kulsoom,' she said, causing both of her friends to forget their argument and look at her. 'I really miss her, and I am so sorry I couldn't be there when she needed me.'

'Oh, sweetie,' Alia cried, reaching for a butter croissant on the coffee table. 'Whatever happened to her was not your fault. It's none of our fault. Kulsoom was…'

'A bit of a bumpkin,' Shabeena finished for her. 'I hate to agree with Alia, but Kulsoom never did fit in our group or any group for that matter.'

'Precisely,' Alia said, biting into her croissant. 'God, where do you get these croissants from, Mona? It's like biting into a piece of heaven.'

'But what happened to her?' Mona continued, ignoring Alia's comment. 'Why did she just vanish?'

'Speaking of which, I keep hearing of people being kidnapped.' Alia shuddered. 'I mean, it was bad enough when terrorism had taken hold of Lahore, but these kidnappings are so random that you can't even tell who might be next.'

Shabeena reached for her teacup. 'They're not that random, actually. We know for a fact that affluent people are the ones being kidnapped and most just get sold to the next highest bidder if the family doesn't pay the ransom on time.'

'Even the rich uncles?' Alia asked, horrified.

'Especially the rich uncles.'

Dread settled like a pit in Mona's stomach. Her thoughts immediately went to Bilal and his devil-may-care attitude, the way he always left the house without a security guard or driver. 'How do you know so much about these kidnappings?' she asked, desperate to know more. If she was armed with all the information, perhaps Bilal would see reason.

Shabeena laughed. 'My dear, the kidnappings are all anyone talks about these days. I swear, it's like a pall has descended on us. Kitty parties used to be such fun once upon a time.'

Before Mona could ask any further questions, Shugufta scurried into the drawing room. 'Bibi, your guest is here.'

Mona looked at Alia. 'What guest?'

Alia just smiled. 'You'll see.'

Mona gaped at them, but before she could instruct Shugufta to let the mysterious guest in, the scent of Chanel N°5 perfume wafted in the drawing room as Humaira Hamid arrived, her sky-high pencil heels clicking on the marble, the silky fabric of her kaftan swirling around her. Her neck shone with glitter, some of which she'd also applied on her eyelids. Perhaps it was a side effect of working with Meera, but Mona couldn't help but notice how Humaira had a perfect catwalk. It was as if she was walking on a ramp.

'Humaira,' Mona began, choking on the perfume as Humaira leaned in for a kiss. 'What a pleasant surprise.'

Humaira beamed at her. 'Well, you can thank your friends for inviting me. It's always such a joy to be in your house, Mona. I love old money.' Her gaze flitted around the drawing room, taking in the surroundings. 'I do wonder why you haven't redone your drawing room, though. I have everything reupholstered twice a year.' She flashed them a dazzling smile as she took a seat next to Mona, and poured herself a coffee. 'It keeps those lazy servants busy.'

As Shabeena and Alia launched into praising Humaira's attire, she waved a hand at them.

'Yes, yes, it's from Karachi. Custom-made, of course. Twenty workers laboured over this embroidery.'

Alia held a hand over her mouth. 'If I am not mistaken, is it the designer who usually puts everyone on a year-long waiting list?'

Humaira smacked her lips. 'The very same. When you're old money, you can rise above the rabble.'

While they were busy, Mona took a moment to get her bearings. Humaira was like a hawk, perpetually attuned to its prey's movements, so it was imperative to put on a good show in front of her.

'I hope you got the invitation for the fashion week,' Mona began, sitting straighter so that her tummy didn't show through her high-neck sweater. 'Meera has arranged for a front row seat for you.'

Humaira bit into a samosa, letting out a small moan. 'I don't indulge in these oily treats in general, but these samosas are something else, Mona. Compliments to the chef. Is it the Filipino one you employ?'

Mona shook her head. 'I've always employed a Pakistani chef.'

'Of course, that must have been someone else, then. Didn't you know, hiring foreign house staff is the latest fashion? And since Lahore is overflowing with money, why the hell not?'

Mona was trying very hard not to roll her eyes. Instead, she crossed her legs and pretended to admire her nails. 'Maybe your Lahore is, Humaira, but if you look outside of your bubble, you'll see that most of the people in the city are struggling.'

Humaira shrugged. 'So? Am I supposed to feel sorry for them? It's not my fault they're piss-poor.'

'Maybe a bit of compassion wouldn't be a bad thing.'

Humaira laughed. 'Please tell me you did not just try to lecture me on compassion. I keep Lahori society together. I keep the engine running so that we don't run out of parties to attend. It's basically a public service, and if that isn't being compassionate, then I don't know what is.'

Mona sniffed. 'I was talking about the poor people.'

'But there are so many of them, and they breed like rabbits. It's their fault that they can't keep it in their bloody shalwars.'

'Mona was just asking about Kulsoom,' Alia said, changing the topic.

Humaira all but spat out her coffee. 'Oh yes, please! Gossip is what I came here for! Let's see... the elusive Kulsoom. I had promised you that I would tell you all about your erstwhile friend, hadn't I, Mona?'

Her tone stung.

'I wouldn't call her erstwhile,' Mona murmured. 'Kulsoom is still very much my friend.'

Humaira raised an eyebrow. 'When was the last time you heard from her?'

Shabeena gave a nervous chuckle. 'Come on, Mona, let's not pretend we were best friends with her. She was only ever an acquaintance. It's okay, you don't need to feel guilty about it.'

Before Mona could reply, Humaira announced, 'Well, she ran away with her gym instructor.'

Mona blinked. 'Excuse me?'

'You heard me.'

'She ran away? When… and why?'

Humaira's smirk was back in place as she sucked the oil from the samosa on her fingertips. It was uncouth, but it wasn't like anyone could call her out for it. 'Apparently, she was in *love*…' She drew out the word. 'Her husband sent her to the gym to lose weight for him, and the fool fell in love with her trainer, sold and pawned off everything she owned and ran away with him. Rumour has it that they're living up in Abbottabad now in some godforsaken house.'

Mona held a hand to her chest. Kulsoom's face flashed before her eyes, and for a moment, she felt something akin to pride. She had broken free of the shackles that bound them all. Turning her attention to the group, she said, 'I had no idea. I just thought that she moved away to Karachi with her family or something.'

Humaira laughed. 'Ha! As if she could go to Karachi. The only reason she's run off to Abbottabad is because nobody knows her there, and I don't know anybody there. Otherwise, I would have destroyed her, or let social media do the dirty work. Karachi, you say. Please!'

'Why?' Mona whispered. 'What has Kulsoom ever done to you?'

'If harlots like Kulsoom were allowed to run free in our society, what kind of precedent are we setting for our daughters? Would you rather Aimen ran away with her gym trainer too, Mona?'

Before Mona could reply, Shabeena hastily cut in. 'Aimen is a saint, but honestly, with the stuff that's going on here, how can they even say that Pakistan is a Muslim country any more? It makes me sick that people get to defy the sanctity of a marriage like this. I hope that Kulsoom suffers for this. She deserves to.'

'Why?' Mona asked. 'Because she's a woman? She was our friend, Shabeena.'

'Because it's wrong, Mona,' Alia replied. 'You don't cheat in a marriage, period. And anyone who does is no friend of ours. That person is a pariah.'

Mona stared at her friend, momentarily lost for words. If anyone in this room knew about her past, they would decimate her. Her thoughts travelled back to that text message, and she involuntarily shuddered. She would be the pariah.

'And cheating is even worse if you're a woman,' Shabeena added, fixing her scarf back on her head once more. 'At least with men, you know it will be over soon. They tire easily, but women? We have a duty towards society, towards our families.'

'Even when you're in an abusive marriage and want to get out?' Mona murmured.

'Yes.' Shabeena's face was devoid of any expression. 'Once you're married, you cannot leave. Only for your funeral should you leave your husband's home.'

'And what if you're not in love with your husband any more, Shabeena? What if your husband beats you and you happen to find love elsewhere?' Mona was breathless. She didn't know what had come over her, and why she couldn't let it go. 'Being married doesn't mean that you have to suffer forever.'

Humaira clapped her hands together. 'Dear me, you ladies certainly know how to make a conversation interesting. I had no idea how fun this tea would be, but I hope I haven't hit a nerve. Who knew you had such liberal views towards love and marriage, Mona? Colour me shocked.'

'I – I didn't mean it like that,' Mona began, realising only too late that she shouldn't have opened up to Humaira. 'I love my husband and have been married for over thirty years. I just meant—'

Humaira patted her hand. 'I know, darling. I know.' Drawing closer, she whispered, 'And although *I know your secret* now, you may rest assured that I will keep it.'

Mona froze, the coffee cup almost sliding off her finger.

I know your secret.

No, she thought. It couldn't possibly be Humaira. What did she even know of her life? Nothing! 'What do you mean?' she whispered back, meeting Humaira's eye. 'Are you threatening me, Humaira?'

Humaira laughed out loud, not bothering to cover her mouth with her hand. 'No need to be so dramatic, darling. I merely meant that I won't tell anyone in our society about the kind of liberal views you hold, although your reaction does beg the question: do you have something to hide?'

'I don't think I need to justify myself to anyone, least of all you.' Mona suddenly rose from her seat. Despite the large bay windows and the sun streaming in, she felt claustrophobic. She needed air. Turning to Humaira, she took a deep breath. 'You must forgive me. I'm just not feeling too well.'

Humaira's smile was as sweet as bitter honey. 'Of course. We're all on the same team, after all. It would be catastrophic if one of us were to become a laughing stock.'

As the discussion turned to the fashion week, Mona watched Humaira closely.

Could she be behind the message?

Chapter 5

Bilal

Bilal buttoned up his shirt, waiting for Dr Shafiq to assess the results of his ECG. Ever since his mother had breathed her last here, Bilal had hated this hospital. But his mother had always been a fan of Dr Shafiq, and if there was one thing Nighat was famous for, it was her stubbornness.

'Dr Shafiq is a good egg,' she used to say. 'He lets me eat pakoras and samosas. There's no other doctor on earth who would allow that. Promise me, you'll never let him go hungry, Bilal. He must be our family doctor forever.'

'You're such a softie, and that is why you're always sick, Amma,' Bilal would reply, to which he'd either get her infamous glare or a sharp poke in the stomach from her walking stick.

'If I am to die, I would like to die in Dr Shafiq's luxurious, muscular arms, Bilal. Would you deny your old mother this one last comfort?'

Looking at Dr Shafiq now, Bilal wondered if the man spent more time in the gym than in the hospital.

Why was Bilal even here?

Dr Shafiq stacked the papers on the desk and set them aside in a neat pile, proceeding to clasp his hands on the desk. 'It doesn't look good, Bilal.'

The sombre expression on his face made Bilal laugh. 'You're joking, right? I feel fine. Just some mild discomfort occasionally, but I'm fine.'

'Having regular angina attacks is not fine. That's your heart screaming for help. You may not survive another major heart attack. It's obvious that the angioplasty we did a few years ago is no longer working as well as it should be.' He looked Bilal straight in the eye. 'I think we need to start thinking about a heart bypass.'

Although fear pierced him, Bilal forced himself to remain calm. 'I'm sure things aren't so dire. My mother lived a very long life, and she had a heart condition.'

Dr Shafiq nodded. 'Yes, she loved fried food, but on the whole, she took care of herself. She didn't take any stress, and she lived a good life even if her knees prevented her from being very active.'

Bilal rubbed his palms together. They were clammy with sweat. He wasn't ready to have a bypass. He'd heard of people dying on the operating table. Arslan was only twelve, and completely unable to look after himself. And Mona? How could she possibly begin to unravel the business side of things if he was gone? Would she marry again? Would his son, Farhan, even come for his father's funeral? It had been over a year since he'd laid eyes on his firstborn.

Bilal took a deep breath. He was going soft in his old age. If this was the end, then this was the end, but he wasn't going to face the excruciating pain that came with a heart bypass. If he was to die, then he'd die on his own terms. 'Can't we do another angioplasty?' he asked.

Dr Shafiq pressed his lips together and shook his head. 'The time has come for a heart bypass, Bilal. I can play around with your medication to help while you come to a decision, but try to take it easy, please.'

'May I at least work, or is that out of bounds too?'

If Dr Shafiq had a sense of humour, he'd only revealed it to Nighat, because he just looked at Bilal blankly. 'Yes, of course you can work. I just advise you to remain cautious.' Tearing a piece of paper from his pad, he passed it over to Bilal. 'Here's your prescription. Just remember, you're not a young man any more.'

'*You're not a young man any more,*' Bilal mimicked Dr Shafiq as he slid into his brand-new Beemer. 'Go fuck yourself, gym bunny.'

That snowflake had no idea what he was talking about. Bilal was built like an ox, always had been. He'd weathered some tough times – hell, he'd survived his wife cheating on him and lived to tell the tale – and there was no way he was going to let a measly little angina attack come in the way. He even regretted that angioplasty because, apparently, it had done nothing for his heart. And besides, it wasn't as if he suffered from angina attacks daily – only when he was particularly stressed. He closed his eyes, trying to steady the beat of his heart. It was in a doctor's nature to get their patients to panic… that was how the leeches made their money. Shafiq had been telling Nighat that she was dying for as long as Bilal could remember, but she'd survived ten years into that initial diagnosis. But then, his mother had been made of stronger stuff.

'A diet of desi ghee, rich buffalo milk cream and parathas as a child is what is sustaining me,' she used to say. 'Not these godforsaken exotic vegetables and quinoa they eat today. Looks like cat vomit to me. And don't even get me started on the taste of avocado. I'd rather chew sawdust.'

Bilal smiled as his driver sped the car down Gulberg's Main Boulevard and towards Mall Road where he was due to attend a major business event. Even though they were officially into winter season, most of the trees were still green. Just as well since they added a bit of cheer to the otherwise cold and dull afternoon. God, he missed his mother more than anything. She would have kept Qudsia in line, and she would have let him know immediately if he was mistreating Mona. Maybe it was paranoia, but he couldn't help but notice how distant she had been with him lately. He'd tried to take things further the other night, but she'd put a stop to it immediately.

Like she didn't even care.

He had told her that he was going to see Dr Shafiq, but she hadn't even batted an eyelid, too busy scrolling through her phone. It was as if her entire life revolved around that thing. The thought made him angrier than it ought to, and anger was one of the things Dr Shafiq had advised against. What would it take for that woman to truly love him? Hadn't he done everything in his power to make her happy, to ensure that she didn't have to lift a finger for anything? He'd even allowed her to work, which wasn't something most people in his social circle were happy with.

'As annoying as she is, she's not your property, Bilal,' his mother used to say. 'The moment you realise that will be the moment your mind will finally find peace. Repeat after me: women are not chattel.'

'Women are not chattel,' he murmured to himself.

As if on cue, Mona's name and face lit up his screen.

The familiar anger reared its head. He swiped the screen of his phone and held it to his ear. 'Yes?'

There was a pause as Mona gauged his tone. 'Just wanted you to know that I won't be home for dinner. I'm going out with friends.'

His hand gripped the seat. 'Am I allowed to ask who these friends are or would that be too controlling of me?'

'Bilal, what is going on with you? If I tell you something, you get offended. If I don't, you still get offended. What am I supposed to do?'

You're supposed to be a loving wife. You're supposed to ask me how my hospital visit went. You're supposed to know that I could drop dead any second.

He said none of those things to her. Instead, he took a deep breath. 'I guess I'll see you before bed, then. I'm heading to Mall Road for a business meeting. I'll be late too.'

There was a brief pause followed by the rustle of papers. 'And how was the visit to the doctor? Anything new to report?'

'It wasn't a bloody cricket match I went to, that I'd have things to *report*.'

'Bilal, I just—'

'Perhaps you ought to focus more on your work, Mona. Obviously, you're the one running the house and not me. Bringing in the big bucks, aren't you? What am I to anyone, anyway? Dispensable, like I've always been.'

Mona sighed. 'You know I can't talk to you when you're like this. Why do you always have to make things so difficult?'

'Let's see, maybe because I am a difficult man?' Bilal made a show of tapping his chin, only to realise that she wasn't there to see it.

'Bilal, what did the doctor say?' There was the merest hint of panic in her voice. 'Is everything okay? Should I have accompanied you?'

So you do care, even if a little bit. However, he was still too angry to indulge her.

'A bit late for that now, isn't it? I've already been.'

Before she could reply, he ended the call, throwing the phone on the empty seat next to him. The satisfaction was short-lived, though, and he felt even worse than before. Why was he like this?

'Drive faster,' he barked at Naseem, his driver. 'What were you doing, eavesdropping on me? Why aren't we at the hotel yet?'

He could see the sweat erupting on Naseem's forehead in the rear-view mirror, which gave him a hint of satisfaction. 'Sahab, I – I promise I wasn't eavesdropping,' Naseem stammered. 'It's just that the traffic is very bad. We will be there in five minutes.'

'Focus on your job or I'll have your hide, Naseem. And stop eavesdropping.'

'*Ji*, Sahab.'

Although he tried to be a good husband to her, sometimes he couldn't be sure Mona even liked him, let alone loved him. She'd be looking at him as if she was looking through him. He knew that was just his anxiety over the doctor's verdict, but Bilal couldn't help but feel insecure. As the car screeched to a halt in front of the hotel entrance and he walked towards the exclusive bar on the sixth floor, hidden from prying eyes, some of the tension in his shoulders eased. Here, alcohol flowed freely, and there was plenty of finger food available too. Bilal's stomach rumbled, and he almost reached for a drink before remembering the doctor's dire warnings.

'No alcohol for you, Bilal. Definitely no beer.'

Screw you, he thought, picking up a can of beer and taking a gulp. He immediately felt better. All around him, wealthy men were mingling, most of them stuffing their faces with food in the process. Pigs, all of them.

Out of the melee, Faheem burst forth with his arms outstretched. 'Bilal, my boy. Thank you for making it here today.'

There weren't a lot of people left alive to call him 'boy', but Faheem refused to die. He'd outlive them all. Bilal looked around, hoping to catch the eye of someone else – anyone else. With his rotund stomach, rancid breath and wandering hands, Faheem gave him the creeps. And sure enough, as they hugged, Faheem's hands clutched his bottom, giving it a squeeze.

'Gaining weight in your old age, aren't you, friend?'

Crushed against his stomach and surprisingly strong arms, Bilal was unable to breathe for a moment. 'I could say the same for you, friend,' he managed to wheeze.

With a final pat on his ass, Faheem let him go. 'Always been straight as an arrow, Bilal, much to my chagrin.'

Bilal breathed in from his mouth, trying not to choke on the garlicky aroma of Faheem's breath. 'Looks like quite a gathering of businessmen you've got here.'

Faheem dipped his head. 'One must do what one can in times of recession. Pakistan is suffering and if I can't use my considerable resources to help my fellow businessmen, then what good am I?'

'And how exactly is this party helping Pakistan? What are we doing here?'

'Mingling! Helping each other out.'

Bilal raised an eyebrow. 'You could help me out by investing in my latest real estate project.'

Faheem's eyes grew dreamy. 'Ah, but what do I get in return for that considerable investment? That, my dear friend, is the million-dollar question.' He threw his head back to guffaw, before pulling in a young man who was passing by. 'You know I only jest, friend. Besides, have you met Basharat? He's the son of our dear departed Elahi Sahab.' Basharat nodded at Bilal but winced as Faheem slapped his bottom as well. 'He's learning the ropes now that his daddy is gone, aren't you, Basharat?'

Basharat gave a meek nod. 'It's been over a decade since Daddy passed away, but naturally, we are very grateful for your support, Faheem Sahab.'

How the mighty have fallen, Bilal thought. There was a time when Elahi commanded the respect of everyone in the city, people bowing and scraping just to spend one minute in his presence. And here was his son, getting humiliated by a creep like Faheem who wasn't even old money.

Faheem wasn't going to invest in his project, not unless he got something in return. And that was a line Bilal was never going to cross. He didn't need to.

As if reading his thoughts, Faheem winked. 'You have nothing to fear from an old man like myself,' he said. 'My needs are more than adequately met by others.' His arms tightened around Basharat's waist. 'I just wanted you to be a part of my little club, but no matter. We'll talk about that investment soon.'

'Faheem, I—'

'I say, have you heard of Nageena?'

Bilal blinked. 'Is that code for something?'

'Of course not, my dear boy. Don't tell me you don't know Nageena, only the most popular female companion of Lahore.'

'Companion?'

Faheem slapped a palm against his forehead. 'Companion. Courtesan. Whore. Must I spell it out?'

Bilal looked away, the noise in the hall suddenly getting overwhelming. His throat was parched. 'I'm not into that stuff any more, Faheem. As you very well know.'

'There are women in bed, and then there's Nageena in bed,' Faheem whispered, his belly bouncing with excitement as he skipped once. 'The moves she knows will have even an eighty-year-old standing at attention.'

'Do you have first-hand experience, then, being an eighty-year-old yourself?'

'Seventy-eight. There's a difference. And yes, I have. You know I swing every which way.' He glanced at stone-faced Basharat. 'Isn't that right, Bash?'

The young man swallowed but gave a tight nod.

Bilal felt sorry for him. He felt sorry for himself. What had Lahore turned into? Had he been like this in the past as well, so lecherous and heartless?

Once Faheem had wandered off to accost someone else in the crowd, Bilal stepped closer to Basharat. 'Does he force himself on you?'

Basharat's cheeks turned pink as he shook his head. 'Faheem Sahab has been very gracious ever since my father passed away. He brought us back from the brink. He paid for my mother's treatment in the United States.' He downed the drink he was holding in one gulp, his eyes tearing up. 'Spending some time with him is a small price to pay for his kindness.'

Basharat couldn't have been more than thirty. Younger than his boy, Farhan. Bilal wanted to reach out and hug him only to reassure him that the world wasn't so bad. But if he did that, he'd be telling a lie. The world was worse... much worse.

'Come to my office on Monday, Basharat,' he said. 'There's a business proposal I'd like to discuss with you.'

Basharat's cheeks were still a bit pink when he replied, 'That's very kind, sir, but as you know, we supply steel exclusively to Faheem Enterprises.'

Bilal waved a hand at Faheem's retreating figure. 'I'll take care of Faheem. You don't have to worry about him. From now on, you'll be supplying steel to my company as well.'

'And does this business come with certain conditions?'

Bilal's eyes widened. 'God, no. Nothing like that. Your father was a shrewd businessman and a good colleague. I'm just doing what I can for his family.' He patted him on the head. 'Give my best to your mother. Tell her that my wife, Mona, often asks about her.'

'Yes, sir. Thank you, sir.' Before Basharat turned away, Bilal saw him rubbing his eyes.

He pulled him back and whispered in his ear, 'And the next time you see that fat bastard alone, give him an *accidental* kick in the balls. That should put those ancient testicles to eternal rest. Creep.'

After that, Bilal just didn't feel like mingling any more. Everywhere he looked, he saw vultures, desperation etched on their features as they talked business and pleasure as if they went hand in hand. As he walked out of the hotel, he couldn't help but marvel at life's cruelty. To see the son of a mighty businessman selling himself to disgusting old men for money had shaken him to his core, and he had already been on edge after the visit to the doctor. It also occurred to him that he had been unnecessarily short with Mona. If he should die, shouldn't he at least be on good terms with his wife? She was only trying to look out for him. At least, that's what he told himself. How could anyone ever be sure with Mona? *Damn it*, he thought. Life was hard enough already for him to be adding to his woes by not talking to his wife. He ought to apologise like a grown-up and take her out for a date night. She deserved that much. Despite what Qudsia said, Mona did work very hard, and deep down, Bilal admired her for it. Never in a million years had he thought that his wife would work and that he'd be okay with it.

Welcome to the twenty-first century, Bilal, he thought with a wry smile as he pulled out the phone from his pocket. He'd take her to the fancy new Italian place in Defence Phase 6, a place that made you feel like you were in Dubai. However, before he could dial her number, the phone slipped from his grasp and skidded across the marble floor, finally coming to a stop against a pair of glittering purple heels.

A woman.

'Fuck!' he said aloud. That was the latest iPhone, a gift from Mona from her own salary. She'd never forgive him for smashing it so soon after she'd bought it for him.

The woman knelt to pick up the phone, her face obscured by cascades of ash-blonde hair, the slit in her dress showing legs that any man would die for. Bilal's breath caught as the mystery woman rose and shifted the hair out of her face. Her sequinned lilac dress hugged her in all the right places, and when their eyes met, it was obvious that she was beautiful, and she knew it.

With a small smile, she drew nearer, Bilal acutely aware that his armpits had started sweating. He tried to look away, but the woman had him rooted to the spot. All he could do was stand there helplessly as she sashayed closer in a perfect catwalk.

'You dropped your phone, sir.'

Bilal blinked as she offered him his phone back, and just like that, the spell broke. Life seemed to return to his legs. 'Thank you, miss.'

He didn't want to know her name. As a matter of fact, he didn't want to have anything to do with this woman. She was trouble. And yet, when he took the phone from her, and their fingers brushed, a shiver went through him.

A small smile still played on her face. 'You didn't even ask for my name. I saved your phone for you.'

Bilal gulped. 'And your name is?'

The woman laughed, a network of lines breaking around her eyes. She wasn't as young as he'd presumed. Probably mid-thirties. Maybe older. 'I have to say that I am a bit offended. Anyone who is someone knows me.'

He didn't like her attitude. Shoving the phone deep in his pocket again, he patted down his suit, hoping nothing else would fall off. 'Well, if you would excuse me, I've got to get home to my wife.'

She licked her lips. 'How quaint. I love it when husbands are so in *love* with their wives.' She pronounced the word as if it was a crime. 'They're the most fun to break.'

'Bibi, I have been married for over thirty years, and I've seen much more of this world than you can imagine, so maybe think before patronising me again.'

She laughed, covering her mouth with a bejewelled hand. 'And he's got a temper too. You must be Bilal.'

Bilal narrowed his eyes. 'How do you know my name?'

'Lahore is a small place, Bilal Sahab. Word gets around.'

'Lahore has a population of fifteen million people.'

'Still a small place.' She extended a hand towards him. 'Nageena. A pleasure to meet you.'

Chapter 6

Fakhar

His hand was slick with the blood of the animal he'd just slaughtered. He wiped it on his shalwar and grimaced. Bloodstains never came out in the wash, but luckily for him, he was going to burn the clothes he was wearing.

'Leave nothing behind for them to find.'

That was the mantra they'd been taught by Sahab ji. Things had got tough lately, and it was imperative that they covered their tracks well. They were always on the run, going from place to place to maintain secrecy. This small shack was where they operated from these days, but it was only a matter of time before they had to move from here as well. The authorities had come down hard against Sahab ji after all the high-profile kidnappings recently and, as Sahab ji's right-hand man, Fakhar had to be extra careful. He still didn't know where all the money went.

Maybe Sahab ji is going to use it all to buy us a new country, *Fakhar thought with a chuckle, but from what he knew, there was a lot of bribery involved as there was no way otherwise that Sahab ji could get away with so much.*

The room smelled of blood and shit. His eye caught the bucket in the corner that was now filled to the brim with muck, steam rising from it and dissolving in the frigid air. The bitch must have pissed in it moments ago.

Fakhar wrinkled his nose. 'Disgusting little gushti. Look at all the mess you've made. For shame. Is your father going to come and clean it for us?' He laughed. 'Oh wait, he's not coming, is he?'

'Please.'

He looked down at the whimpering mess of a woman in front of him. Her designer outfit was in tatters. Gucci, that was the brand she wore. Fakhar knew because he liked to follow these brands on the internet, not that anyone here knew about it. They'd label him as a West sympathiser in an instant and probably lock him up to piss and shit in a bucket as well. He shuddered.

That would not *be his fate.*

Like a pack of rabid wild dogs, some of the boys had ripped her jacket open earlier to help themselves to the bounty within, but Fakhar had pulled them back.

'Don't you dare rape her!' he'd hissed. 'Not everything is a free-for-all. We might still get a ransom for her, so she must remain untouched. Do you think her family will thank you bastards for harming her?'

'Sahab ji uses them,' one of them said, a boy of fifteen. 'He uses them and when he's done, they're in no fit state for anything. Utterly useless.'

'What's your name?' Fakhar asked.

The boy drew up his chin. 'Shabbir.'

Desire ran through him like hot blood as he watched the boy's defiance. Fakhar would enjoy teaching this boy a lesson. He would whip that defiant mind into submission, and then he'd subject him to the biggest insult of all. He shivered, already anticipating the things he'd do to him, but for now, the boy needed to be put in his place.

Fakhar gave him a backhanded slap, hard enough to draw blood.

Shabbir squealed like a piglet.

'Shut up. It's Sahab ji who feeds your worthless mouth, and you have the nerve to question his behaviour? He has never touched anyone. Now get out of here, or I'll have your hide.'

The woman brought her palms together in silent gratitude, and Fakhar smiled back at her.

'You're safe here, Bibi,' he whispered, for now... too bad about the Gucci jacket he couldn't save.

What she didn't know was that in case nobody came for her or a deal wasn't struck, she'd just be sold to the highest bidder, but not before he'd had some fun with her.

And since a deal hadn't been struck in the time frame provided, it was time to have that fun now. He may have liked designer brands, but Fakhar abhorred seeing them on Pakistani women. To be brazen enough to show the female body like that was basically inviting punishment. The woman held the rags close to her chest now to hide her exposed breasts, her eyes wild with terror as Fakhar advanced on her. He almost giggled when he caught a flash of her pink bra. But then she opened her mouth and screamed.

For a moment, Fakhar was afraid that her wails would catch the attention of Sahab ji. He didn't like unnecessary torture. In fact, he despised it and if he knew of all the crimes Fakhar had committed in his name... well, Fakhar chose not to think about the repercussions. But then he remembered that Sahab ji wasn't even here, so there was nobody to hear this woman's screams, and besides, what Sahab ji didn't know couldn't hurt him. He left everything to Fakhar when he went gallivanting into the city, never suspecting what happened behind his back because, by the time he returned to check on things, the hostages had either been dispatched to the next highest bidder or returned to their families. Fakhar had tried to remain trustworthy for the most part, but when it came to matters of the flesh, he was powerless. And it wasn't like Sahab ji was a saint himself. He was the one who abducted these rich people, so whether they were taken advantage of was beside the point. 'Don't worry,' he cooed, kneeling in front of the woman. 'I won't hurt you. If you relax, you might even enjoy it. I've been known to be gentle with pampered women.'

Her face was streaked with dirt from being trapped in the room for days, and she smelled rank, but her eyes shone in the semi-darkness and what beautiful eyes they were. Fakhar closed his eyes and groaned, willing himself not to climax then and there.

She scrambled back until she hit the cemented wall – it was a small room, after all. Shaking her head, she began crying. 'Please don't. My family will pay the money.'

Fakhar shook his head too, mirroring her. 'We gave them five days, but they didn't cough up a single rupee, and now the deadline has passed. Sahab ji is very particular about his deadlines.'

'It takes time to get everything organised. Nobody has so much cash sitting around. If you wait a few more days, they will pay you. Please don't hurt me.'

Fakhar smiled. 'Someone else has paid us more for you, and soon you'll be their problem.' He licked his lips. 'I will take you to them myself once we've had a little fun.'

Those beautiful eyes widened with horror. 'You've sold me?' She clapped her hands to her mouth. 'Don't you have a mother or sister? How could you do this to a woman?'

She was openly weeping now, which made him wince, and on top of that, she had mentioned his mother, which made Fakhar's head spin. He didn't like to hear the sound of weeping – it reminded him of his childhood when his father would beat his mother to within an inch of her life, after which he would advance on Fakhar, walking stick in hand, his eyes wild and streaked with red.

Despicable old cripple.

He turned his attention back on the woman. 'It's either me or those wild dogs who were here earlier. You don't want them tearing you limb from limb. They won't be so gentle, I can tell you that.' She flinched, and that's when he went in for the kill. 'There now, Bibi. Everything will be fine. Just let Fakhar do his thing, and I promise you, everything will be fine.'

Her screams when he began were like music to his ears.

Chapter 7

Mona

Mona held the phone a foot away from her ear as Meera continued shouting. 'I can't believe that the bastard has been cheating on me. And with someone much older than him. I swear I will kill Zarrar.'

It must be one of the models due to walk in the fashion week, Mona figured. Spending the kind of time they did together, it wasn't uncommon for models to hook up with each other occasionally. 'You're just making a big deal out of it, Meera,' she said. 'You never told him you two were exclusive. Or did you?'

'Of course we were exclusive. Do you think I'd share my prize with someone else?'

Mona closed her eyes. 'He's a person, Meera. He's not your plaything. You can't say this sort of stuff. Hell, you can't even think it. It's wrong.' She had a headache setting in, and with Qudsia sitting in the corner, knitting, her ears trained on their conversation, Mona knew she had to cut this short. She stood up and walked towards the window, looking out at their sprawling lawn, illuminated at night with dozens of lights. In the eyes of most people in Lahore, they were a privileged family with regular holidays abroad, an army of servants and not a care in the world for bills. It was all true. Mona acknowledged her privilege, but that didn't mean that she didn't have problems. Her thoughts flitted to that text message, but she pushed it out of her mind. There had been no more messages since that day, and she was beginning to wonder if it had all just been a mix-up.

In any case, she had more pressing matters to deal with. Bilal still hadn't returned despite saying he'd be back in time for bed. Arslan had gone to bed hours ago.

'That's not the point,' Meera cried, reminding Mona that she was still on the line. 'The point is that he cheated on me and there is no way I am going to allow him or that slut to walk the ramp now.'

If Zarrar and his girlfriend went public with the kind of discrimination Meera was planning, she would be dead meat on social media. 'Listen, take a breath. Why don't you sleep on it, and we'll revisit this when I'm in the office tomorrow?'

'I want him to drop dead, Mona. I want to slice off his prick. I want to drink his blood.'

'You need a stiff drink, my friend, and an early night. Early for you, at least.'

'I can't believe he would cheat on me with someone who is not that much younger than I am. I would have expected him to at least go for a girl.'

Mona glanced at Qudsia before speaking. 'God, you're so ageist, but I have to say this is interesting. Who is this woman?'

'Not a woman. Call her a cougar.'

'I thought you were a cougar.'

Meera laughed through her sobs. 'Mona, this is not the time for jokes.'

69

'Made you laugh, though, didn't I? Also, you haven't made it to the age of fifty-three only to fall to pieces over someone like Zarrar.'

Meera blew her nose. 'Forty. Officially, I'm not a day over forty.'

As Mona caught the headlights of Bilal's Beemer enter the gates, she exhaled. He was back. 'Listen, I've got to go now. Bilal is here, but what did you say the name of that model was who is going out with Zarrar?'

'Screwing Zarrar, you mean? Yeah, her name is Nageena. A bitch if there ever was one.'

Nageena, she thought as she pressed the red button to end the call. *What a strange name!* Although her job was mostly to look after the PR side of things, she did keep track of the models that came and went through the agency. She'd never heard of anyone called Nageena.

Bilal's entry immediately cut that line of thought because, from the way he staggered, it was obvious that he was drunk. Qudsia stood up, clapping a hand to her mouth. '*Astagfirullah*. Has it come to this now? Is this a house for drunkards and whores?'

Mona ended the call and rushed to her husband, putting an arm around his waist. He reeked of alcohol. 'Bilal, where have you been?' she whispered, breathing through her mouth. 'You are absolutely wasted.'

'Shut up, woman,' he slurred, pushing her away. 'I don't need your fake concern. I don't need anyone's concern.'

Qudsia held the edge of her dupatta to her nose. 'I can smell the spirits from here. Oh, if my mother was alive, what would she say?'

'Your mother enjoyed the occasional drink herself, Qudsia,' Mona replied, enjoying the look of horror on her sister-in-law's face.

'She did not.'

'Red wine all the way for her.'

'You're a liar, Mona. Maligning the good name of my dead mother. How dare you?'

'I think I'm going to be sick,' Bilal murmured. 'I must have downed an entire bottle of whisky.'

'*Uff tauba*, what a den of sin this house has become,' Qudsia cried. Turning to Mona, she added, 'Are you happy now? You got what you wanted. If you had even tried to behave like a wife, he wouldn't be in this state. Leaving his elderly sister to look after him while you go prancing God knows where with that *gushti*, is it any surprise it has come to this?'

'If you haven't noticed, I've been home for ages,' Mona hissed. 'Why don't you go to bed, Qudsia? It's not like you're helping.'

Qudsia shrugged, unpinning her hijab. 'I'll leave, but I am warning you, Mona. You are failing in your duty as a wife, and there will come a time when you will regret it.' With her hair uncovered, she suddenly looked fragile, even though she wasn't. Qudsia was always ready to breathe fire. She ran her fingers through her sparse grey hair and stalked off without another word.

'What's got into you?' Mona whispered to Bilal, holding on to his shirt and trying not to choke on the stench of spirits. It was strange that something she hadn't been able to live without years ago nauseated her today. 'Must you make a scene, Bilal? Are you a child?'

Bilal looked at her, then. There were bags under his bloodshot eyes, and his white stubble was overgrown. He looked like an old man.

Mona swallowed the lump in her throat. 'Oh, Bilal.'

'Where were you when I needed you today? You never have time for me.'

'I told you I was at work, but I got home earlier than I had thought. The dinner plan with my friends was cancelled. I was hoping we could have dinner together despite the appalling way you behaved with me over the phone.'

Bilal snorted, dragging his feet towards the staircase. 'Give me a break. When was the last time we had dinner together, just the two of us? You know what the funny part is? I was planning to take you out to that Italian place in Defence to make up for my behaviour earlier.'

'Then, why didn't you just ask?'

Bilal didn't push her away as she clung to him. She counted that as a small victory.

'Because I knew you'd say no. Your answer to everything these days is a resounding no. Someday soon, when I die and people ask you if you'd like to see my face one last time, you'll still say no.'

'Enough with the theatrics. You're drunk, and tomorrow morning, you'll be so embarrassed for speaking to me like this.'

'You're the one who should be embarrassed, Mona.'

'Excuse me?'

Bilal's expression grew hard, savage even. He was beginning to look more and more like the man she'd known for decades and not the man he'd been since Ali.

Please don't say anything you'll end up regretting, she thought, but it was obvious that Bilal was on a collision course.

'Maybe you'll get a toy boy to play with after I'm gone or maybe...'

Mona stopped breathing. 'Go on, spit it out. Or maybe what?'

Bilal shook his head, running a hand over his face. 'Forget it, I'm just wasted.'

'Maybe what, Bilal?'

'Given how you're always absent, maybe you already have one. A nice strong man to keep you satisfied, eh? If I remember correctly, you're good at that sort of thing.'

His words knocked the breath out of her. After all those declarations of love, was this what he really thought of her? Mona pushed him away with all her might, and he hit the wall laughing. 'You disgust me. How dare you, Bilal? After all these years, how bloody dare you?' She blinked rapidly so that he wouldn't see the tears. More than anger, it was the dismay that hit her. 'I think I'll sleep in the guest room tonight. I can't even look at you.'

Bilal gave her a mock bow. 'By all means, my dear. That's what you do best. You just up and leave when things get the least bit inconvenient for you.'

The smirk on his face made her say the one thing she knew would hurt him. 'Thank your lucky stars your son is asleep. If he were to see you like this, he'd be so disappointed to know that his father is a mere shadow of the man he thinks he is.'

She was pleased to see his face crumple before she slammed the door of the guest room shut.

—

It had been a few days since that drunk incident with Bilal, and they hadn't spoken since, Mona living out of the guest room and spending as much time as she could at the office. Surprisingly, even Qudsia had kept her distance, perhaps sensing the tension in the house. However, as Mona sat at the dressing table, getting ready for another stressful day at the office, she heard the sound of Qudsia's flat heels outside. *Here we go again*, she thought, grunting in assent when her sister-in-law asked for permission to come in.

'I know how busy you are with the fashion week today,' Qudsia said, as she stepped inside, holding her hands behind her back. She'd ditched the hijab today and just had her head covered with a dupatta. 'I can look after Arslan for you. Perhaps we can go watch a movie together. I'll ask Aimen too.'

'She's supposed to come for the fashion week,' Mona snapped. 'You really don't need to look after Arslan either, Qudsia. Shugufta can attend to him.'

Qudsia was silent as she played with the hem of her dupatta. 'To be fair, it was Bilal's fault the other night. He was way out of line. To come home so drunk and take it out on his wife was uncalled for.'

'You seemed pretty convinced it was my fault,' Mona replied, applying some eyeliner. 'Everything seems to be my fault around here.'

There was another pause. Mona could see her in the mirror as Qudsia's eyes flitted around. 'Well, I am sorry,' Qudsia said finally. 'I didn't know you'd end up sleeping in separate rooms as a result. I don't like it.'

'That's not your fault, Qudsia,' Mona whispered to herself.

'What was that?'

Mona closed her eyes as she rummaged inside her emergency make-up bag for her blush. Her proper make-up was all in the other bedroom where Bilal was still snoring. 'I said that I forgive you,' she said. 'You don't need to worry about us.'

Qudsia looked close to tears. 'Will you kiss and make up?'

Despite herself, Mona smiled at the expression. 'Wherever did you hear that from?'

'Aimen told me it's how fashionable people talk,' Qudsia murmured. 'I just want there to be peace in this house. Bilal is not as young as he used to be. He really ought to take better care of himself. You ought to—'

And they were back to square one. Mona sighed and turned around. 'Won't you come for the opening night, Qudsia?'

Qudsia shook her head. 'Den of sin. I wouldn't be caught dead in a place like that. I'm sorry, I know it's your work and that most of Lahore's elite love this sort of thing, but it's just not for me. I'd rather stay at home and pray. For you and Bilal.'

Apparently, theatrics ran in the family. Nighat had been like that, and so were Bilal and Qudsia. Before leaving the room, Mona paused and gave Qudsia a quick kiss on the cheek. 'Everything will be fine. You should focus on your own health too. You're much older than us.'

Her eyes widened. 'Is that an insult?'

Mona sighed. 'Just concern, Qudsia. I'll see you tomorrow, I suppose, as it will be a late night.'

She didn't wait for Qudsia's response, hurrying out of the house and into her waiting car. Instead of sliding in the back seat, she snatched the keys from Bashir and took to the driving seat. If Bashir was surprised, he had the good sense to keep it to himself.

As she drove down the Kalma Underpass, Mona held on tight to the steering wheel. Keeping busy was the only way she could stop thinking about what Bilal had said.

You're good at that sort of thing.

It wasn't the words, but the way he had said them, his voice full of contempt, as if he hated her. All these years and he still hated her. That more than anything broke her heart. It had been three days since they'd exchanged a word, and what had surprised her the most was that, this time, he hadn't reached out to ask for forgiveness.

What is going on with you, Bilal? What happened to being in love?

She tried not to ponder on Bilal's erratic behaviour as she turned into Johar Town where the fashion week was taking place. They had organised a glittering opening ceremony in a fancy hotel that was to be attended by the entire elite society of Lahore, and people had even flown in from Karachi and Islamabad to be present. Mona had been working overtime at the office, confirming attendance with everyone's secretaries, sending out invitation baskets and giveaway bags, mostly keeping her cool except for that moment yesterday when she had snapped at a politician's assistant.

'Madam Shumaila hates to cause inconvenience,' the assistant had said, 'but you said that the chocolates would be Godiva, and they're not. They're just regular chocolates you can get from anywhere.'

'Maybe it's because Godiva is proving difficult to import,' Mona had replied in a measured tone. 'I assure you that the chocolates you received cost just as much.'

'But they're not Godiva,' she had cried, not clocking the danger in Mona's voice. 'Madam was very particular about it. She only ever nibbles on Godiva.'

'I'm sure Madam can make do with the chocolates we've sent. They're delicious.'

'She really can't. We can only accept—'

'Godiva,' Mona had finished for her. 'And since she's been so brutally robbed of Godiva, maybe she can stick these ones up where the sun doesn't shine.'

It still embarrassed Mona when she thought of the silence that had ensued before the assistant put the phone down. Of course, Meera then had to fly in the Godiva chocolates from Karachi just to salvage the situation. Only the best for Madam Shumaila, the politician from some backwater town of Punjab, but seeing her pearls and statement handbags, you'd think she was from Lahore or Karachi.

Mona hated blaming menopause for the outburst, but she couldn't exactly tell Meera why she was on edge, not when there was a fashion week to get through and Meera's own problems with Zarrar. As if on cue, Meera threw her arms around Mona as soon as she arrived at the hotel.

'I am so glad that you're here, Mona. Only you can save me from myself.' Her face was tear-streaked, the kohl smudged everywhere. 'God help me, I just proposed to Zarrar.' A whimper escaped her. 'And he said no.'

'Oh, Meera.'

'I am doomed,' Meera cried. 'I will die alone, and on my gravestone, it will say *Here rests Meera, who gobbled up four husbands and didn't even live to tell the tale.*'

Mona looked at the event organisers rushing around, erecting stages and flower arrangements. It was too loud for them to be overheard, but she still dropped her voice. 'Listen, you need to push the thought of Zarrar from your mind. It's the opening night of the fashion week. Are you really going to let someone like him eclipse something we've been working on all year?' She took a hold of Meera's shoulders, realising with a pang that they were all bones. 'Meera, get a grip. Look around you, this is your night. Our night. The cream of the city is coming, and we can't have you falling to pieces. This is your time to shine.'

'Only if you're with me,' she whispered.

'Always,' Mona replied, hugging her. As they broke apart, Mona tried not to let her tears show. They really had come a long way since their Kinnaird College days. In many ways, Meera had been her constant over the past decade, the only shoulder she could cry on when she was mourning Ali. She couldn't imagine a world without her.

Meera wiped her tears away with the back of her hand. 'Did you know that Nageena will also be at the opening night?'

'Nageena?'

'The horrible woman Zarrar is seeing. She's what everyone is talking about these days. She'll be here as someone's plus-one, so there's nothing I can do to stop her from entering the premises. I just hope she isn't contracted by some designer to walk the ramp in the coming days.'

'I don't even know what she looks like,' Mona murmured.

'Just think expensive plastic surgery gone wrong, but the men love her. Word on the street is that she can charge a million rupees for a night. A night that doesn't even include sex. And here she is, seducing my poor Zarrar.' Meera ran her fingers through her hair and arranged it in a messy bun. 'I hope she gets kidnapped by one of those gangs. That would show her.'

'That's not a nice thing to say, Meera. Besides, Lahore is pretty safe now.'

Shrugging, Meera turned away, heading towards the dressing rooms. 'I don't care. And Lahore isn't as safe as you think. These ransom gangs are always on the prowl.

We got rid of terrorism only to be saddled with this new terror.'

Mona watched her friend leave, the familiar fear she'd felt all those years ago returning. Everyone had heard of the kidnappings, of course. In a matter of months, things had got out of hand, with these gangs picking up people without warning and whisking them out of the city and to areas unknown. Rumour was that most of them ended up in the western parts of Pakistan, after which the demands for ransom commenced, most of the victims being sold multiple times to rival gangs before their families could even be notified. She shuddered, looking up in silent thanks that Bilal had the money and resources to hire the best security guards to look after them.

But as the threat of terrorism had abated, they'd all grown lax, often heading out of the house with just a driver. Mona checked her phone, but apart from a few messages in group chats, there was nothing.

Nothing from Bilal.

Then, so be it. She threw the phone in her handbag and followed Meera into the dressing rooms where they had to take a final look at the models and schedules before getting ready themselves.

—

Hours later, and the dressing rooms were still in a state of disarray. Most of the supermodels from Karachi were resting upstairs in their rooms, their clothes hanging uselessly on the racks. Each outfit cost a whopping two million rupees, and Mona was afraid that in spite of the security they'd hired, someone would end up stealing them. Thankfully, the jewellery designers had sent their own security staff with the decadent sets. Mona didn't even want to think how much those things cost. If those ransom gangs knew about the kind of treasure the fashion week was harbouring, they'd ditch extorting the business people in an instant and focus their efforts here.

An involuntary shudder went through her.

Meera was still at the makeshift salon getting ready, but Mona had put on a sequinned black dress with a long trail. It did a good job of accentuating her trim upper waist while hiding the fat she had accumulated in her lower abdomen over the years. Looking at herself in the mirror, she thought she looked pretty good.

'Ma'am, are you sure you're not walking the ramp?'

The effect was immediate. Her cheeks coloured as she turned around to see who had addressed her. Zarrar stood smiling at her, a peculiar expression on his face like he was seeing her for the first time.

She turned her attention back to the full-length mirror. 'What are you doing here, Zarrar? Shouldn't you be getting ready for the show?'

'It's full of silly butterflies who think this fashion week is going to change their lives.'

'Isn't that why you're here?'

She could see him smirking in the mirror. 'No, I'm not here for that. My father has shitloads of money already. I'm just here to make friends.' He took a few steps towards her. 'If I may be so bold, ma'am, you're looking very beautiful tonight. I never realised.'

'That I am beautiful? Oh, my bad luck!' Mona all but rolled her eyes. 'Does Meera know you're here?' She turned to give him a wry smile. 'Yes, I know about you two. And I also know you're seeing someone else, so please don't waste your time with me.' Holding up her ring finger, she added, 'I am married.'

Zarrar smirked. 'Since when has that stopped anyone?'

Mona froze. 'What makes you say that?'

He shrugged. 'Plenty of married women out there looking for a quickie. Men like me are more than happy to comply.'

What a sleazeball, she thought. What did Meera ever see in him? 'Is that what you tell every woman you meet?'

Zarrar tilted his head, running a finger down his sharp jawline. 'I can tell you're a bit of a lost cause, but I'll have you know that I've charmed women who charge for their services to sleep with me for free... if you get my drift?'

She did know. He was talking about Nageena. All of a sudden, Mona felt sick. This was exactly why she kept herself away from this part of the modelling world. It sickened her that everything was thought to be on sale. Making a mental note to abstain from these events in future, she proceeded to leave the room, pausing only for a moment to say, 'Stop being a creep, Zarrar. You're the reason why people are so wary of considering modelling as a profession. Grow the hell up.'

The banquet halls had been divided into five main stages where simultaneous fashion shows were being held. Of course, the largest stage was devoted to Haque's show, who was also headlining the opening night. Most of the people were coming in to see his latest bridal collection, something he deliberately kept under wraps until the day of the fashion week. Chequebooks would be out tonight, and people wouldn't hesitate to splurge on outfits that cost as much as a small house in Lahore. Mona's wedding ring caught on one of the sequins in her dress, which made her glance down and look at it. Really look at it. Was it a good idea to wear such a thing in Lahore, where even the merest hint of skin set tongues wagging? Since hitting fifty, she'd stopped wearing sleeveless out of fear of judgement but also because she was too vain. Her arms weren't how they used to be, and she didn't want anyone noticing the change. However, today she'd let Meera goad her into wearing not just a sleeveless dress but one with a halter top. She looked back in the mirror to see if the skin had folded over the back of the dress, but it was all good.

In soft lighting, she could be mistaken for someone in her early thirties. The thought made her smile and improved her mood enough to be able to face the sudden onslaught of guests. The photographers arrived first with their collection of cameras, old and new, which they set up across the red carpet. They were followed by some of the less popular influencers, who spent a lot of time making videos of the place, posting them with the designated hashtag before the big influencers arrived and stole their thunder.

The dresses they wore had been provided by various participating designers who had given away dresses in exchange for exposure, and judging by the smiles on their faces, Mona was sure that the influencers had received gift vouchers too. Thankfully, dealing with influencers wasn't her responsibility, and given the horror stories she'd heard about some of them, Mona was keen to keep it that way.

Before long, other guests started arriving too, the photographers going haywire for an influencer who had assumed the status of a minor celebrity. Mona watched with interest how the girl posed in front of the camera, blowing kisses in their direction, but as soon as she turned away, there was a scowl on her face.

'I need more gift vouchers if I am to get through this event,' she barked into her phone as she walked by. 'Meera Siddiqui is loaded. Get more money out of her, or I won't post a single story on my Instagram.'

Mona didn't have time to ponder over these words because, at that moment, someone waved at her.

Her heart fell as Humaira walked up to her in an all-black Hervé Léger bandage dress that reached just above her knees. The fact that she'd walked through the hotel lobby in this dress in a place like Lahore was admirable in itself. Women had been killed for less.

'You look amazing, Humaira. Thank you for coming,' Mona began, extending a hand, knowing there would be a clever retort from her.

Spreading her arms, Humaira went in for a hug. 'Oh, darling, so do you. Thank you for inviting me.' Tugging at the skin on Mona's back, she added, 'Is that a back boob? Isn't this dress a bit too fitted for a woman of your age and figure?'

Here we go again, Mona thought, but she assumed a neutral expression as they parted. Humaira was here on her invitation, and it wouldn't do to insult her guests. 'Careful, Humaira, you wouldn't want to be branded as ageist.'

They laughed, but Humaira's expression hardened. 'Honey, you mustn't put words in my mouth. It's not about being ageist, it's just a matter of wearing what looks good on you, and, believe me, this just doesn't look that great. And showing those arms? A strict no-no.'

Mona twirled around. 'I've been told I look great.'

A bemused expression came over Humaira's face. 'By whom? The hundred-year-old fossils that you seem to have invited to this plush event? Did you run out of people that you had to resort to inviting the riff-raff?'

'The riff-raff you're referring to are billionaires.'

'But not old money. They don't have class. But if you're happy about wearing these sorts of dresses, then good for you.'

Mona arched an eyebrow. 'Didn't you say only days ago that fifty was the new thirty?'

Before Humaira could reply, someone said, 'I think you look fabulous, my dear.'

That was a voice Mona hadn't heard in a while. She whipped around to find Shahida Elahi, her erstwhile nemesis, wrapped in a black Banarasi saree, smiling at her. Meera must have been very persuasive because Shahida hadn't been known to venture out of her house since the death of her husband and the downfall of their significant empire. From what Bilal had told her, Shahida's son was struggling to hold the business together. However badly she'd treated Mona in the past, it *was* all in the past now.

Mona squared her shoulders and air-kissed Shahida, reaching out to take her hand as well. 'It is very nice to see you after all this time, Shahida.'

Instead of gaining weight like doctors had advised her years ago, Shahida seemed to have lost some more. Her face was all sharp angles, and when she smiled, her teeth looked rather large for her face. 'A pleasure to be out and about after so long,' she said, looking around at all the familiar faces of Lahori society, most of whom were pointedly ignoring her. 'I see Lahore hasn't changed one bit.'

Mona shook her head. 'I'm afraid not.'

Standing on tiptoes, Humaira seemed desperate to be introduced, so Mona felt compelled to do the introductions. As expected, Shahida wasn't impressed and didn't even bother with pleasantries.

'One would think you were under house arrest, given how rarely you venture out,' Humaira said. 'Surely, your house can't be that interesting that you spend all your time there.'

Shahida sniffed. 'When you have a house as big as mine, you'll find that there's always plenty to do.'

'You'll find that my house is bigger, Shahida.' There was an edge to Humaira's voice, which Shahida clocked, but chose to ignore.

'I am sure it is, darling. And I am sure you've filled it to the brim with every expensive thing you could find.'

'You bet I have.'

'That only proves my point.' Shahida allowed herself a thin smile, which she directed at Mona. 'Some people still haven't learned that less is more.'

Mona smiled back as she watched Humaira's face turn red.

'At least I wear all the latest fashions and don't have to rely on clothes I bought fifty years ago. This Banarasi saree has seen better days.'

'It's vintage, Humaira, but I don't expect you to understand.' Turning away from her, Shahida leaned into Mona. 'I only came because your husband has been kind to my son, and I wanted you to know that from now on, you have my support. Always.'

And with that, she glided away, leaving Humaira frothing at the mouth. It was a mark of how times had changed for Shahida that she no longer had a group of sycophants accompanying her. She walked alone now, but she did so with dignity, with her head held high.

Mona was saved from making more conversation with Humaira by the arrival of Shabeena and Alia who waved at her as they walked down the red carpet. The photographers, ever hungry for influencers and celebrities, largely ignored them, but it didn't look like her friends cared. Shabeena had removed her headscarf for the occasion, revealing blonde-streaked hair, while Alia was equally well dressed in a fully embroidered dress.

'Well, look at you two,' Mona cried. 'I am so happy that you came.'

There were so many diamonds on her throat that Alia was shimmering. 'Forget about me. It's Shabeena who is stealing the show.'

Shabeena tried not to let the smile show on her face. 'Well, thank you, but if you must know, covering your head isn't a requirement after menopause. I'm past sixty and allowed to let my hair down once in a while.'

'Are you allowed to get blonde streaks after turning sixty too?' Alia asked with a straight face, to which they burst out laughing a moment later.

Shabeena played with the dupatta wrapped around her shoulders. 'Maybe I ought to cover my head, after all. It feels a bit awkward.'

'And take away the ancients' eye candy? Don't you dare! Look at how the ninety-year-olds are watching you. Would you deprive them of such a rare pleasure at their age?'

'*Astagfirullah!*' Shabeena turned away from them and started chatting with Humaira.

Before Mona could stop her, the phone in her hand pinged.

Her heart fell. It was a text message, not a WhatsApp. She quickly swiped down, expecting another cryptic message, but it was just a text from the telecom company.

She sighed, lifting her elbows a bit to dry the dampness in her armpits. Why was she letting that random text message govern her life like this?

'Don't worry about her,' Alia said, mistaking Mona's distress for concern over Shabeena. 'It's exquisite fun to torture her, but I do love her to bits. I am so glad she's let her hair down tonight, although we were worried for a moment while driving over here that we wouldn't make it.'

Mona glanced up, the text message forgotten for a moment. 'Why?'

Alia looked around before lowering her voice. 'If we didn't have a car with guards behind us, we could have been kidnapped. We were in one of the quieter streets of Shadman, and all of a sudden, half a dozen men came and surrounded our car. I think they were after our diamonds, but with the stories you hear, who knows?'

'These gangs are really getting out of hand.' Mona clutched the diamond choker on her own neck, once again grateful for the fact that they had the money to keep guards.

'I wondered if they wanted to rape us, but Shabeena assured me that we were way past that age.'

'One is never past *that* age,' Mona replied, standing on tiptoe. 'Not in this country, at least. These people don't seem much better than the terrorists we used to have marauding the city back in the day.'

Alia shuddered. 'Don't remind me. I live in constant fear that we will go back to living like that. I used to worry every day that my husband wouldn't return home from work.'

'I'm glad those days are behind us,' Mona whispered back. 'It broke my heart to see Shahida Elahi arrive all alone. If it hadn't been for that terrorist attack, her husband would still be alive.'

Alia craned her neck. 'How on earth did you manage to bring Shahida Elahi out of retirement? That old bird hasn't stepped out in society for ages.'

Bilal and his small acts of kindness. He hadn't told Mona that he was helping out Shahida's son and that just went on to show that her husband believed in actual kindness and not just the optics. He had been unkind and abusive for so many years that this side of his personality still caught her off guard. Kindness was something she'd never thought Bilal capable of, and yet, here he was being just that.

As Mona surveyed the hall, she couldn't help but feel a sense of déjà vu. This was exactly the sort of event where she had first seen Ali, a young man trying to succeed in the cut-throat world of modelling. With a pang, she realised that, had he lived, he'd be about forty now.

In his prime.

Life could be so cruel. He had missed seeing his son grow up – his beautiful son with those ocean-blue eyes everyone fell in love with.

Mona shook her head. Arslan was Bilal's son, and he always would be. Nothing could change that. But where was Bilal when you needed him? Why hadn't he arrived yet? Was he even going to come? The questions swirled in her head as another more frightening thought occurred to her. Maybe he was punishing her.

No, she thought. *He wouldn't dare do this today. He wouldn't dare.*

He knew how important this day was to her. Her thoughts were disrupted by the arrival of Meera, arm in arm with Zarrar. Wearing a diaphanous dress that left very little to the imagination, she gave a flying kiss to the frenzied photographers, throwing an arm around Zarrar's shoulders, pulling him close.

Don't kiss him in front of the cameras, you foolish woman. You'll never get away with it. But true to her reputation, Meera planted a big wet kiss on Zarrar's cheek before winking at the paparazzi and walking away. Mona wondered if her friend was drunk.

'Just nervous,' Meera said when Mona finally caught up with her. 'I act out when I'm nervous.'

Mona took a hold of her arm. 'Have you forgotten where you live, you fool? This is Pakistan. What are you wearing? What are you *doing*?'

Meera pulled her arm away. 'You mean the country where women are still treated like shit? Where young children are raped and thrown in gutters? Yes, I think I am making a statement in that country.'

'Meera, you are supposed to be the smarter one. Please don't throw away your reputation like this.'

Meera closed her eyes, teetering on the towering heels she was wearing. 'You're right, of course. I shouldn't have had those drinks, and I shouldn't have let Zarrar persuade me to wear this slutty dress.'

'You let Zarrar persuade you? Why does that man hold so much sway over you?'

Meera opened her eyes. 'He's too good in bed. I'm afraid I'm quite in love with him, Mona.'

'He's a creep. He would flirt with a statue if he could.'

Meera spread open a shawl she had across her arm and wrapped it around her shoulders. 'Happy now? I've covered up. The way you make it sound, one would think that every single extremist in the country was after me.'

Mona smiled. 'That's not to say that you weren't slaying it in that outfit. I just worry for your safety.'

Meera sucked in a breath through her teeth. 'I was just desperately trying to act young for Zarrar. He really brings out the worst in me.' Falling in step with Mona, she reached out to take her hand. 'I'm glad you're always around to help me see reason. Have you met Shumaila, the politician?'

Mona groaned. 'That Godiva lover? No, thank you. She'll probably ask me for more chocolate.'

'She's right there, look! Would you deprive that poor woman of some more Godiva?'

'That poor woman loots Pakistan enough as it is. She hardly needs more chocolate from me.'

Shumaila was in a shimmering saree with her secretary running after her, and when she looked in their direction, Mona pointedly looked away.

To hell with you and your infatuation for Godiva.

Meera squeezed her arm. 'Now, let's go and welcome Samir Haque properly, or that asshole won't agree to do another show with us.'

Samir Haque was, of course, just as obnoxious as Mona had expected. Wearing an expensive Tom Ford suit and followed by a long line of admirers, he extended a hand in Mona's direction.

Mona made to shake his hand, but Samir pulled it out of her grasp. 'You don't shake Samir's hand. You kiss it.'

Mona's eyes widened. 'Are you serious?'

Beside her, Meera was shaking with barely concealed laughter. 'Kiss it, Mona. Kiss the royal hand.'

Samir Haque stood with a haughty expression, looking down at both of them. 'I don't shake hands with people. It's too pedestrian. Either you kiss my hand or just don't greet me at all.'

Mona turned to Meera. 'Is this really happening?'

Meera shrugged while wiping the tears from her eyes. 'I'm afraid so.' Pointing to her damp cheeks, she said, 'Tears of happiness at your arrival, Samir. Thank you for gracing us with your royal presence. The models are backstage, getting ready for your show.' In a swift gesture, she bent down and kissed his hand.

'Lovely.' Satisfied, Samir Haque turned again towards Mona, his hand out. He tilted his head a fraction and raised an eyebrow. 'Well?'

'I'm not kissing your hand.'

'She is *not* kissing your hand.'

Mona's heart rose at the sound of Bilal's voice. She turned around to see him standing behind her, wearing his best suit and looking like something out of an Armani ad. He had even gone to the trouble of wearing a tie and dyeing his hair so that the grey looked muted.

Mona pressed her hands together, blinking back tears. 'Bilal, you came.'

'Of course I came.' Bilal's expression was still stern. 'Why wouldn't I come for your big day? I was just caught up in traffic, and before that, I had to put Arslan to bed. You ought to have told me that the event was in Johar Town. Do you know how hard it is to get here from Gulberg, especially with the roadworks?' He turned his attention towards Samir Haque once again. 'And what are you, a relic from colonial times? Why the hell would you want my wife to kiss the hand you probably had up your arse all day?'

Mona took a step in front of Bilal. 'He doesn't mean it, Samir,' she added hastily. 'Don't mind him.'

'Of course I mean it,' Bilal said. 'Look at the state of the guy. He's a bloody clown asking people to kiss his hand. What he needs is one tight slap across his face.'

Samir's hand flew to his chest. 'Excuse me, sir? Just who do you think you are?'

'I'll tell you who I am.' Bilal attempted to push his way past Mona, but Mona held fast. 'What are you doing, woman? Let me talk to the guy.'

'Won't you come with me backstage to check all the preparations, Samir?' Meera wheedled. 'Your team needs you there. You're our headline event, as you very well know.'

Perhaps sensing impending drama with Bilal that probably wouldn't translate well for him, Samir Haque just sniffed and nodded. 'Perhaps it is for the best that we go backstage now. But maybe you ought to take a good look at your guest list for next time and weed out the' – his eyes surveyed Bilal from head to foot – 'offensive undesirables.'

'Why you little—'

It took all the strength Mona possessed to keep Bilal from launching himself at their lead designer for the fashion week. Once Samir had vanished backstage, taking an entire contingent of his fans with him, she turned to Bilal. 'Have you gone nuts? That guy is the whole fashion week. People have come from as far as Dubai to see his show.'

Bilal ran his fingers through his hair, unsettling the gel. Somehow, that made him look even more appealing. Deep within her, there was a yearning, a knotting in her stomach that was a familiar and yet unfamiliar feeling. With a jolt, Mona realised what it was.

Desire.

The last time they'd had sex was over a year ago, and that too out of a sense of duty. Over the years, their marriage had veered away from physical intimacy, mostly surviving on the emotional bond they shared as well as the love for their children.

Taking Bilal's arm, she fell in step with him and guided him towards the far corner of the hall that was less crowded. 'Thank you for being my knight in shining armour.'

'An ageing knight now, but it's always a pleasure, madam.'

Her hand slid down his arm and tickled his palm. Without warning, he grasped it. 'And here I was thinking that my knight was still young enough for certain things.'

A lopsided grin spread across his mouth. 'Are you flirting with me, madam?'

She returned the pressure on his hand. 'If you behave, who knows, maybe you might end up getting lucky tonight.'

A low groan escaped his lips as he closed his eyes. 'I'd forgotten how seductive you can be.'

She nudged him in the ribs. 'Are you accusing me of being a seductress, sir?'

'I say we ditch this event and jump in the car. Perhaps even do it in the car. That would be a first for us.'

Mona laughed. 'Stop it, Bilal. I draw the line there. I would never do it in a car even if my life depended on it.'

'And what if mine depended on it?'

'Speaking of which, what did the doctor say? You were so focused on avoiding me that I didn't dare ask.'

Bilal glanced at her, the edges of his mouth turned down. 'I am sorry for what I said. I didn't mean it. It's just that I find it very difficult to apologise even when I desperately want to.'

'You didn't answer my question.'

Bilal laughed. They had paused in front of the empty food table, away from prying eyes. He took both her hands in his own and looked into her eyes. 'I am fine, Mona. It's nothing you need to worry about. I just need to exercise more, I think. That's the only thing holding me back from peak health.'

'The only thing holding you back from a wild night right now is this event, I'm afraid.'

He groaned again. 'Don't rub it in.' Holding her by the arms, his thumbs stroking the bare skin around her shoulder blades, he leaned in. 'Remember, I'll be undressing you with my eyes all evening.'

She gasped, but before they could continue the conversation, there was a flurry of activity as everyone rushed towards Hall 1, where Samir Haque's show was about to begin.

'Ugh,' Bilal said, as Mona pulled at his hand. 'If watching that entitled little brat's show is the price I have to pay for your company tonight, then so be it.' However, before they could step into the hall, he held her back. 'Aren't you forgetting something?'

Mona frowned. 'What?'

'Look, our daughter has just arrived.'

And sure enough, there was Aimen hurrying towards them, the tail of her dress in her hand, her heels clacking on the marble floor. But it wasn't Aimen that caused Mona to exclaim in surprise. It was the person walking behind her.

'Qudsia!' Mona cried. 'What are you doing here?'

Fully covered in a delicately beaded beige abaya, Qudsia looked stunning. 'Yes, here I am,' she said in a dull monotone. 'Aimen insisted that I put make-up on, so I asked her to do it for me.' She touched her face. 'Is it too much?'

Mona clapped her hands together. 'You look beautiful.'

Qudsia snorted. 'Let's not go that far. That ship sailed long ago.'

'Qudsia, you do look rather stunning,' Bilal echoed. 'After all, this is my sister we're talking about. Of course she'd be pretty.'

Despite herself, Qudsia couldn't help but smile. 'Oh, stop it, you two.'

Mona leaned in to air-kiss her daughter, but then went ahead and planted a small kiss on her forehead. 'Thank you for bringing your aunt. I can't begin to tell you how happy I am to see my family here.'

'Of course,' Aimen whispered back. 'You might not be able to see it all the time, but we all love you very much.'

'Before you ask, I called one of my friends to come in to babysit Arslan,' Qudsia said. There was a gleam of admiration in her eyes as she looked around. 'It must have taken some planning to come up with all this. I have to say I am glad I came.'

'Wait till you see how we've decorated the stages.' Mona paused, looking back at Qudsia. 'There will be music, though.'

Qudsia tutted. 'I wasn't born yesterday, and just because I'm religious doesn't mean that I don't enjoy my music.'

Bilal spread out his arms. 'Well, today has been a day full of surprises. Lead the way, wife.'

True to his reputation, Samir Haque's show brought something new to the fashion week. With the stage set to reflect a small village in southern Punjab complete with earthenware kitchens, steel utensils, *charpais*, and what were actual wheat stalks pulled from a nearby field, even Mona, who had been part of the plan from the start, felt transported. With Saraiki folk music blaring from the speakers, models walked down the runway in ethnic bridal outfits, most of them holding an earthenware pot or a bamboo fan for effect.

They had been worried about objectifying life in rural Pakistan for such a commercial business event, but Samir Haque's office had been adamant. Either they did it his way, or he would not be participating at all.

'I'll wring his neck if this fashion week goes belly-up in the press,' Meera had shouted a few weeks ago. 'Who does he think he is?'

However, judging by the way she was smiling today, it was obvious that Samir's gamble had paid off. The smug expression he wore suggested as much. The audience was rapt, especially the people in the front row. For a moment, Mona's heart swelled as she looked at her family sitting there in support of her. Catching her eye, Bilal gave her a thumbs up and stood up.

Mona yelped as he crossed the ramp to walk over to her, drawing disgusted looks from the audience and models alike. It was very poor form to leave a show in the middle, but Bilal looked like he couldn't care less. He only seemed to have eyes for Mona, and when he finally extricated himself from the crowds surrounding the stage, there was a small smile playing on his face.

Mona frowned at him, shaking her head in exasperation. 'Samir Haque will never forgive you for walking out of his show. Did you see the faces of his models?'

'Good,' he replied. 'I did it on purpose. That stuck-up *kanjar* ought to realise that the world doesn't revolve around him. *Kiss his hand?* He could kiss something of mine, and it's not going to be my hand.'

Mona punched his shoulder. 'Oh, Bilal, you do go on. You simply could have waited. The show ends in a few minutes.'

'And miss the chance of spending time with my beautiful wife?' He nudged her. 'Is this sleeveless dress for my benefit?'

'It's a halter top, if you please.'

'And what's to stop me from having my way with you right now?'

Mona wanted to laugh, but she kept her face impassive. 'That would be most unwise, especially in the presence of hundreds of people.'

Bilal threw a hand across her shoulder, rubbing the skin on her upper arms. 'I perform better in front of an audience. And at this point, I'd do anything to steal that asshole's thunder.' Leaning close to nibble on her ear, he whispered, 'So, what say?'

Mona's exclamation was drowned out by a collective cheer from the audience as Zarrar walked down the ramp in an unbuttoned dull gold sherwani, his naked chest shining with glitter.

Bilal wrinkled his nose. 'What has happened to this profession? I don't remember people being so sleazy in the past.'

Mona laughed. 'Trust me, it's always been like this. And this little fool tried to flirt with me today.'

The moment the words left her mouth, she knew she'd made a mistake. Bilal's hand slid away from her shoulder. 'Oh yeah? And what did he say to you?'

Although it was dark, she could see that Bilal's expression had hardened. It was obvious that her words had reminded him of Ali. Mona swore under her breath. She ought to have known better. Reaching out, she patted his forearm. 'It was just innocent flirting. You know what young men are like.'

She was just going from bad to worse.

Bilal turned away. 'Yes, I know. But of course, when they have faces and bodies like that, who could resist?'

'I'm fifty-three years old. I think I'm beyond this sort of nonsense. And, if you must know, I gave him a piece of my mind.' She pulled at the front of the dress she was wearing. 'Perhaps I ought to stick to shalwar kameez in the future. If this is how you're going to react to situations like this, then I'd rather not risk it at all.'

'Don't ever apologise for your attire, Mona. You're not the problem. These bastards are.'

And with that, she noticed just how far they had come as a married couple. The same Bilal who used to beat her for wearing provocative clothes was defending her right to wear whatever she wanted today. It was often said that people didn't change, but looking at her husband now and how hard he was trying not to let his jealousy get the better of him, she realised that people could change. If they wanted to.

Bilal took her hand. 'Let's get out of here. We'll check into a hotel and see where the night takes us. It's about time we did something fun. Qudsia can look after Arslan. She'd love to.'

For once, Mona agreed with him. The now familiar desire she'd felt for him earlier stirred inside her again. 'Let me see if I can get away without Meera noticing.'

She wished she hadn't pulled her phone out to leave a message for Meera. She wished she had just taken Bilal's hand and gone to the hotel for a rare, carefree night. These thoughts swirled in her head the moment after she swiped down to see that there was a text message waiting for her.

> Did you think I'd forgotten about you? About the dirty secret that you've kept hidden all these years? And just to reassure you that this isn't a spam message, I am talking about your son, Arslan.

She froze, blinking her eyes in rapid succession as she took in the message. She read it several times, but the text didn't change. Of course it didn't.

Before she could think about what to do, her phone rang, the words *Unknown Number* filling her screen. This person was calling her now? With her stomach feeling like there was a fire burning in there, she rejected the call.

Her screen lit up again.

Mona turned her phone off and threw it in her clutch as if it had scalded her.

'What is it?' Bilal said. 'You've gone very pale. Are you all right?'

Her bottom lip trembled as she attempted to hold back the tears that threatened to break out. *Who could it be?* Was this some kind of sick joke? Her eyes scanned the crowd, desperately searching for someone who could be looking at her, someone who might have reason to harm her, but there was no one. All eyes were on the models that were still walking. Even Qudsia, who had sworn that she had no interest in fashion, was gazing awestruck at the bridal outfits, whispering in Aimen's ear as she clapped.

After all these years, who could it be?

'Mona!' Bilal said loudly, shaking her out of her reverie. 'What's up with you?'

She looked around and found his face. It took a few seconds for her to focus on him, another few to actually realise what it was she was looking at. Her mouth opened and closed like a fish out of water. 'Nothing,' she murmured finally. 'I – I just realised that I'm supposed to stay here until the end.' She ran her fingers through her hair, disturbing the pins holding it in place. 'I'm sorry, Bilal. I have to take a rain check.'

Bilal took her hand. 'But where are you going?'

Mona was just seeing red. She pulled her hand out of his grasp. 'I need some air. I'm sorry, it must be the menopause.'

'Mona!' Bilal called after her, but she had already broken into a run, hurrying backstage.

Someone knew her secret, and now they were out to get her.

She whimpered as the potentially devastating ramifications of that text message hit her. Her life could be over in a matter of minutes if that person chose.

Chapter 8

Bilal

He watched her make a beeline for the backstage, leaving him standing alone in a corner. He clenched and unclenched his fists as he tried to ignore the sting of rejection. Mona was known to run hot or cold at the drop of a hat, but this sort of behaviour was strange, even for her. He had put aside all his grievances and come here to support her, hoping that they could mend ties and maybe have a nice night out. The way Mona had been dropping hints all evening, he was expecting things to heat up in the hotel later tonight, but the way she had abandoned him now made him think otherwise.

Perhaps it was all a game to her now that she knew how much he loved her and would do anything to be with her.

He *did* love her, and he *would* do anything to be with her. But the question was, did she? Bilal knew that he had a lot of ground to cover before Mona could completely forgive him, but he liked to think that she could at least meet him halfway. They hadn't had sex for more months than he could remember. They said that a man's libido weakened with advancing years, but even today, like clockwork, he felt the stirrings of desire every morning. He never acted on that feeling, knowing that his wife had plenty of stuff to keep her occupied and that intimacy was perhaps the last thing on her mind while she went through the menopause, but how much longer did she expect him to wait?

Sure, there were other ways of relieving himself, but he was sick and tired of that. And it wasn't like he was getting any younger. According to Dr Shafiq, he could drop dead any minute. It wasn't that he was afraid of dying… he just worried about his family. And Mona didn't know the first thing about real estate, and neither did Farhan and Aimen. If he died, his family might as well be on the streets in a few months.

As the audience erupted in a round of applause for Samir Haque as he walked down the ramp with a famous actress who had modelled for his collection, Bilal pinched his nose and looked up. He wouldn't be caught dead with tears in his eyes, especially not at this tacky event with that insufferable designer. His bottom lip curled with disgust as he watched Samir Haque extend a hand in the actress' direction. For a moment, she looked like a deer caught in the headlights. She looked around as if unsure of what to do, but then one of the other models whispered something in her ear, and her eyes widened. Her lips barely brushed Samir's hand before she recoiled, blinking rapidly as if she couldn't believe what she'd just done.

'So, Bilal, we meet again.'

It was a voice he had heard before. A shock of ash-blonde hair was the first thing he saw before his eyes slid over the woman's deep-neck dress that left little to the imagination. Even though her hair was partially covering her chest, Bilal had to admit that it took some guts to wear something like that in a country like Pakistan. None of this helped in jogging his memory, though. He had no idea who this woman was.

Following his gaze, the woman arched an eyebrow and threw her hair back, bunching it together. 'I know I ought to be grateful for all God has given me, but honestly, this hair can be such a nuisance sometimes.'

'Not to be a nuisance myself, but I really can't remember where we met.'

Her face fell. 'And here I was thinking that you'd be thrilled to see me again. The moment I saw you, I ran straight over.' She clucked her tongue. 'In a sea of mediocrity, you shine like a beacon, sir, but what a pity that you can't recognise me.'

'I guess you must not shine like that said beacon, then.'

The woman gasped, placing a hand on her chest. 'Are you flirting with me?'

Bilal snorted. 'Quite the contrary, madam. I have no idea who you are.'

'You wound me.' The way her eyelids trembled and she drew in small breaths, it was obvious that she was prone to theatrics. They may have looked good on someone half her age, but on her, they just looked comical.

'If you will excuse me, I need to look for my wife.'

Before he could turn away, she reached for his forearm. Surprisingly, her grip was firm, and when she smiled, there was a sharp edge to it. 'Your wife won't perish if she has to spend a few more moments away from you. She's had you her entire life. Right now, I am speaking, and when Nageena speaks, men listen.' Recognition must have shown on his face because she smiled wider, her face losing some of its severity. 'I see you finally recognise me.'

'You're the woman who gave me my phone back in the hotel lobby.'

Nageena performed a curtsy. 'The very same. But tell me, what is a man like yourself doing at the fashion week?'

Bilal spread his arms. 'It's a free country, but if you must know, my wife helped organise the event, so I'm here to support her.'

'Don't tell me you're married to Meera Siddiqui.'

Bilal's mouth curved into a smile. 'I'm married to Mona.'

Nageena nodded slowly. 'I'm sure I've seen her around, but honestly, it's kind of hard to notice anyone when you're under the golden glare of Samir Haque.' She let out a sudden laugh. 'Did you kiss the royal hand too?'

Without warning, they started to laugh. He couldn't remember the last time he'd laughed with such abandon. 'Good one,' he wheezed. 'But unfortunately, I wasn't afforded the opportunity to kiss the royal hand. My wife was, but I ruined it for her by preventing the kiss from happening.'

'So, you like to be in control, do you?'

His smile widened. 'And what could you possibly mean by that?'

Smiling and maintaining eye contact with him, Nageena reached for his hand. Her palm was warm as she brought it to her lips, and she broke eye contact only when she closed her eyes and kissed the back of his hand. 'There now, I have kissed the real royal hand.'

Bilal suppressed a moan. What was happening to him? Thoughts of Mona came crashing into his head like waves, and he snatched his hand back, looking around to see if anyone had noticed.

No one had.

Now that the show was over, people were beginning to stir, most rising from their seats and mingling. If Mona were to see him with this woman, all hell would break loose, and he hadn't even done anything yet. From what

Faheem had told him, Nageena had quite the reputation in Lahore and even by talking to her right now, he was implicating himself. But he had to admit that the woman was drop-dead gorgeous. Perhaps it was the earlier desire he'd felt for his wife, but looking at Nageena and her raw feminine appeal now, something in him stirred. He took a deep breath. 'It was nice meeting you, but I must head back to my wife.'

For a moment, her eyes flashed, but then she pouted, tapping her painted nails against her jaw. 'Oh, Bilal Sahab, there is nothing sexier than a man who is devoted to his wife.'

Before he could reply, he spotted Faheem in the crowd. Their eyes met, and he waved at him, waddling in their direction. Bilal felt like a trapped animal.

Faheem took the better part of five minutes to greet him and slobber over Nageena, leaving disgusting damp marks on her cheeks from his incessant kissing. The fat bastard even had the nerve to cup Bilal's ass again when he went in for a hug.

Bilal closed his eyes.

Lord, give me strength.

'Faheem Sahab,' Nageena cried, wiping her cheek, a look of disgust crossing her features. 'When will you stop assaulting women like this? My face is smeared with your stinky saliva.'

Faheem held a hand to his heart. 'Nageena, my dear, how you hurt me. You didn't seem to think I was stinky last night when we were together.'

'*Raat gayi, baat gayi*, Faheem Sahab. My mood changes like the wind. Our friend, Bilal, is the new flavour of the season.'

Faheem assumed a look of mock surprise. 'Bilal, what is this? I thought that wife of yours had finally managed to tame you, but here you are, up to your old antics again.'

Ignoring Faheem, Nageena leaned into Bilal, sliding a piece of paper into his coat pocket. 'Call me when you're free.'

And just like that, she glided away from them, leaving the scent of her Chanel perfume in her wake.

'God damn it,' Faheem groaned. 'That woman gets a rise out of me every time.'

Bilal almost gagged at the image in his mind and turned his attention to the crowd around him. The piece of paper in his pocket weighed heavy. In the past, he'd always taken the initiative with women, so it was a bit of a surprise to have someone like Nageena hit on him.

You've still got it, Bilal, he thought with a smile. He wouldn't be calling Nageena, but it felt nice to be desired sometimes. Maybe he'd tell Mona just to see her reaction. He looked around for her in the sea of unfamiliar faces, but she was nowhere to be found.

Chapter 9

Mona

The valet brought their car to the hotel entrance, but as she slid inside the Beemer, Mona realised that she was still breathless from her walk down the lobby. She was wheezing like a ninety-year-old woman. Casting an anxious glance at her husband tipping the valet, she reached into her handbag for Arslan's spare asthma spray, but then thought better of it. Bilal would notice, and right now, the last thing she needed was him asking questions.

She'd switched her phone off immediately after reading the message, but even then, her gaze kept getting drawn to it. Her heart thudded in her throat as she ran the words in the text message over and over in her head.

> Did you think I'd forgotten about you?

This person knew about Arslan, and this information in the wrong hands could be devastating. Her family would never recover from the scandal. She thought of the pride in Qudsia's eyes today as she'd seen the event Mona had organised, and it made her want to cry. Qudsia would never forgive her. Aimen's husband would divorce her if he found out. Maybe they'd even question the legitimacy of Farhan and Aimen. The toxicity of Lahori high society was bottomless.

And Bilal...

Bilal would never be able to show his face in public if this secret got out. If there was one thing Pakistani men couldn't tolerate, it was to be made a laughing stock of, and that's exactly what Bilal would become.

A laughing stock.

She turned to look at him and, without warning, let out a strangled cry.

His head whipped in her direction. 'What is it?'

She shook her head, swallowing back tears. 'Eyes on the road, Bilal.'

He looked away, but not before reaching out to squeeze her hand. 'That mood you were in earlier seems to have evaporated. I was expecting us to get some action tonight.'

The mere thought of sex made her want to throw up. 'I'm sorry, I think I'm just exhausted.'

Bilal's finger clenched the steering wheel tighter. 'Is it that, though? You seemed perfectly okay a while ago. Something happened to you while we were talking during the show, and you just withdrew.'

'It's nothing,' she murmured.

'We've been married for more than thirty bloody years. Give me some credit, woman. I know something is off.'

Mona rested her head against the seat, her gaze drawn upwards. At this time of the night, the grey padding looked charcoal. Almost black, like her mood. 'Well, forgive me for not meeting your expectations. Hasn't that always been the case?'

'Hey, don't get mad at me. I'm just concerned about you.'

She took a deep breath and lowered the window. It was suffocating inside the car. Even though all she got were mouthfuls of smog when she extended her head out of the window, it was still better than festering in the stagnant air of Bilal's disappointment.

He took a handful of her dress and pulled her back. 'Have you lost your mind? You want someone to slice your head off?'

At the moment, she couldn't think of anything better. How liberating it would be for life to end right now, with her secret intact and the world unchanged. Out of frustration, she banged her head against the headrest.

'Honestly, what is going on with you, Mona?'

To throw him off the scent, she mustered a smile on her face when they arrived home and took his hand, guiding him upstairs. It didn't take long for Bilal's concern for her to go out of the window and get replaced by pure lust. Although she'd come to enjoy the intimacy whenever it happened, this time she couldn't take her eyes off the black spot on the ceiling. With clammy hands, she held on to Bilal's back as she watched the spot grow larger, spreading its wings like a Rorschach inkblot until all she could see was black in her vision. She gasped with fear, which Bilal mistook for pleasure, and responded by quickening his thrusts. As the darkness enveloped her completely, the urgency of his desire and her fear became one, and Mona closed her eyes, letting herself sink into oblivion.

But sometimes, even oblivion was not enough. After what seemed like mere minutes, Mona woke up to an alarm ringing. It was Bilal's phone. She peeled herself away from Bilal to swipe at it but missed a couple of times.

Next to her, Bilal groaned. 'Shut that thing off, will you?'

Mona shook her head and focused on the phone in her hand, finally managing to swipe up the small white circle that silenced the alarm. She'd used his phone for the alarm to avoid switching hers on. The day hadn't even begun, and she already felt nauseous. Who knew what horrors awaited her today? As she pulled off the covers, goosebumps erupted all across her skin. Despite the heating, there was something about Pakistani homes that turned them into iceboxes in winter. *Must be the concrete*, she thought, fully aware that she was only trying to distract herself from the messages.

'Don't forget we are hosting a dinner for Aimen and her husband tonight,' Bilal murmured, snuggling into the duvet. 'I know how you struggle to remember things that don't concern you, but this is our daughter. We show up for her.'

Mona took a deep breath. 'I should know. I gave birth to her.'

'Only trying to help...' His voice was muffled, but Mona caught a hint of his usual playfulness in it, and the knot in her stomach loosened ever so slightly.

For a moment, she wondered why life couldn't go back to the way it was, when her only worry was her fluctuating weight and waking up early for Arslan.

As if on cue, Bilal echoed her thoughts. 'If you're tired, I can take him to school.'

He was going to make her cry. 'I'm fine,' she replied, bunching up her hair into a ponytail. 'I've been doing this for a long time and today ought to be no different.' She poked the duvet. 'I did notice last night that you were panting a lot.'

There was silence for only a moment, before he said, 'That's what usually happens when you're in the thick of it, Mona. You get breathless. It's completely normal.'

'Have you been to see the doctor again, though? You never really told me much.'

'I'm fine!'

Before she could leave the bed, Bilal reached out and grabbed her hand. His head emerged from the duvet, eyes sleepy and hair tousled. If it wasn't for her state of mind at the moment, she'd have acted on the desire she felt just then. Judging by the small smile playing on his face, he seemed to be thinking along the same lines. 'As enjoyable as last night was, I'm up for more if you are.'

Mona found herself laughing. Pulling her hand from his grasp, she rose from the bed. 'Don't push your luck.'

—

At work that day, Meera held her head in her hands, a steaming mug of coffee on the desk in front of her. The office was empty, with most of the team still at the venue of the fashion week. For a moment, Mona wondered if the opening night had been a failure. In her distress, she hadn't even bothered to switch on her phone, let alone check Instagram and Twitter.

'Was it a failure?' she asked Meera, who hadn't looked up.

Meera groaned. 'I'm so hung-over. I feel like my head could split open right now.'

No stranger to hangovers herself, Mona reached out to pat her arm. 'It happens. Just get that coffee in yourself, pronto. And knock back a few paracetamols.'

'And I slept with Zarrar again.' She removed her hands from her face, revealing bloodshot eyes. 'And before you scold me, I know that I'm making a mistake. The man is bad news,' she whimpered, 'but, Mona, he is so good in bed.'

'Oh, Meera.'

'At least the opening night was a success.' She slid her phone across the desk towards her. 'Did you check Instagram? The fashion week is all people can talk about.' The thought of her phone tightened the knot in Mona's stomach. As she flicked through the photos, Meera seemed to perk up. 'Did you know we received over three hundred queries this morning for Samir Haque's exclusive bridal designs? Say what you will about him, but the guy knows how to cause a stir.'

'Only if you kiss the royal hand,' Mona said drily.

Meera threw her head back and laughed. 'God, that royal hand. It smelled of expensive oud, by the way, so not an entirely unpleasant experience, although his palms were very damp. Sopping wet, actually.'

'Ew, Meera!'

'Well, I am serious. You could clean my car's dusty windshield with all that moisture from Samir's palms. Maybe even mop the floors too.'

Mona covered her ears. 'I don't even want to picture that image in my head. You've put me off the royal hands forever, if such a thing was even possible.'

Taking another gulp of her coffee, Meera sat up straighter. 'I can't deny that I didn't notice the way Bilal stood up for you and point-blank refused to let you kiss Samir's hand.'

'I wasn't going to kiss it, anyway.'

'But you have to admit that it was kind of hot.' Meera smirked. 'There's something about a man taking control that gets me a bit weak in the knees.'

The mention of Bilal brought thoughts of that text message back. Taking a deep breath to settle the frantic beating of her heart, Mona scrolled through some more photos on Meera's phone. Most of the usual suspects had been photographed, and there was even a photo of Shumaila with her mousy little assistant. Apart from Samir Haque's show, there were a dozen others that had taken place last night, but looking at the designs now, Mona could see why Samir ruled the roost. There was a peculiar timely and timeless quality to his outfits that buyers of haute couture loved. His were the kind of outfits you could wear for any occasion and they'd still look fashionable.

'I say, Meera,' Mona began, glancing up from the screen briefly. 'You've never told anyone about Arslan, have you?'

Meera narrowed her eyes. 'What about Arslan?'

Mona paused, not meeting her friend's eye, focusing instead on the pastel-pink wall behind her. 'About who his real father is.'

It was a sign of how well they knew each other that Meera didn't overreact or accuse her of anything. Instead, she leaned forward, the frown on her forehead deepening. 'What makes you say that? Has anyone asked?'

It was right on the tip of her tongue. The text messages. She could tell Meera and maybe, just maybe, she would feel less alone, less likely to implode. But they still had the rest of this fashion week to endure, and Mona knew that she couldn't do this to her friend. Not now. So, instead of coming clean, she just smiled. 'Just asking because I know how much you like to gossip, and who knows, you may have blurted something out.'

Meera leaned back against her chair, but the frown was still there. 'Well, it's good that you're joking, but I still don't know why you'd ask me this question out of the blue. Of course I've never told anyone. I could be blind drunk and I'd still not betray your trust. Not now, not ever.'

'Of course,' Mona replied. 'Just me being emotional, I guess.' She thought of veering the conversation back toward safer ground and was about to mention Samir Haque again when she froze. The phone in her hand trembled, and it took an immense effort of will for her not to drop it like a hot coal.

There, right in front of her, was a face she recognised in one of the photos.

No, she thought. *It cannot be. It must be a trick of the camera.*

But no matter how much she tilted her head to re-examine the photo, everything stayed the same.

'What is it now?' Meera asked. 'You look like you've seen a ghost.'

Mona handed the phone over to her. 'Who is this?'

Meera opened a drawer and drew out a pair of reading glasses. Her eyes bulged. 'Don't you dare tell anyone that I need these.' She took one glance at the photo and tutted. 'Oh, it's' – she frowned again – 'it's... why, it couldn't possibly be.' Their eyes met. 'He looks remarkably like Ali, doesn't he?'

Mona let out the breath she was holding. 'It does. It looks like him. What is going on?'

Meera held up a hand. 'Hang on, now. Let's not panic. I'm sure there's a perfectly reasonable explanation. This is from Ayesha Amjad's show, so let me pull up details of the models that walked for that show.'

Mona could see stars in her vision. All thoughts of the text messages vanished from her mind. It couldn't be a coincidence that the moment she'd mentioned Arslan's real father, he had appeared before her.

Meera was scrolling through some more photos while glancing at her laptop screen. For several moments, Mona sat in suspense, sick to her stomach as Meera's face grew paler. And then, all of a sudden, she sat up. 'Aha!' She turned the laptop screen in Mona's direction. 'This is Hashim Akhtar. At thirty-nine, he's slightly older than our usual models and has an uncanny resemblance to Ali, but I can assure you it's not Ali unless they've figured out a way to bring people back from the grave.' She handed her phone back to Mona. 'Look at these photos. You can tell the difference easily here.'

And she was right. Looking at the photos now, Mona couldn't help but feel embarrassed. Hashim Akhtar only had a passing resemblance to Ali. She didn't know if she was relieved or disappointed.

—

When she arrived at the hotel for the second day, she made a beeline straight for the backstage.

As usual, it was a fright. Clothes that workers had probably spent weeks making by hand lay strewn on the makeshift couches with chemises and undergarments scattered on the floor. Sweaty make-up assistants rushed between the celebrity showstoppers, ignoring most of the models completely. It was absolute bedlam, and Mona wasn't sure what exactly she was doing here. All she knew was that she wanted to take a look at Hashim Akhtar herself. She had to be sure.

It was silly because she had visited Ali's grave so many times over the years, and still, here she was, trying to make sure that he was actually dead.

Of course he is, you silly goose, she thought. If Bilal knew what was going on in her mind, he would kill her. She hadn't dared to switch on her phone since last night in case there were more messages waiting for her, but watching the chaos of the backstage unfold in front of her, she knew that nothing was forever. Not even blissful ignorance. Her thumb pressed the button, and her phone vibrated to life.

The sound of a slap brought her back to the present. She turned towards the row of seats where a make-up assistant stood clutching her cheek, her face beetroot red.

'Not this, you stupid bitch,' the woman in the seat cried. 'If you think I'm going to wear this cheap-ass make-up, then you don't know me at all. Bring me the Dior products.' She pushed the assistant. 'And, if you bring this cheap make-up within five feet of me again, I'll put it all on you and make you join the circus.'

'Yes, madam,' the assistant whimpered.

'Bring me Shaista,' the woman snapped. 'Tell her that Nageena is not the kind of woman who makes do with inexperienced make-up assistants. I want the real deal. It's either Shaista or I will not be today's showstopper.'

So, this was Nageena. Although she had covered herself with a sheet, Mona could tell that the woman had a good body. She seemed to be a decade younger than her, but definitely over forty. The fine lines around her eyes said as much, although these days one couldn't tell with all the fillers people used.

As Mona approached, Nageena looked up and gave her a small smile. 'I wasn't aware that designers were starting to invite women over fifty as showstoppers as well. Colour me impressed. Pakistan is finally moving with the times.'

Mona's friends said that she looked young enough to be in her early forties, but she'd always known that she looked her age, and Nageena had just proved it. Blinking once, Mona returned her smile. 'I'm not walking the ramp. I'm helping out with the PR for the fashion week.'

Nageena raised an eyebrow. 'Then what are you doing backstage, if I may ask? This area is strictly for models.'

Her question brought Mona back to the reason she was here. Her eyes scanned the place. Still no sign of Hashim. She'd checked his schedule, and he was supposed to be doing this show, so where was he? Turning back to Nageena, she smiled. 'Just checking if everything is all right. I'll be leaving shortly.' She didn't like the way Nageena was looking at her, so she added, 'Now, if you'll excuse me.'

'And your name is?'

'Mona Bilal.'

Recognition dawned on her features. 'When you say Bilal, do you mean that handsome real estate tycoon?'

'The very same,' Mona replied stiffly. How on earth did Bilal know someone like Nageena? He'd been so devoted to her for years now that she had almost forgotten that, back in the day, Bilal had cheated on her regularly. The thought still pierced her like a hot needle. Bilal wasn't the same man any more, and there was probably a perfectly good reason why he was friends with Nageena. And so what if he was? Mona was not going down that rabbit hole again.

'You're very pretty,' Nageena said, but her face was drawn as if someone had shoved a bunch of stones into her mouth. 'You're also lucky to have him as a husband. Such a man.'

'Excuse me? How do you know my husband?'

A satisfied smirk spread across her mouth. 'So, he hasn't mentioned me? I wonder why…'

'Maybe because he didn't think it was important enough.'

That wiped the smirk off Nageena's face. 'Look at that. Fancy rich lady has got quite a tongue on her.'

Mona stared at her in the mirror. 'She has claws too, so you had best watch yourself.'

Perhaps sensing the heightened tension between them all of a sudden, Nageena pulled off the sheet covering her and stood up. Mona barely caught the short white dress she had on before she was overwhelmed by Nageena's fruity perfume as she embraced her.

Mona stood with her arms hanging to her sides, too shocked to return the embrace.

'You mustn't mind me,' Nageena whispered. 'This is my brand of humour, and having spent decades in this industry, my manner has become a bit brittle. I really admire Bilal as a person, and it is a pleasure to finally meet his wife.'

What a strange creature, Mona thought. Before she could return the hug, Mona saw him. Standing at the other end of the room with his back to them, Mona knew it was probably Hashim Akhtar, but the resemblance with Ali took her breath away. It was like a punch in her gut. The same back, the same hairstyle, the same love for tweeds.

'Excuse me,' Mona said, extricating herself from Nageena and edging past her.

A flash of anger crossed Nageena's features. 'Nobody treats Nageena like this.'

Mona found that she could hardly breathe. Who was this guy? As she watched, he proceeded towards the exit that would lead him outside and into the crowds of people. She'd never find him again. She looked back at Nageena. 'I'm sorry. I have to go, but we'll catch up again soon.'

But Nageena was like a dog with a bone. She fell in step with Mona, a surprising feat considering the towering heels she was in. 'Why are you in such a hurry?'

Mona ignored her, picking her way through the sea of chairs, bumping into models and assistants, but never losing sight of the retreating figure of that man. She increased her pace.

'For God's sake,' Nageena cried. 'What is up with you? I can't keep up in these heels.'

'Then don't,' Mona snapped. 'Why are you following me?'

'Because I like to know about everything and everyone.'

'Is that so?' Mona pointed ahead. 'Then tell me, who is that man in the grey coat?'

Nageena squinted in the distance but didn't slow down. 'Why, that's old Hashim, of course.'

Mona stopped, almost colliding with an assistant carrying a tray full of drinks. *They are drinking in here?* What on earth was going on backstage? She rounded on Nageena, panting slightly from the brisk walk. 'How can you be so sure?'

Nageena cupped her hands to her mouth and screamed, 'Hashim!'

The man in the grey coat swivelled around, and Mona's stomach fell.

It wasn't Ali. Of course it wasn't.

Although handsome, Hashim looked more like a sibling of Ali's than the real deal. But she knew that Ali only had a younger brother, and this man was too old to be that.

He smiled, waving at Nageena and coming straight at them.

Mona bit her lip. She wasn't prepared for this. She had only wanted to check if he was Ali or not; she had no interest in chatting with the guy.

Up close, Hashim was even more handsome, the way the hair fell over his forehead and his grey eyes glimmered. He air-kissed Nageena twice before holding her at arm's length. 'To what do I owe this honour?' he said. 'It isn't every day that someone as grand as Nageena calls out my name.'

Beside her, Nageena blushed. 'I see you've lost none of your charm over the years.' She gripped Mona's arm and thrust her forward. 'My friend here is the wife of Lahore's biggest real estate tycoon, but just now, she only has eyes for you. The poor lady just ran a marathon trying to get to you.'

Hashim glanced at Mona, the skin around his eyes crinkling. 'And does the rich lady have a name?'

This time, it was Mona who blushed. She extended a hand in his direction. 'Mona Bilal.'

Hashim took her hand in both of his, cocooning it in his warmth. 'A pleasure, madam. Now, what can I help you with?'

Nageena screeched with laughter. 'Don't you go flirting with the woman, Hashim. For starters, she's too old for you, and she has a very handsome husband. I doubt she's interested in you in that way.' Giving Mona a surreptitious smile, she added, 'Unless, of course, you are?'

'Nonsense,' Mona replied. This was most unlike her. She wasn't going to get wrong-footed by people who were much younger and less experienced than her. She removed her hand from Hashim's grip and jutted out her chin. 'It's just that you reminded me of someone I knew once.'

Hashim gave her a pleasant smile. 'May I ask who?'

Something about his manner disarmed her. Could he be related to Ali? 'He was another model, but this is ancient history. I don't even…'

She froze, realising too late that Nageena was hanging on to her every word.

A smile was playing on her mouth. 'Well, don't keep us in suspense. Who does Hashim remind you of?'

Mona sniffed. 'No one, but thank you for your help.' She turned to Hashim. 'Nice to meet you.'

Although they didn't shake hands, Hashim gave her another warm smile. 'I really hope our paths will cross again, Mona Bilal.'

'I doubt they will,' Mona replied.

'Lahore is a small place. You never know.'

Mona turned away without another word to the two of them. Coming here had been a gross misjudgement on her part; she was too old to let impulse dictate her actions. Nageena was a self-proclaimed gossip. It was hard to say what she would construe from Mona's behaviour tonight, but if there was one thing Mona was grateful for, it was that she hadn't been foolish enough to say Ali's name out loud. There was no use in dredging up the past. Ali's chapter was closed, and if it hadn't been for those blasted text messages, he wouldn't be on her mind so often. It was all in the past, it had been for many years, and as she rushed to be home in time for dinner, Mona realised that this was the most she had thought of Ali in months.

Her relief at there being no new text messages or unknown calls was short-lived as her car entered the gates of her home. Aimen and her in-laws were already here. The fact that there hadn't been a single call or message from Bilal for the past couple of hours meant that he was furious with her. Despite his repeated reminders, she was late for dinner at her own house.

There could be no greater embarrassment.

The heels of her Louboutins clicked loudly on the marble as she hurried towards the dining room, the maids pausing in their activities and bowing their heads as she passed them.

'How many times have I told you all not to bow your heads like this?' she snapped. 'I'm not a queen!'

'*Ji*, Bibi,' they murmured in unison, their heads still bowed.

Mona didn't have time to give them another lecture, she was late enough as it was, but it was entirely possible that these ideas were fed to these poor girls by Qudsia. There was no other explanation.

A hush descended as she opened the sliding doors leading into the dining room. The only sounds were of Zahid and his mother eating. Like Bilal, they hadn't even bothered to look up.

Sitting at the head of the table, Qudsia made a show of checking the watch on her wrist. 'Oh, Mona, we waited for you, but you were so obscenely late that we had to start dinner without you.'

Aimen rose to meet Mona, giving her a quick hug before sliding back into her seat. Mona followed suit, taking the empty seat opposite Bilal. After a moment, he looked up, but his face was expressionless. Avoiding eye contact with her, he speared a piece of lamb on his fork and brought it to his mouth.

From the set of his shoulders, Mona could tell that he was angry. And rightfully so. It was very unlike her to forget such an important dinner, but what else could she have done? She had to go and see Hashim Akhtar. She wouldn't have been able to rest otherwise. 'I'm sorry, I got caught up with some work,' she announced.

'I reminded you this morning, Mona,' Bilal said. 'And again in the afternoon. Surely, you could have planned your schedule so that it didn't clash with the dinner?'

'Bilal, I—'

'You do know about the kidnappings going on. So many people from affluent families have been abducted for ransom. If you're going to be late, the least you could do was call ahead and inform us, so we didn't worry. It is very unlike you to be so irresponsible.'

'Irresponsible? Me?' Mona stared at her husband. There was no way she was letting him get away with this bullying. 'If you were so concerned, you could have just phoned me again. Of course I know about the kidnappings. That's all anyone ever talks about these days.'

'Oh, it's all water under the bridge, Bhenji,' Shama said, shovelling forkfuls of pasta in her mouth. 'Bilal Bhai and Qudsia Apa kept us well entertained.'

'Apa?' Qudsia echoed.

Shama gave Qudsia a sympathetic look. 'What else am I supposed to call a woman who is so many years older than me?'

Mona enjoyed the look on Qudsia's face at being called an older sister. Shama probably had years on her.

'We were just talking about Bilqees, our maid,' Shama continued. 'The slut ran away with one of our drivers.'

Mona turned to Aimen, her disagreement with Bilal forgotten for a moment. 'Wasn't she your personal maid?'

Aimen nodded, pushing food around her plate. 'She was. I am barely coping without her. She handled everything. There's no one to dress me in the morning now.'

Mona pinched her mouth. 'Surely, you can survive without a maid, Aimen. I haven't raised you to be completely useless.'

'I like that my wife is used to comfort, Aunty,' Zahid spoke up, his mouth full of God knows what. 'It is a sign of prosperity when the ladies of the house can't even be bothered to lift a finger.'

'It's a sign of laziness,' Mona replied, to which she got elbowed in the arm by Aimen.

'Ammi, be quiet!'

Zahid laughed. 'Oh, Aunty, I see that this new-age nonsense has got to you as well. There really is nothing wrong with women spending time at home. Look at my mother, Shama Begum. While my father worked, she meekly spent all her days at home, cooking food and attending to her children. And when my father hit the jackpot, who do you think benefitted the most?' He pointed at his mother, whose face shone with pride. 'My darling mother. She rules the roost now. She makes all the decisions, and if Aimen is patient, she too will rule one day.'

'A noble thought,' Qudsia added. 'I have to say, it is refreshing to see someone young upholding our traditional values.'

Zahid beamed. 'And I intend to pass these values on to my children.'

'If they ever materialise,' Shama muttered. 'It's been years.'

Beside Mona, Aimen went rigid. 'Well, we're trying—'

'I did not ask you for details of your intimate life, Aimen. I was just making a statement.' Shama folded her arms across her chest and looked away.

'A lot of people are taking their time when it comes to having kids,' Bilal said, putting his cutlery down. He had been angry from the start, but his eyes were blazing now. Nobody picked on his daughter in his presence. 'And sometimes, the problem can lie with the man as well, especially when he is so visibly overweight.' As if realising what he'd just said, he looked across at Zahid. 'Of course, I mean it generally. I am sure God will bless you two with many kids in the fullness of time.'

Shama pushed away her plate. 'Well, one can certainly hope so. People keep asking me if I have any good news to share, but I just have to sit and give them vacant smiles. It goes against the natural order of things.'

'Like Bilal said, being overweight sometimes plays a part in this too,' Mona began, but when she caught Bilal's glare, she looked away, and changed tack. 'I read about it in a few magazines.'

Shama looked around. 'Well, it's a good thing your daughter isn't overweight, then. Imagine if we also had her weight to consider.'

Mona opened her mouth to protest, but then thought better of it. There was no point in reasoning with people like Shama. Instead, she watched with distaste as Zahid dug into a bowl of kheer with gusto, flecks of sweet rice sticking to his upper lip.

How her daughter managed to endure this man's touch was beyond her.

Shama smiled at her son. 'Have some of the ice cream too, Beta. Nothing can fill that baby-shaped void in your life, but food does help.'

Mona had always known Shama to be a controlling and manipulative woman, and this latest display only reinforced that belief. She had had reservations about the *rishta* from the start, but Nighat had been adamant. Zahid's father had been a decorated civil service officer and had amassed a huge amount of wealth over the years. He also had immense agricultural lands down in Sindh.

'He sent his son to an excellent Ivy League college in the United States, and they are a very liberal family,' Nighat had said all those years ago before Aimen was even engaged. 'Your daughter will want for nothing.' When Mona had continued to express reservations, Nighat had looked at her straight in the face. 'Mona, I know what difficult men are like. My husband was one and my own son is one as well. I know what they're like. So trust me when I tell you that Zahid is nothing like that. I can tell. Your daughter will live like a queen.'

Except that Zahid had probably gained a hundred pounds since then and done nothing with his fancy degree. He simply danced to his mother's instructions like a grown-up baby. A complete waste. The only silver lining was that they had so much money that Aimen really did want for nothing.

Qudsia gave Shama a tight smile. 'I really am glad that Bilqees ran away when she did. I shudder to imagine what kind of damage she could have caused to the family's reputation otherwise. We ought to count our blessings, don't you think, Shama?'

As Shama launched into another tirade against Bilqees, Mona caught Bilal squeezing his sister's hand in gratitude.

She'd prevented the dinner from descending into chaos by changing the subject.

Mona reached for Aimen's hand. It was cold and clammy. All she wanted to do right now was to smash all the dishes on Shama and her son's heads. For her daughter's sake, she hoped there would be a baby soon because Shama didn't look like the kind of woman to wait around forever.

'It's a sad state of affairs when we can't even control the behaviour of our maids in this country,' Shama said, spooning some kheer into her mouth. 'If the lower classes are behaving this way, can you even imagine how bad things must be in the upper circles?'

Even Bilal rolled his eyes to that. 'Shama ji, love is not a crime. Even poor people are allowed to love. I don't understand what's so wrong with what Bilqees has done.'

Shama's nostrils flared. 'I'd arranged for her to get married to someone in my village, and the slut ran away with the driver. She was engaged. She shamed the family.'

'She had nothing to do with your family, Shama ji.'

Shama banged a fist on the table. 'Silence! Are you trying to tell me that it is okay to have vulgar sex before marriage, Bilal Bhai? Are you even Muslim?'

Qudsia had clapped her hands to her mouth, but Bilal was unfazed. 'You can't control everyone, Shama ji. You can't control human nature. Sex is the most natural thing in the world.'

'So, am I to understand that it is also okay for married women to sleep around, then? Because it's human nature?'

'I didn't say that.'

'Then what were you trying to say, Bilal Bhai?'

'Bilal—' Mona began, but Zahid cut her off.

'Women at the office flirt with me all the time,' he said, looking at all of them proudly.

'No, they don't,' Aimen replied. 'I've told you a million times, Zahid, that if a woman speaks to you, that doesn't mean she's flirting.'

'If talking constituted flirting, then I'd say Shama ji and I were just now furiously flirting,' Bilal said, a small smile playing on his face.

'*Astagfirullah*, Bilal Bhai,' Shama replied, touching her ears.

Zahid pointed at himself, poking his index finger into his fleshy chest. 'They're attracted to me, Uncle. To my beauty.'

To everyone's surprise, Qudsia let out a laugh, hastily masking it as a sneeze and covering her mouth. 'Sorry, just my allergies.' Her eyes watered as she suppressed her laugh.

Shama wasn't amused. With a solemn expression, she announced, 'I tell you what, if I ever found out that someone in my family had slept around while married, I would cut ties with them immediately.'

In that instant, Bilal's eyes met Mona's, and her heart fell. She knew that they were both thinking about her past... about Ali. But what Bilal didn't know was that there was even more reason to be concerned now that her past had come back to haunt her.

Whatever little appetite she had was gone now.

That night, as Bilal washed up in the bathroom, Mona lay in bed, burying her cold toes in the duvet. Over the years, the sounds of splashing water and Bilal's trimmer had grown on her, to the point that if she didn't hear them, the day felt incomplete. She knew that in a few minutes he would emerge from the bathroom in his dressing gown, smelling of mint toothpaste and aftershave. He would give her a small kiss on the cheek, and if she cared to take things further, she would lean into him and he would, as always, be ready. Most nights, she just whispered good night to him as they took their respective positions in bed and called it a night.

She was texting Meera when her phone lit up with an unknown number.

She pressed a hand to her mouth to stop herself from crying out. This was the second time this person had called her. What did they want from her? Water was still running in the bathroom, so at least Bilal was busy. Mona looked around the room for answers, but if the walls had any answers, they kept them to themselves.

She watched the screen, the little green phone icon dancing at the bottom, urging her to swipe right. With her heart pounding in her ears, she realised that, at any moment, the phone would stop ringing. Did she dare face this person head-on?

It was now or never.

Closing her eyes, she swiped right and held the phone to her ear.

She didn't know what she was anticipating, but whatever it was, it wasn't silence.

And then, as she strained her ears, she heard it... deep breathing.

Deep, measured breaths.

Although this person hadn't made their intentions clear with the text messages, hearing them breathe over the phone somehow cemented everything, making her realise that whatever this was had just become even more serious.

'Hello?' she said, hating how weak her voice sounded. 'Who is this?'

There was no sign that the person had even heard her. The deep breathing continued as before.

'Hello?' she tried again.

The water stopped running in the bathroom, signalling the fact that Bilal would soon be out. The sudden silence sharpened the sound of the breathing. For someone tormenting her with the messages, this person sounded very calm and composed. But then, that's how these people operated. They treated this like regular work. Perhaps it wasn't personal at all.

Bilal was clattering around in the bathroom now, presumably putting all his lotions and aftershaves in their proper place. He would be out in seconds, and she didn't want to answer any questions about why she was on the phone at this time of the night.

However, before she could end the call, a faint sound of squawking broke through the monotonous breathing. Birds – no, it sounded like a parrot of some sort.

They must be outside somewhere. Mona wracked her brain for places in Lahore that had parrots. Who was she fooling? Lahore was a city of almost fifteen million people – maybe more – and there were probably hundreds of places where parakeets could be found. It was like looking for a needle in a haystack. She shook her head, focusing on the breathing pattern. Maybe she could glean something from it. But the breathing was the same as ever. Unchanged.

There was another loud squawk – it sounded like a parrot, but wasn't – and then the line went dead.

'Hello?' she said again, knowing full well that it was futile.

Tears threatened, but she gulped them down, putting the phone aside as the door to the bathroom clicked open.

Reconsidering, she grabbed it again and pushed past Bilal. He gave her a searching look, but she ignored him. There would be time later to apologise for being late for the dinner.

Locked in the bathroom, she turned on all the taps, allowing the rushing water to drown out the sound of her sobs. It was all getting to her, which was probably what that person wanted. Mona looked at herself in the mirror, her face swollen from the stress she had been carrying for weeks, her eyes red-rimmed with unshed tears.

Maybe she ought to tell Bilal. He would know what to do. Why hadn't she thought of that before? She knew why, of course. He wasn't well, and no matter how much he tried to prove that he still had the health of a young man, he had a heart condition that was only going to get worse. And her relationship with Ali had almost broken him then, so she couldn't be sure what rehashing it all would achieve now. Despite his reassurances, she'd noticed him wheezing like an old engine when they were intimate, and the thought that his heart might be getting weaker chilled her to the bone. She would never be able to forgive herself if the burden of these messages gave him a heart attack. She'd rather die than subject him to that torture.

But you will need to eventually, a voice said in her head. *It's not like you're getting any younger. All this stress isn't healthy for you either.*

As if on cue, her phone lit up with a new text message. It was from an unknown number.

With her heart in her throat, she clicked it open.

> Three million rupees in cash. Bring the money to Thokar Niaz Baig on Sunday at noon. If you tell anyone about this – even Bilal – your secret is out, and your life will be over.

The astonishing figure didn't even register in her mind at first. All she could think of was that somehow the blackmailer knew about Bilal and that she had just been thinking of telling him. How had this person managed to read her mind?

Against her better judgement, she replied to the text.

> If I give you the money, does this stop?

The reply arrived almost immediately.

> It stops. Three million and I'm gone. You have my word.

Mona sighed. The word of a blackmailer. She didn't have this kind of cash on hand. There was plenty in her bank account, but she shared it with Bilal, and such a big withdrawal would surely alert him. Would this money really end this torture? Three million was a very small price to pay if it meant that she'd be at peace again. The faces of Bilal and Arslan flashed before her eyes, the kind of future Arslan would have if this secret got out. She thought of her daughter, Aimen, who was already struggling with a cruel mother-in-law. Would her marriage survive this?

Even Farhan, sitting in London, wouldn't be unaffected by this. As the eldest son, he'd get dragged into the drama too, and since London was the second home of most of Pakistan's elite, Mona knew that they wouldn't hesitate to drag her son through the mud if they got the chance.

By the time she unlocked the bathroom door, stepped into the chilly bedroom and approached a snoring Bilal, she'd made her decision.

Chapter 10

Bilal

There were many things he regretted in life, but none as much as his friendship with Faheem. It was inconceivable how this odious man had weaselled his way into Bilal's life, to the point that he could even able to ruin weekends by suggesting useless trips.

He put his hand on Bilal's thigh and squeezed. 'I know Sundays are for family, but believe me when I tell you, this plot of land is worth it.'

Bilal looked out of the window as they sped down Canal Road, watching young children jumping into the frigid water and splashing around. The water was murky brown and absolutely filthy, but the children didn't seem to mind. Even their mothers were unconcerned as they did their laundry on the banks of the canal, leaving the clothes out to dry on the grass and bushes. Sometimes, Bilal wondered if being poor was better than being rich with the burden of the world on one's shoulders. If it wasn't for Arslan, who kept him entertained and on his toes, he didn't know where he would be.

He'd almost given up on trying to understand his wife. All these decades of being married, and he was still no closer to figuring out the enigma that was Mona. Her moods changed like the weather. She blamed it all on the menopause, but surely, that couldn't mean that she should be temperamental all the time. But then, what did he know about the female anatomy? And he wasn't about to ask Faheem.

Instead, he asked how much longer they'd be.

Faheem leaned over and ruffled Bilal's hair. 'Did you know that you pout like a teenager?'

Bilal shot him a dirty look, running his fingers through his hair and setting it back in place. 'I don't pout, Faheem.'

'You're pouting right now. Just look at yourself.'

'You'd be better off focusing on the road instead of on me.'

Faheem sighed. 'What can I do when the person sitting next to me is so irresistible?'

'Ha ha,' Bilal replied. 'Drop the act, man. It isn't funny any more.'

Faheem's voice grew solemn. 'Who said I was joking? Who's to say I'm not taking you to my secret lair to have my way with you?'

Looking at Bilal's shocked expression, he threw his head back and laughed.

'Oh, Bilal, you need to stop being so predictable and uptight. Just relax, will you?'

Pushing eighty, Faheem would be lucky to lay a finger on Bilal, let alone have his way with him, but Bilal remained silent.

'You know, Nageena keeps asking about you,' Faheem began, his various chins wobbling as he helped himself to some roast chickpeas they'd bought from the roadside. 'I told her you're a busy and married man, but the woman is relentless.' He glanced sideways at Bilal. 'I've already told you, she knows her stuff.' With that, Faheem let out a massive burp, diffusing the smell of undigested chickpeas into the car.

Bilal gagged, pulling down the window and letting the cold air blow across his face. 'I don't want to hear about this,' he murmured. 'I'm fine the way I am.'

'You mean you're happy being unhappy?'

'Why does she want me when she knows I have no interest in her?'

Faheem sniggered. 'Why does anyone want you? I hate myself for the very same reason.'

'But, I—'

'Just look at it with an open mind, will you? There is no harm in having a bit of fun on the side. It's not like you have to marry her. I doubt Nageena wants to be saddled in marriage with anyone either. Just buy her nice things and have some fun. You look like you need it.'

Bilal was about to tell Faheem that he knew nothing of his life, but it seemed like Faheem had read his mind.

Holding up a hand, he said, 'I see enough to know that your sex life is very dysfunctional. You have to understand that women over fifty don't even want it.'

Bilal blinked once. 'Wow. And I thought you could sink no lower, Faheem.'

Faheem shrugged. 'Well, it's true. They just want to focus on their children and friends after a certain point. Sex takes a backseat for women here, but not for men. We want it till we drop dead.'

'God, you're such a misogynist. It's not a good look, Faheem. I wonder what your wife thinks about all of this.'

'Gulrukh is very happy in her bubble. She spends six months a year in London buying things for our numerous grandchildren. What she doesn't know won't bother her.'

Bilal looked ahead, squinting in the sun. 'Don't you ever feel that it's wrong? All this cheating?'

Faheem shrugged. 'Why should it be wrong? It's not like I'm marrying them. It's just innocent fun. And, let me tell you, Gulrukh is very happy that the sex is over. She never really liked it, anyway.'

Without warning, Bilal laughed. The man was barking mad. 'Were you a woman in another life that you know so much about them, Faheem?'

'Laugh all you want, but the next time your wife turns you away, you'll remember my words. And you'll remember good old Nageena and her warm, wet embrace.'

Bilal shuddered. 'If you say so.'

As it turned out, the plot of land Faheem showed him wasn't that bad at all. It had potential, and Bilal could see himself developing it into a proper high-rise apartment building. As land prices had shot up, people in Lahore were starting to look at investing in apartments, and that's what Bilal wanted to capitalise on. He'd always believed in being an innovator, and right now, innovation was required in the real estate market.

He couldn't believe he was doing this, but he found himself patting Faheem on the shoulder. 'Thanks for bringing me out here today, Faheem. It's a good piece of land.'

Having finished the chickpeas, Faheem was now busy digging into a corncob he'd bought. 'I told you,' he said between bites, chewing noisily. 'But you never listen to poor Faheem. It's like I don't even exist for you. If I hadn't brought you to Thokar Niaz Baig today, you wouldn't even have known this land existed and then...'

Bilal didn't hear a word of what Faheem said next. For a moment, he thought he was hallucinating, but there it was, clear as day: Mona's white Beemer. There could be no doubt about it since he had memorised the registration number by heart. He craned his neck, searching for his wife sitting in the back like she usually did, but there was no one. There was just a single person in the car, and that person was driving it. As the sun caught the blond streaks in the driver's hair, Bilal knew that it was his wife who was driving.

How strange, he thought. *You haven't driven a car for ages!*

But, here she was, driving her Beemer all alone. A flash of rage overtook him as he marvelled at his wife's stupidity in travelling alone. Had she forgotten that most of the kidnappings in Lahore were taking place in Thokar Niaz Baig? Mona had lost her bloody mind; there was no other way to explain this bizarre behaviour.

He turned to look at Faheem, but it didn't seem like he'd noticed anything. Letting him yap on about the plot of land they'd just seen, Bilal pulled out his phone and dialled Mona's number.

He saw her pick up the phone from its holder on the dashboard and hold it up.

His stomach dropped as she set it aside, ignoring his call.

Bilal called her again, his heart rate picking up.

This time, she picked up. 'Hi, sorry I didn't see your call earlier. What's up?'

'Where are you?' he asked, glancing at Faheem before lowering the volume on his phone. The old buffalo was silent now, ears trained towards the phone. Faheem was a shameless gossip, but Bilal wouldn't be giving him any fodder.

'Oh,' Mona replied, trying to add some cheer to her voice. 'I'm actually just heading to work. Sorry we couldn't speak properly this morning.'

We never speak properly nowadays, he opened his mouth to say, but one look at Faheem and Bilal closed it again. 'It's Sunday,' he said after a moment.

'So? You had work too, didn't you? The fact that it is Sunday didn't seem to bother you.'

'Meera is working you too hard.'

Mona sniffed. 'No more than usual. Now, was there something you wanted to ask me? Because I am kind of busy.'

He couldn't bear it any more. 'With what?'

'Work, what else? What's got into you today? Do I need to be worried?' Mona sounded completely unfazed.

'Where exactly are you at this moment?'

'Out.'

'Out where?'

'Why do you care?'

He slammed his fist against the dashboard. 'Where the hell are you right now? Answer my question!'

She was silent for so long that he thought she had ended the call.

Bilal closed his eyes. He shouldn't have let his temper get the better of him, especially not in front of Faheem. He sighed. 'Look—'

'I am not bound to tell you my whereabouts, Bilal. I am not your slave.' Her voice was quiet, but there was barely concealed anger there. And tears. 'I am in Garden Town, heading to work. Don't raise your voice against me ever again.'

And with that, she ended the call, leaving Bilal gulping for air like a fish out of water.

Faheem was smirking as he asked, 'Trouble in paradise?'

Bilal didn't respond. He was seeing dark spots in his vision, his forehead starting to sweat. He wasn't sure he felt too well. Wiping some of the sweat from his forehead with the back of his hand, he blinked several times. 'I'm just feeling a bit nauseous.'

Faheem reached out and squeezed his arm, but this time there was nothing sleazy about the gesture. He seemed genuinely concerned. 'Are you sure you're okay?'

Bilal pounded a fist against his chest, trying to get rid of the all too familiar pain that had erupted there. 'I – I'll be fine,' he murmured.

Maybe she's sick, he thought. *Maybe she's come to see a doctor.*

On a Sunday? That was preposterous.

They were on their way back to Gulberg by the time it finally sunk in that Mona was lying to him. He wondered how long she'd been doing it for, and more importantly, what exactly she was hiding?

Chapter 11

Fakhar

The fact that Sahab ji had summoned him the moment he got back indicated just how angry he was. Fakhar wondered who had blabbed to him. It must have been that silly boy he'd had fun with. The woman couldn't have done so, since she'd been dispatched to her new captors days ago. Both the woman and the boy had been so forgettable that Fakhar didn't even remember their names.

Plastering a smile on his face, he knocked on the battered wooden door and entered. The door creaked as it opened to reveal a small room with just a neatly made bedstead upon which Sahab ji sat. Fakhar immediately lowered his gaze. 'Salam, Sahab ji. So good to see you back all hale and hearty.'

There was pin-drop silence in the room except for the sound of the tennis ball being bounced on the concrete floor.

'We don't shit where we eat, Fakhar,' Sahab ji murmured, his voice quiet, but deadly. 'You had no business subjecting those people to such torture.'

Fakhar would have liked to disagree, seeing how Sahab ji abducted these people from their homes and then sold them off, but he kept his mouth shut. He had to be careful about this. If Sahab ji turned him away, there would be nowhere for him to go, and he knew that people with tastes like his almost always ended up either in jail or dead in a ditch. He didn't want either fate for himself, so he kept quiet, keeping his head bowed, not meeting Sahab ji's eye.

'You know, I do think there is something dreadfully wrong with you in the head,' Sahab ji continued. 'Have you no remorse for what you did to that poor boy? He needed stitches. You're lucky that you're under my protection because our authorities take a very dim view of men who torture women and children like this.'

'The little shit was asking for it, Sahab ji,' Fakhar said. 'I only gave him what he wanted. And he's no kid, let me tell you that.'

'You mean he was asking to be raped?'

'You don't know these people like I do, Sahab ji. A firm hand is what they need.'

He stole a glance at Sahab ji to see that his eyes were blazing as he sat on the charpai with his legs spread out, tennis ball in hand. He was gripping it so hard that his knuckles had turned white.

'You presume that the man who employs your sorry ass knows so little about the world, do you? These people were under my protection, and you violated them. I spend a lot of money keeping this operation running. I am planning to expand it, to become something more than a common kidnapper. And you — you flout all the rules?'

Fakhar bit his tongue. Although Sahab ji provoked both fear and admiration in him, sometimes, he could be very dense. In Fakhar's village, people got raped every day. What was so special about it? Consent didn't matter. That was what he'd been taught his entire life, that it was a man's world out there.

'Rules are meant to be broken,' he whispered, realising too late that he'd said it out loud.

Sahab ji's face grew stormy. 'What did you just say?'

'Sahab ji—'

Without warning, Sahab ji aimed the tennis ball at him, catching him in the face. Fakhar howled, clutching his right eye as pain seared through him. His vision went blurry, the area around his eye tender to the touch. If he lost the eye, he would need to wear an eyepatch forever.

'Don't test me again, Fakhar, I am warning you.'

Fakhar threw himself at Sahab ji's feet. 'Forgive me! Forgive me, Sahab ji! I will never do anything without your permission ever again. I promise.'

'I ought to dismiss you or, even better, kill you.'

Fakhar wept, tears streaming down his face as he bent to kiss Sahab ji's boots. The taste of leather and dirt filled his mouth, but he didn't care.

Sahab ji kicked him away. 'Stop slobbering all over me, you creep. You're sick, but you're also useful, so maybe I will keep you around for a bit longer.'

'Yes, Sahab ji, please, Sahab ji—'

'But you will be punished. For as long as I please.'

Fakhar held his palms together, silently begging for mercy that didn't come.

Sahab ji's face was a mask of disgust. 'I'd suggest marriage to tame your sick mind, but I have a feeling you're well beyond it at this point.'

Fakhar almost laughed at that. Marriage. He didn't know of a more obsolete concept. But for Sahab ji, he dipped his head. 'Whatever you say, Sahab ji.'

Marriage was what his parents had, but that hadn't saved his mother. Fakhar still remembered the numerous beatings, the sick and ugly games his father played. He had been only nine years old when he'd witnessed his father beating his mother so brutally that the sound of her screams reverberated around the entire hut.

Smack, smack, smack.

The sound of the flat leather shoe against Maa ji's bare skin made him close his eyes in fear. Usually, these beatings stopped after a while, but that day, his mother had made the mistake of going to the butcher's all by herself, with her face uncovered. Even worse, she'd smiled at him, showing her brilliant white teeth as she bade him goodbye.

'The butcher has told everyone that you are a whore,' Abba Jaan shouted, as the shoe landed against Maa ji's naked back. He had stripped her of her kameez, so that she was only in a short undershirt.

'I only bought meat,' Maa ji cried. 'Apart from thanking him, I didn't utter a word.'

Smack.

'You're a liar, Meena! I know you spread your legs for him. I can smell him on you.'

'You smell the meat, which I was carrying. And the butcher stinks of it. Do you honestly think I would sink so low?'

'Shut up! How dare you talk back like this? I see now that I've given you a free rein for too long. It's all my fault. Go easy on women and this is how they repay you.'

'Ji, you're not thinking clearly,' Maa ji whimpered. 'The village folk are just trying to get in your head. This is what they thrive at.'

The beating stopped for a moment, but Fakhar didn't dare open his eyes.

'Not thinking clearly, eh?' his father murmured. 'You dare say that to me, Meena? You dare?'

Fakhar thought that just because his eyes were closed, he'd be invisible, but of course, he wasn't.

Drunk on the power these beatings gave him, Abba Jaan shouted, 'Fakhar! Come here this instant!'

Fakhar kept his eyes closed and shook his head.

'Let him be,' Maa ji replied, her voice barely more than a whisper. 'Let him have a normal childhood.'

'I said come here, or I will drag you here,' Abba Jaan growled.

Fakhar had opened his eyes, then, and stepped forward. Seeing him approach, his father let the shoe fall from his hand, and in its place, he picked up a leather whip he reserved only for special occasions. Fakhar had only seen it get used once, and that too on someone who had swindled his father. The man had received ten lashes, enough to ensure he never walked straight again.

Fakhar mewled, his vision going blurry with unshed tears.

A playful smile spread across his father's mouth. 'Since you're cowardly enough to watch your mother get beaten, let me offer you a choice.'

'He's only nine,' Maa ji said. 'Let him go outside and play.'

Abba Jaan shook his head. 'I will stop beating your mother if you agree to take her place. You'll get only one lash, but if you refuse, I'll give your mother twenty lashes.'

Maa ji's breath caught in her throat. 'Twenty?' she echoed. 'Do you mean to kill me?'

Abba Jaan spread his arms. 'The choice is yours, Fakhar.'

Maa ji's gaze locked with Fakhar's. Her eyes implored him. He knew she wasn't strong enough to endure twenty lashes and he could make her pain go away if he agreed to that one lash. Abba Jaan probably wouldn't even hit him that hard, he knew that much. He was a son, after all... the prized son who would carry his name forward.

'Fakhar,' Maa ji said, her voice scratchy from the pain. 'Fakhar, please...'

Fakhar didn't want his mother to get twenty lashes, but then he thought of the soft skin on his back and how much that one *lash would hurt him, and his mind made the decision before his heart could intervene. 'I don't want to get beaten.'*

His mother gasped, but Abba Jaan's face gleamed with triumph. 'I am impressed. You're an even bigger coward than I thought. You'd let your own mother suffer like this?'

Fakhar looked away and Abba Jaan laughed.

'Look at that, Meena. You've been raising the devil's spawn. Even I wasn't like that. I loved my mother.'

Maa ji's eyes were hollow as she rose to a sitting position with her legs tucked underneath her. 'I hope you kill me with these lashes. If I can't even step out to get food without being beaten to within an inch of my life, why am I even alive?'

'Save the theatrics, Meena. You only have yourself to blame' – *Abba Jaan bared his teeth* – *'and perhaps little Fakhar for being such a wimp.'*

Fakhar witnessed his mother receive every single one of those twenty lashes, never flinching, never regretting his decision, not even for a second.

Better her than him.

He watched his mother stagger towards the charpai *when Abba Jaan was done and collapse on it, ribbons of flesh hanging off her back, but Fakhar's heart didn't thaw.*

Better her than him.

Ten days later, she died of an infection, howling in pain, but Fakhar didn't shed a single tear.

Better her than him.

–

It was cold and dark in his small prison cell, but there was hay on the floor, a heavy blanket to curl up in and his comforting thoughts that kept him going. Soon, Sahab ji would tire of punishing him and let him resume his duties. He'd heard from the chatter outside that they would be targeting Lahore's business community again and the thought brought him immense pleasure. He despised watching those men in their expensive suits and fancy cars, strutting around like they owned the place. They probably did, but it was time now to take it all back from them.

Soon, Sahab ji would need him again because he was hopeless at this. He didn't have the guts Fakhar did. Sahab ji hadn't been brought up by someone like Abba Jaan, who, despite being a cruel and despicable man, had taught him one valuable lesson: the importance of self-preservation.

The door of his cell opened, letting in a sliver of light and warmth. Fakhar exhaled, his breath a cloud of mist.

To his utter delight, it was the boy who brought him a meal, the one he'd molested. Shabbir, that was his name, Fakhar remembered now.

Poor Shabbir still walked like there was a pole lodged up his backside. 'Sahab ji has asked for food to be brought to you. He thinks death by starvation is too good for the likes of you.'

Fakhar licked his lips. 'If the food is as hot as you, consider me game.'

A look of revulsion crossed the boy's features. 'You stink like the pig you are, Fakhar, and you will die like one.'

Fakhar shrugged. 'I just taught you a lesson, Shabbir. You don't get to rape people and not expect to be treated in kind. That's something I learned very early on in my life.'

'I wouldn't have raped her,' Shabbir hissed. 'I was only jesting.'

Fakhar smiled. 'Were you? Well, then, I am sorry.'

Shabbir spat in the bowl, tendrils of spit and phlegm landing in the daal, before he slid the tray in his direction. 'I hope you enjoy your meal.'

Fakhar made sure Shabbir was watching as he dipped the naan exactly where the spit swam and put it in his mouth. 'Delicious.'

He took another mouthful as the boy gagged on his way out of the cell.

Chapter 12

Mona

She'd done it. She'd gone against everything she believed in and paid off her blackmailer. There were a thousand books and films on the subject, on how the blackmail never ended. Mona used to laugh at the people who thought that paying money would help get rid of their problems, whereas it was obvious that the person would just come back to demand more when they needed it.

And yet, she'd gone and done the same. It had been a few weeks since she'd pushed the bag of money through the gate of an abandoned house on Raiwind Road, near Thokar Niaz Baig. She was such a mess of nerves that she'd botched the phone call with Bilal, and he hadn't been the same with her since. There was a haunted look to him these days, and whenever she'd emerge from the bathroom in her nightie, his eyes would travel all over her, not in lust or admiration, but what looked like suspicion.

If he thought she was having an affair, he couldn't have been more mistaken. She was in her fifties, for crying out loud. Not that it had stopped Meera, but who was Mona to judge? When she saw him glare at her for the umpteenth time as he helped Arslan with his homework, something in her broke. Despite all his faults, this man had been trying to do his best by her ever since Arslan was born. The weight of her guilt was almost too much to bear. She blinked away the tears and cleared her throat. 'Can I talk to you?'

He looked away, focusing on the workbook. 'About what?'

The coldness in his voice even made Arslan look up. 'Alone, please,' Mona said.

Bilal refused to look at her. 'I'm trying to help Arslan with his biology homework, Mona. And besides, why the sudden desire to speak to me after snubbing me for weeks?'

Mona puffed out the breath she was holding. 'If you would only give me a moment—'

'You can go, Dad,' Arslan said in a small voice. 'I can manage.'

It broke Mona's heart to see their son frowning at his workbook, trying not to break into tears. Perhaps Bilal noticed the toll their argument was taking on Arslan, for he finally met her eye. 'Okay.'

However, just as he rose from the sofa, he collapsed on it again. 'Oww,' he muttered, clutching his chest.

In one swift motion, Mona was kneeling in front of him. 'What is it?'

Bilal's forehead was beaded with sweat, and he was breathing tightly as if it hurt to move his chest. 'I'm fine,' he said, closing his eyes briefly before opening them. 'Must have eaten something that's causing this heartburn.'

Mona's gaze travelled to the left side of his chest. 'Bilal, is this to do with heartburn or something else?'

'I said I am fine, woman. Stop scaring Arslan. Look how pale he's become.'

It was true. Poor Arslan was trembling as he watched the man he'd always seen as a strong and authoritative figure lying back on the sofa with his eyes closed. Mona reached out and took Bilal's hand in her own. It was clammy, but he returned the pressure.

'Shouldn't we go to the hospital?' she tried again.

He closed his eyes and shook his head. 'I'm fine. It's just heartburn from eating too many pakoras. Don't you have places to be?'

'My place is here with you.'

She could sense the anger he'd been holding on to deflate out of him. 'I'm sorry I've been such an ass.' He massaged his chest. 'Damn those pakoras. Better now, though.'

That was what his mother used to say. He was just as stubborn as her.

And that was when she decided. Bilal could never know. She wouldn't tell him anything about the blackmail. Her guilt was hers alone. There was nothing to be gained by worrying him, and she had already paid the amount that had been demanded, anyway.

—

As they eased into March, and there was still no contact from the blackmailer, Mona started to relax. Just a tiny bit, but enough that she was attending social engagements again.

For many days after making the payment, she couldn't sleep, always dreading another demand for money. However, no further demands had come. She would check her phone every morning with her heart in her throat, but lately, she'd grown more complacent and no longer viewed her mobile phone as an object of great danger. So, it was in a much lighter mood that she arrived at the engagement ceremony of Alia's daughter at their sprawling mansion on Canal Road. Her spirits lifted even further when a cool breeze caught her hair and swirled it in the air. Mona closed her eyes and let it, not bothered at all about the careful blow-dry being ruined. This right here was what life was all about. Living in the moment. It was a beautiful March day, and in the absence of the grey blanket of smog that usually choked the city, everything looked and sounded liberating. Even the birds seemed to chirp with renewed vigour, and Mona smiled as she pulled the edge of her velvet kaftan out of the car and proceeded towards the lawn.

However, her hard-earned sense of equilibrium was disrupted as soon as she entered the event space. The place was in an uproar. A crowd of people had gathered near the stage, and the rest of the guests were whispering to each other, some making videos on their phones, no doubt selling them to the social media rags for a tuppence. A frantic Shabeena fell into her arms, sobbing uncontrollably.

'What is it?' Mona asked, her hands beginning to shake. 'What's happened?'

'Oh, it's ruined. Everything is ruined,' Shabeena sobbed. 'There will be no engagement.'

Mona pulled her back by the shoulders. 'What's going on, Shabeena?'

Shabeena's scarf had fallen off, and her lips were chapped where she'd bitten into them. 'Fahad... Alia's husband... oh, Mona, he's been taken. He's vanished.'

Mona stopped breathing. She didn't need to ask who had taken Fahad. Everyone knew it, and everyone dreaded it. He'd been taken by the gang. 'What was he doing without security?'

'Alia sent him to pick up their daughter's jewellery, being too busy herself. And with the entire staff caught up with the arrangements, Fahad went out alone. It was only a five-minute drive, but that's all it takes for them to kidnap you. They were watching him.'

'What on earth are the authorities doing if not catching these criminals?'

Shabeena shook her head. 'It's not that easy. This gang operation is like a Hydra monster. You chop off one head and two sprout in its stead. These gangs are getting wealthy on the ransom money, and if a family doesn't pay the money—'

'The person is sold to the highest bidder,' Mona finished for her.

'And they know exactly how much people are worth. One family ended up paying five times the original ransom amount before their person was returned to them.'

A cold fear gripped Mona, and she pulled out her phone to call Bilal before remembering that he was at home. Still, she wrote him a quick message telling him about what had happened. He probably wouldn't reply to her. In his own words, he found it difficult to apologise or make up even when he desperately wanted to.

There would be time later to figure things out with Bilal. Right now, her friend needed her. She pointed atced the crowd of people. 'Is Alia in there somewhere?'

Shabeena nodded, finally pulling the scarf back on her head. 'The poor thing fainted the moment she heard, although I don't know if it was due to her husband being taken or the diamond necklace that she lost along with him.'

'This is hardly the time to joke, Shabeena.'

Shabeena shook her head, eyes brimming with tears. 'I'm not joking. God, no. That's what the people are saying. The necklace cost a fortune.'

Mona took her friend's hand, and together, they made their way towards the crowd, brief snatches of conversation reaching them as they moved past the loud ones.

'This is what happens when you broadcast your wealth to the whole world.'

'The diamond necklace was apparently worth forty million rupees.'

'Took him straight to Thokar Niaz Baig and then out of Lahore, presumably. That was the last location on his phone.'

Mona sucked in a breath.

Thokar Niaz Baig.

That's where she'd left that bag of money the other day. She'd lost count of the number of times Bilal had warned her against venturing out alone, and that's exactly what she'd done. It was pure dumb luck that she hadn't been picked up then and there.

Surely, her blackmailer was acting independently, because the alternative was extremely terrifying. If this was a gang operation, then she was done for.

The world spun around her, and she had to lean on to Shabeena for a moment.

Shabeena patted her shoulder. 'I know, darling. I know.'

Of all the people in the world, it was Humaira who was kneeling next to a semi-conscious Alia, who lay propped up on pillows, a glass of juice in her hand. As she looked up, her gaze locked with Mona's, and she wailed.

'They've taken him! They've taken him and the necklace. My daughter is ruined.'

'Now, now, let's not be so dramatic,' Humaira said. 'I've told my husband, and he's assured me that he's in touch with the authorities and they might just catch those rascals before they can get out of Lahore. They've put up barricades on all entry and exit points.'

Mona pursed her mouth. Like that had ever helped. Lahore was huge, and they could just lay low somewhere in the older parts and wait it out – that is, if they hadn't already left the city.

She knelt down next to Alia as well and ran a hand over her forehead. It was burning. 'Perhaps we ought to shift you inside the house.'

Alia grabbed Mona's hand. 'No! I won't move until I have news on Fahad. And no matter what happens, the engagement has to go on. We'll pretend nothing is wrong.'

Humaira reached out to squeeze Alia's shoulder. 'Don't be silly. You can't hide something like this. Everyone is bound to find out, and besides, I've already called your daughter's in-laws and told them the news. They won't be coming.'

'You what?' Mona and Alia said in unison.

Humaira shrugged. 'I did you all a favour. You would have been a laughing stock.' She looked at the people making videos. 'You already are.'

'That was not your decision to make, Humaira,' Mona said. 'It's a family matter.'

Humaira blinked. 'Oh, I'm sorry. Are you telling me that you believe in family values all of a sudden?'

'What is that supposed to mean?'

'Just that the last time we sat together, you were pretty vocal about women being allowed agency over who they decide to be with.' With a smirk, she added, 'If I am not mistaken, you seemed pretty okay with married women leaving their husbands for gym instructors.'

That drew gasps from the crowd.

'A married woman sleeping with other men? *Haye haye*, what is this new devilry?'

'If she likes loose women so much, maybe she's one too.'

'Is there any difference at all between us and the West at this point?'

Mona held a hand to her chest to calm herself. Her breathing was ragged, and after kneeling next to Alia for all this time, her knees were killing her. If anyone was ever to find out about her secret, she'd be over. There would be no going back, and with people like Humaira reigning Lahori society, the only option open to her would be suicide.

'That's not what happened,' Shabeena spoke up. 'Stop putting words in her mouth.'

Humaira rose, brushing imaginary dust from her heavily embellished gown. 'And a desperate sixty-year-old has-been is going to tell me what happened and what didn't?'

'Just leave, Humaira,' Mona whispered.

'Careful, Mona. You do not want me as your enemy. You won't survive a day in Lahori society. Don't forget who came to support you at your stupid little fashion week.' Her eyes swept the crowd. 'And who didn't.'

She was right, of course. Humaira could decimate her whenever she wanted. All the money in the world wouldn't be able to save her from her wrath. And her friends understood that. Lahori high society thrived on gossip and taking down people. Alia pulled on the hem of Humaira's gown. 'Thank you for everything, Humaira. You're a gem.'

'Yes, you are,' Shabeena added, still a bit red in the face.

'Yes, you are,' the crowd echoed.

Humaira smiled as she surveyed her army of sycophants. 'And, Mona? What would you say?'

Mona pressed her lips together and looked away. She would not give her the satisfaction.

Humaira, however, was relentless. 'Mona?'

In the end, Mona decided that a feud with Humaira was just not worth it, especially since the person she was fighting for had already capitulated. Hating herself, she said, 'You're a gem, Humaira.'

Humaira bent forward with her right ear held out. 'Sorry, I didn't catch what you said.'

'You're a gem, Humaira,' Mona said again, louder. 'A gem!'

Humaira's smile was benevolent. 'Lovely!'

If Mona was hoping for a respite back home, she was sadly mistaken. She felt a hint of foreboding as her car crunched against the gravel upon entering the gates. Darkness had descended, and she realised only now how late it was. Too much time had been spent trying to console Alia. And that was all they could do because her husband's fate was in the hands of the gang now. Any moment now, there would be a demand for ransom, and if Alia didn't comply and supply them with the required amount, they'd just sell her husband to the next highest bidder. What a rotten world it was.

Inside, the house was shrouded in darkness. The sound of her heels on the marble floor echoed as she made her way down the foyer and towards the stairs. She'd put her feet up in the guest room and try to calm her mind before facing Bilal.

She'd almost reached the foot of the stairs when she heard a rustle behind her.

'So, you've finally returned.'

Mona clutched her chest. 'Bilal, you almost gave me a heart attack. Don't do this to me, not at my age.'

Bilal laughed, a mirthless and bitter laugh. 'Age is just a number, isn't it, Mona?'

As her eyes adjusted to the darkness, she made out his outline on the sofa, his eyes shining like a cat's.

'What are you doing, sitting in the darkness like that? Where's Qudsia?'

'Gone to sleep,' Bilal replied. 'They all have. It's become a bit of a habit for you, missing out on family time.'

Mona gripped the bannister to steady herself. It had been a long day, and she had very little patience for Bilal right now. 'After what Alia has been through, my being late should be the least of anyone's worries. I texted you about it.'

Bilal's face was illuminated as he turned on his phone. 'And I got your text. It's just that I couldn't tell whether Fahad had actually been kidnapped or you were simply lying to me.'

'Why on earth would I lie to you, Bilal? What's got into you?'

Bilal rose from the sofa, his knees cracking as he drew himself to his full height. In the darkness, he looked terrifying. Mona held on to the bannister, not trusting herself to stand on her own. All of a sudden, she was exhausted.

She did not have the headspace for an argument right now.

Bilal advanced on her. 'Ever since Arslan was born, I have been nothing but honest and devoted to you. I agree that I had issues in the past... I was not a good husband, but I loved you then, and I love you now. The problem is that I'm not sure if you feel the same way.'

Mona closed her eyes. 'Bilal, I am tired. Can we please not do this today? I am emotionally spent. I have never lied to you either. Not for many years now.'

As he approached her, she saw tears glistening on his cheeks. 'Then why did you lie about your whereabouts the other day? I saw you driving alone in Thokar Niaz Baig, and you pointedly denied it.'

Mona was grateful for the darkness, which would at least mean that Bilal wouldn't see her face drain of colour. She shook her head. 'I don't know what you're talking about.'

Bilal shifted his head to one side. 'What were you doing in Thokar Niaz Baig, Mona?' he asked softly.

How does he know? She took a few steps back. Should she tell him about the blackmail, about everything? Surely, coming clean was better than the alternative.

Before she could say anything at all, Bilal was in her personal space, his face inches from hers. His breath reeked of alcohol. 'I've been watching you for weeks. You're distracted. You're never present, and there's always an excuse when I want sex. Who are you seeing?'

Mona took another step back. 'How dare you!'

'I'm sorry. I should have rephrased it better. Who the hell are you fucking, Mona?'

Tiny droplets of spit landed on her face as Bilal shouted in her face.

She pushed him away. 'Have you lost your bloody mind? How dare you insinuate something like that? If that's what you think I am doing, then you don't even deserve to know the truth. The reason I never said anything was because I feared for your health, which doesn't appear to be as fragile as I had thought.'

Before she could turn away, Bilal grabbed her arm. 'Don't you dare pin this on me. Like you've ever cared about my health. You don't even accompany me to the doctor.' His grip took her back fourteen years when he would do that to her on a regular basis. His strength hadn't diminished. He was still built like an ox.

'Get your hands off me, Bilal. You are drunk, and you are completely out of line.'

'You answer me right now!'

Mona pulled her arm from his grasp. 'Go to hell, asshole.'

The way his eyes blazed, she knew that he would raise his hand against her. She knew it was coming. In a way, she wanted him to, only for him to realise the kind of animal he really was, that it was impossible to tame someone like him.

However, before he could say or do anything, a small voice broke into the darkness.

'Dad?'

It was as if Bilal had been punched. All of his aggression evaporated out of him, leaving him deflated. They both turned to see their son peeking from behind a wall.

'Arslan, my darling boy,' Bilal cried, his voice sweet but measured. 'What are you doing up? I put you in bed hours ago.'

'I heard voices.'

Bilal held up his hands. 'We were just talking.'

Mona rounded on him. 'Were we?'

Bilal's mouth tightened into a grim line. 'Mona, stop it. The kid is scared.'

'Perhaps the kid should see the kind of monster his father has become. Besides, he's almost a teenager, Bilal.'

'You were fighting,' Arslan said, still half hidden behind the wall.

Bilal opened up his arms and embraced Mona. 'See, we are hugging now. We were just talking about something.'

Indecision flickered on Arslan's face. He was old enough to call bluffs, but still young enough to be lulled into a false sense of security. 'Are you sure you weren't fighting?'

Bilal laughed, squeezing Mona into a bigger hug. The smell of alcohol mixed with his cologne made her head spin. 'Well, do you want me to kiss your mother now just to prove my love?'

'Yuck, Dad. I'm outta here.' And just like that, the sullen pre-teen was back.

As Arslan retreated to his bedroom, Mona pushed against Bilal's chest. 'Get off me.' Turning on her heel, she rushed towards the main door.

'Mona, wait! Where do you think you're going at this time of the night?'

'I'm going out.'

Bilal ran after her, trying to take her hand. She brushed him off.

'Don't touch me.'

'Listen, I'm—'

'If you tell me you're sorry one more time, I swear I'm going to smack your face, Bilal. Enough is enough. Don't come after me.'

'It isn't safe. You saw what happened to Fahad.'

She hated the tears sliding down her face. How many more times would she allow him to hurt her like this? 'Well, then you can rest easy when I've been kidnapped. At least I won't be having any affairs.'

'Please don't be like this.' He reached for the back of her dress, but Mona was too fast for him. In an instant, she was out of the door.

'Just piss off, Bilal.'

She didn't allow her heart to melt at the sight of him standing alone in the doorway, looking crestfallen. Instead, she sped off in her Beemer, the tyres screeching against the driveway. She wiped her tears away with the back of her hand and increased her speed, not even slowing for the speed bump. The impact lifted her a few inches from her seat, her head hitting the roof of the car, but she didn't care. At this time of the night, Gulberg was dark and deserted. She quickly turned on to Main Boulevard, speeding down the eight-lane artery that ran through the entirety of Gulberg. Cars honked at her for speeding, but Mona was beyond caring. Perhaps it would be good if she were to just perish in a road accident. Bilal would cry for a few days, until his eye caught a younger, more beautiful woman. Her kids would probably cry for longer, but Aimen was pragmatic, and it wouldn't take her long to fill the mother-shaped void in her life with something else. Farhan didn't even live in Lahore any more, so Mona wasn't sure how much he'd feel her loss. Arslan would probably not even notice his mother's death. He only had eyes for his father. And Qudsia? Well, she would probably celebrate her death and distribute sweets.

Mona picked up her phone to call Meera but then thought against it. The poor woman had enough going on in her life. She didn't notice when she went from Main

Boulevard to an obscure corner of Gulberg, a shadowy circular street set around a sprawling park. Due to the power outages, the area was plunged into darkness. Not a single soul was in sight and the park in front of her was pitch-black, looking almost other-worldly. Like a black abyss that could swallow her whole. She parked at the entrance to the grounds, and in the comforting embrace of darkness, Mona finally let go and cried.

She cried about the abuse she had suffered in life.

She cried about the blackmail she'd endured.

She cried for being born a woman in this godforsaken country.

In the end, it was the fact that she'd broken into hiccups that prevented her from crying any more. It was also due to the hiccups that it occurred to her that she had no idea where in Gulberg she was. She had never been to this park before, but what was more frightening was that the power was still out. Only one house had a small light glimmering at the gate. For some reason, that made her feel even more vulnerable.

The velvety silence of the night was broken by the patter of raindrops on her windscreen. Rain in March, the one thing Lahore was most famous for and the one thing that arrived every year like clockwork. A reminder that life goes on no matter what. That thought calmed her nerves a bit.

Perhaps it was the blackmail that had made her so emotional. Maybe Bilal wasn't as bad as she was making him out to be. Well, she *knew* he wasn't bad, and she also knew that coming out here all alone in the dead of night was not a good idea.

She was about to turn the key in the ignition when a pickup van parked right behind her. Of all the parking spots available, the van had chosen the worst possible one. She honked at whoever was behind the wheel when another similar van parked right next to her. And then a third on her other side. None of them had their headlights on. With the park's boundary wall in front of her and these vans flanking her, she was trapped. Her breath caught in her throat as the penny dropped. This was no coincidence. With mounting horror, she watched the doors to the vans open to reveal men in black, their faces covered by scarves. Even without the scarves, it would have been impossible to make out their features in the dark.

It was obvious what was about to happen to her. In a swift motion, she locked the car doors and did the only other thing she could. She turned on her Beemer's headlights and honked.

Immediately, the men scrambled, hands over their ears as they regrouped. A couple of lights flicked on in the distance. With one hand firmly pressed on the heart of the steering wheel to continue the honking, Mona rummaged inside her bag with the other. Her fingers brushed against her phone, and she pulled it out. All her grievances against her husband were forgotten as she pressed on his name.

The call connected just as something hard crashed against the car, cracking the window right next to her. Mona screamed, lifting her hand off the steering wheel, her head whipping sideways to see a hooded figure staring at her. In one hand he held a revolver and in the other a rock.

'Mona?' Bilal sounded like he'd just woken up. 'What's wrong? I nodded off on the sofa. Where are you?' A second later, it appeared to dawn on him. 'Have you not returned?'

It was his voice that made it all real. This was really happening. She was going to be dragged out of this car and then to somewhere in western Pakistan to be bought and sold like cattle. This was the end. What broke her heart was that she hadn't even made up with Bilal.

Ignoring the tears streaming down her face, she drew in a shaky breath. 'Bilal, I think I'm being kidnapped.'

'Mona, what? What are you saying? Where are you?'

'Bilal, I am so sorry.'

'Where the hell are you, Mona? I'm coming now. I should never have let you go.'

'Somewhere in Gulberg, I don't know… I'm sorry. I should have listened to you.' She was crying again now. 'Bilal, they're going to break into the car.'

Bilal was shouting at the guards, and in the distance, she could hear a car start. 'The tracking people are giving me your car's exact location. I'm coming. Just hold on for a couple of minutes. I'll be there before you know it.'

'It's too late,' she whispered as she watched the men gather around her car again.

Everything was silent now. Even the rain had stopped.

'Mona, I swear if they take you, I will wring their fucking necks.'

As Bilal said those words, another rock was launched at her window, this time shattering it completely.

Mona screamed again, the phone almost sliding out of her grasp. The man closest to her bent down to her level, his electric-green eyes taking her in. He nodded at the phone in her hand, as if asking her permission, before ripping it out of her hand.

'We're taking her,' he said into the phone.

'*Bhenchod*, listen to me. If you hurt my wife, all hell will rain down—'

Bilal's voice was abruptly cut off as the man ended the call and threw her phone somewhere in the grass.

'Don't you dare come near me,' Mona said, packing as much venom into her voice as she could. 'I won't come willingly. I will scream.'

The man's eyes gleamed with mischief, and despite the scarf covering the rest of his face, Mona knew he was laughing at her. He held up the revolver and aimed it at her face. With his other hand, he beckoned her towards him.

She had no choice. There were more than a dozen of them here, and if she didn't go willingly, they'd probably just kill her out of spite and leave. Or maybe not. Killing her wouldn't get them a single rupee. However, before she could think ahead, the man had reached into the broken window and unlocked the doors. In an instant, all four doors were opened, and Mona was dragged out of the car. Her knees hit the ground hard, sending pain shooting up her legs while a hand went up against her mouth to stop her from crying out. Her eyes watered from the grip the men had on her arms. A couple of them ran their hands all over her body for good measure, pausing over her breasts and, later, her stomach.

'This one likes to eat,' one of them muttered, digging his fingers into her lower abdomen.

'She's still in pretty good shape,' said another. 'Better than some of the younger ones we've been getting. Besides, the older they are, the more experience they have.'

'Don't,' another warned them. 'Sahab ji doesn't like this.'

The man with his hands on her breasts squeezed once more – hard enough to make her gasp – before returning his grip to her arms.

Mona closed her eyes to the humiliation. She wondered, *would death be better than this?* She'd been counting the minutes since Bilal had been on the phone with her, but she'd lost track now. It could have been seconds ago or hours ago. Every second here seemed to drag an eternity.

Just when she thought that it couldn't get worse, it started raining again. They were drenched in a matter of seconds. As the men debated which van to throw her in, Mona looked into the deserted street. A few curtains stirred as faces peeked out, but in classic Lahori fashion, nobody raised a finger to help. She wasn't surprised. Even if there were any private security guards here, they wouldn't help her. It didn't fall within their purview.

'Throw her in the black van,' someone shouted. 'You can fondle her some more on the way. One more minute here, and the police will be fondling us instead. This bitch was on the phone with someone.'

Before they could move her, however, the sound of bullets being fired filled the air, puncturing all the tyres of one of the vans.

The men fanned out, shouting at each other in confusion.

'Get her into the other van!'

'There won't be any room for the rest of us.'

'Do you think Sahab ji gives a rat's arse about you? You don't matter. It's the woman that matters.'

Sahab ji… the name that was spoken in terrified whispers by Lahore's elite. Sahab ji was after the rich, everyone knew that. However, the moment his men tried to drag her towards the van, a volley of bullets fired again from somewhere in the darkness.

The men squawked like a bunch of terrified geese.

'If you value your lives, you will leave the woman and go.'

Mona looked up from her dazed state. 'Bilal?' she cried out. Had he really arrived so quickly? No, it couldn't be. She couldn't allow herself to hope. This was probably just her mind playing tricks on her. She let her head sink low again.

Each time the men tried to inch her closer to the van, the bullets started. It was obvious that it was a race against time now.

'If you hurt the woman, I will kill you all.'

The pressure on Mona's arms eased as the man let her go. She fell head first on the ground, her face only narrowly missing the mud. Her hands and clothes, however, fared much worse, but she wasn't too worried about that. She'd take getting drenched in mud over being kidnapped any day. Her heart leapt as she heard the men shout at each other and then retreat towards the remaining pickup vans. Mona watched them pack in like sardines before screeching away in a cloud of exhaust fumes.

She didn't breathe until the vans had turned a corner. It took her several tries before she was able to sit up. Reaching out to her car's door for purchase, she attempted to stand up.

'Bilal, you saved the day,' she murmured, marvelling at his bravery. 'A moment later, and they would have taken me.'

With the vans gone and her own car's headlights smashed, Mona could hardly see anything, so when a hand appeared to help her up, she took it gratefully. Something felt wrong about the hand, but she dismissed it. This was Bilal, her husband.

'Whatever happened to your voice, Bilal?' she chided him. 'You didn't quite sound like yourself. As a matter of fact, you sounded like—'

'Like what, Mona?'

She froze, blinking once. Twice. Despite the cold, sweat broke across her forehead. Whatever she had meant to say died on her lips.

No, it cannot be.

She tried to wrench her hand away, but his grip was too strong.

'I asked what I sounded like to you, Mona?' There was mischief in his voice, as if it hadn't been over a decade since they had talked, as if he hadn't been dead and buried for all those years.

'Ali?' she cried, wondering if she had hit her head somewhere. If not that, then this had to be a dream. He had been buried right in front of her eyes.

'There wasn't much of him to bury,' Meera had told her all those years ago. 'What you saw being carried to the grave was mostly padding.'

Even though it was wet, she could have known that hand anywhere.

'Ali?' she said again, hoping she was wrong. She couldn't do this again.

'Look at me, Mona.'

Even after all these years, all it took was a second for her to recognise him. Behind the mass of hair, it was the same Ali. With her other hand, she traced his features, that aquiline nose he had been so famous for, the neat eyebrows that everyone thought he plucked regularly, those lips that had met hers so many times.

A fierce sense of nostalgia gripped her, and she whipped her hand away, causing him to laugh.

'Don't worry, it really is me.'

'How?' she whispered. 'Why?'

His chest rumbled with laughter. 'We're meeting after more than a decade, and this is all you have to say?'

Her vision grew blurry as the tears finally arrived. She hoped Ali would mistake them for the drizzle that was still falling. In the distance, the sound of sirens rang out, getting louder by the second.

'They're coming,' they both said in unison, and then laughed.

'Twelve years and we can still read each other's thoughts,' Ali said.

'How are you alive, Ali?' Mona said at last, the first full sentence she'd spoken since seeing him. 'Why didn't you ever tell me?'

'I will tell you everything. Meet me at midday on Saturday at the Royal Fort. I'll tell you everything.'

'Why there?' she asked.

He raised an eyebrow. 'Would you rather be seen in Gulberg? There are plenty of gardens in the Royal Fort where we can just pretend to be tourists and, if anyone asks, you're there to sightsee.'

He tried to pull his hand free, but Mona discovered that she couldn't let go. She still didn't know whether this was all real or just an elaborate dream, but she didn't want him to go.

The smile was still on his face as he said, 'I need to go now. Let go.'

'I can't,' she replied. 'I don't want to.'

'We'll see each other soon,' Ali whispered, finally freeing himself and walking away. He turned around after a few steps. 'And, Mona?'

She looked up at him, not trusting herself to speak this time.

'You're still just as beautiful as you were twelve years ago.'

As the sound of the sirens grew louder and a bunch of police cars arrived on the scene with Bilal's Beemer on their heels, Ali vanished in the darkness somewhere, leaving her standing alone. Just like he'd done twelve years ago.

She allowed Bilal to wrap her in his warm embrace.

'You're shivering,' he remarked, tightening his arms around her. It dawned on her that he was weeping. Her husband, who'd never shed a tear in her presence, was crying for her. 'I'm sorry,' he whispered in her hair. 'I am so so sorry. I should never have let you go out like that. I could have lost you, Mona.'

Cocooned in his warmth, his jacket smelling of the Montblanc cologne she'd come to love, Mona had a moment of weakness. 'About Thokar Niaz Baig, I was going to—'

'Shh,' Bilal cut her off. 'We will speak no more of it. I trust you completely, Mona. I am so sorry.'

She buried her face in his chest as police officers encircled them and the rain beat down on them once again. All she could think of, however, was what Ali had said to her before leaving:

You're still just as beautiful as you were twelve years ago.

She began the onerous task of putting on make-up, pausing at regular intervals to make sure that everything had blended well. Sitting in front of the dressing table, she watched her face for ages, touching the skin along her jawline. There were places where it sagged a little now, but there was little she could do about it.

You're still just as beautiful as you were twelve years ago.

'You look beautiful,' Bilal said.

She started, twisting around on the stool to look at him. 'I didn't know you were up.'

Bilal smiled. 'I've been watching you put on your make-up.'

Mona closed her eyes for a moment before opening them. 'I look old, and I feel old too.'

Bilal raised himself up to a sitting position. 'If you're fishing for compliments, I've got plenty for you.'

She turned away, gazing at her reflection in the mirror once again. 'Isn't it strange that we believe life to be so fleeting, but when you come to think of it, it's not that fleeting at all.'

'You seem to be in a strange mood.'

Mona bunched up her hair in a ponytail, but then reconsidered and let it down. 'Wouldn't you be in a strange mood too if this had happened to you? To be manhandled by strange men and almost taken to western Pakistan. I can't think of a worse fate.'

Bilal thrust the covers off and padded over to her. 'Hey,' he murmured, running his hands down her arms. 'I was just trying to lighten up your mood. It killed me what those men almost did to you.' There was a spark in his eyes as he added, 'I won't let them get away with it. I am working with the police to find out who exactly is running this heinous gang.'

'If I know anything about our police, I'd say they're complicit.'

Bilal shook his head. 'They came, Mona. They came as soon as I called them. This gang has them just as rattled as us. They just ferry the victims out of Punjab to God knows where. It becomes impossible to track them. And then, they just sell them like cattle if the families are late with the ransom. I almost think they want them to be late. It's all a sick game for them.'

Mona shuddered, grateful for the warmth Bilal's embrace offered her. 'My heart goes out to Fahad. There's still no sign of him.' Her voice broke. 'When they were about to take me, all I could think of was Arslan and how he would grow up without a mother.'

Bilal grazed his lips on the side of her neck. 'It's over now. You're safe.'

'Is it, though? Do you think we will ever truly be safe in Pakistan?'

Bilal wasn't deterred. He kissed the top of her head. 'Pakistan is safer than ever. Don't let these criminal gangs get to you. They exist everywhere in the world. The trick is to take the necessary precautions. I'm just so relieved that you're safe.'

'I wouldn't be if it hadn't been for—' Mona blurted out before closing her mouth.

Like a predator, Bilal was instantly alert. 'Hadn't been for whom? Who are you talking about?'

Mona met his eyes in the mirror, hoping he couldn't feel her heart pounding. There was no way he could know about Ali. He would never understand. Even she didn't understand. Had she really seen Ali or had that been an apparition?

He was no apparition; she knew that, of course. Ali had saved her life, but what had he been doing there in the first place? Dozens of questions swirled in her head, each more outlandish than the last, but she couldn't give anyone the slightest indication that something was awry. If her blackmailer were to somehow find out that Ali was alive, there was no telling what might happen.

'You,' Mona said to Bilal. 'I meant if it hadn't been for you, I wouldn't be safe.'

Satisfied with her response, he tightened his grip around her.

Ali was alive. The thought still sent a shiver down her spine. Despite trying not to, her mind kept travelling back to all the time they had spent together. She remembered the innocent young man she'd first seen on the ramp, walking in that horrendous parrot-green outfit that exposed his chest. She remembered all of their subsequent meetings, how seeing his face would get her all light-headed, how his merest touch would make her breathless. She remembered the feel of his hand on hers, the weight of his body on hers.

Mona gasped, shutting the lid on her concealer so hard that it slipped out of her hands, shattering on the floor.

Bilal withdrew his hands from around her and knelt to pick up the ruined make-up.

Mona knelt down with him, busying herself with scooping up the viscous nude-coloured liquid. 'Bilal, stop it. You don't need to clean it. I can manage.'

He took a hold of her hand and squeezed it. 'Look at me.'

She hoped he couldn't see her blushing. 'What?'

'I want you to take a guard wherever you go now.'

'Well, duh, Bilal. Of course I will. I have no interest in being kidnapped again.' Her hands were dripping with concealer, so she rose to go to the bathroom.

'It's just that you're way too precious, Mona, and if something were to happen to you, I don't think I could keep going. Not for anyone. Not even Arslan.'

'Oh, Bilal.' Even now, his tenderness sometimes surprised her.

Chapter 13

Bilal

He was doing the one thing he thought he would never do: meeting Meera Siddiqui alone. When he arrived at the bustling cafe, she was already seated in a far corner. As he approached, an impish smile spread across her face, and she rose to shake his hand. 'Well, colour me surprised. I never thought I'd live to see the day when Bilal Sahab would ask to meet me.' As they took their seats, she added, 'To what do I owe this honour?'

Bilal looked around. 'You certainly chose the noisiest cafe.'

'That's Lahore for you, darling. We may not have money to fulfil our most basic needs, but we definitely have enough to drink overpriced coffee in cafes. And, of course, to have as many babies as physically possible. We're obviously in a competition to fill this land with starving children.'

Bilal wrapped his arms across his chest. 'God, Meera. I'd forgotten how crass your sense of humour can be when the mood strikes you.'

Meera laughed. 'Lighten up, Bilal. We are getting way too old to be serious all the time. I mean, at least you are. I'm still forty.'

'You've been forty for many years now.'

'Hmph, says the man who's pushing seventy.'

'I am not pushing seventy!' He shook his head, wondering if this was all a mistake. This woman wasn't going to help him at all.

Perhaps noticing his disappointment, her face assumed a serious look. 'Tell me, what's going on? Why have you asked to meet me? If I remember correctly, this is the first time we are meeting without Mona being present?'

Bilal nodded. 'Thank you for keeping this between us. I didn't know who else to turn to. Mona and you go back a long way. You've known her longer than anyone else, so it was only natural that I came to you.'

'Alia and Shabeena are good friends of hers too.'

Bilal laughed. 'I wouldn't talk to them if my life depended on it. They're shallow and conceited. Typical high-society types.'

Meera was smiling again. 'Go on. What's the big secret that only I am allowed to know?'

Bilal took a deep breath. There was no point beating around the bush. 'I think Mona is having an affair again.'

The smile vanished from Meera's face. 'Good God, Bilal! Of all the things I was expecting you to say, this wasn't it. An affair? Have you lost your senses completely? Don't you trust your wife at all?'

He bristled. 'Of course I trust her. I have never suspected her. Well, until now, anyway.'

'That's such bullshit. You only started treating her well after Arslan. You made her life hell in the past, so if she's having an affair, I say you bloody well deserve it.' Meera was panting and had to dig into her bag for a bottle of water, which she downed in one go. 'You men think that you can just prance in with your accusations and we'll indulge you?'

Now that he'd said it out loud, he could see how stupid it sounded. He regretted even contacting Meera in the first place. 'I'm sorry, I shouldn't have said anything. I sound crazy.' He spread his palms on the table. 'You're right. I'm a jerk. I should go.'

But he knew that Meera wouldn't let him. The look on her face said as much. Now that she'd calmed down, her body language had changed. She bit her lip. 'Well, sorry for that outburst, but you had it coming. I *have* seen how you've changed over the last decade or so, which is the only reason I agreed to meet you today. If you had been the old Bilal, I would have told you to fuck off, and you would have deserved it.'

He couldn't dispute that, so he just hung his head.

'But…'

He looked up. 'But?'

For the first time during their meeting, Meera looked uncomfortable. She ran her fingers through her dyed brown hair and covered herself with a scarf when she caught the men around them staring at her. 'I can't say that I haven't noticed that she's distracted… almost as if she's hiding something.'

Bilal raised an eyebrow. 'Like an affair?'

'No, Bilal. For the last time, not an affair! She keeps harping on about how old she feels and how much her joints hurt. Is that the kind of woman who would be having an affair? No, it's not that at all. There's something else she's hiding. If anything, she seems terrified that someone will discover what happened in the past.'

'That was ages ago. Why worry now?'

Meera looked like she wanted to be anywhere but here. 'Look, I've already said too much. Perhaps there's nothing to it. Mona can have brief spells where she likes to avoid people. Remember, she avoided me for decades because of what I did.'

Bilal leaned back against the chair, his hands bunched into fists on the table. 'But I didn't even do anything. Why punish me by being so distant?'

This time, Meera did roll her eyes as she stood up. 'Because she's human? As much as we love her, I think it's best to give her some room to breathe. Stop thinking about it, Bilal. You look like you need a break yourself.' As if taking pity on him, she reached out to pat his arm. 'Mona loves you. Always has and always will. Ali was merely a distraction, and he's gone. Now, if you will excuse me, I need to be back in the office where *Mona* is waiting for me.' Bilal looked up, but before he could say anything, Meera gave him a tight smile. 'Of course, this will stay between us, but this is the only secret of yours I'll ever keep. Don't make it a habit.'

'Thank you,' Bilal whispered.

'I like this version of you, Bilal. This is what a real man looks like. Never change.' And with that, she was gone, leaving the scent of expensive perfume in her wake.

For a long time after that, Bilal sat where he was, resting his chin on the back of his hand, gazing into the distance. Although Meera had told him what he had wanted to hear, for some reason she'd left him feeling even more concerned for Mona than ever.

What on earth could be going on in her life?

Chapter 14

Mona

Although it was late March and the weather had warmed up considerably, Mona couldn't stop trembling. The sun beat down on her back, and the light jacket she wore was warm, but it was as if a chill had penetrated her very bones. Of course, most of it had to do with the fact that she would be seeing *him* again.

Ali. Just thinking his name sent a fresh wave of shivers down her spine. It was noon, and that's when he'd said he would show up. Both the time and location were of his choosing. If Mona was surprised that he'd chosen such a public place, she didn't say. Right now, she wanted nothing more than to see him again. One more time.

After the gang nearly kidnapping her, Bilal had been keeping an ever-watchful eye on her movements, and she wasn't allowed to go anywhere without a guard. So it was fortunate, really, that he'd flown off to Karachi for the weekend and there was no one to enforce his rules. Instead of her usual Beemer – the one he'd put a tracker on – she had taken out one of their ancient Toyota Corollas. Not only would it not stand out in a place like this, but it also didn't have a tracker on it, as far as she knew. Venturing out on her own was a risk, but what else was she to do?

'Tariq will accompany you, bibi,' one of the guards had said to her as she started the Corolla. His forehead was creased with worry. 'Bilal Sahab was insistent.'

'I'm just heading out for a moment,' she'd replied, mustering a smile. 'I'll be back before you know it. Besides, you're all needed here.'

'But, bibi—'

'I said I'll be back shortly, Imran,' she'd shot back. 'Don't forget you work for me as well and when I tell you something, you listen. I have spoken to Bilal about this.'

Imran had gone red in the face as he bowed his head, which was why she hadn't even looked in the direction of the guards as she drove out of the house, knowing full well that if Bilal asked, they'd tell him exactly what she'd done. Thankfully, there had been no texts or calls from Bilal yet, which meant that the people in Karachi, bless them, were keeping him busy.

The spires of the Badshahi Mosque rose in the distance while the Royal Fort's imposing beige gate stood sentry in front. There were many lawns in the area, and, fortunately, Ali had chosen one that wasn't very crowded. In fact, it was quite empty, and for that, she didn't know if she was grateful or terrified. After the incident at the park, empty places spooked her, and as her heart rate climbed, she closed her eyes and took deep breaths. It was going to be fine. Nobody would dare attempt to kidnap her in broad daylight and definitely not from the Royal Fort.

Ali had made a good choice. In this city of the Mughals, there were plenty of places to hide, but nothing was better than hiding in plain sight. Or so they said. She didn't want to even think what would happen if anyone from her social circle was to see her right now, sitting alone in front of the Royal Fort. She took out a scarf from her bag and covered her head, but then reconsidered and stowed it back.

Back at home, she'd pulled out her jeans and Western shirts after what seemed like years. The length of the shirt hid her thighs, and the jacket did the rest. With her hair down and sunglasses perched on her head, Mona had caused Qudsia's eyebrows to almost vanish in her hijab. 'Did you run out of your own clothes that you're wearing Aimen's?'

Mona had known that she was baiting her, but she had too much on her mind to be offended. 'It's a free world, Qudsia. Even if I am wearing Aimen's clothes, what's it to you?'

'Just that you're in your fifties, and people will talk.'

'So what?' Mona had snapped. 'What do you want me to do, kill myself? Just because I'm in my fifties doesn't mean I'm not allowed to live any more.'

Qudsia had held up her hands. '*Haye haye*, just go wherever it is you're going. I was simply looking out for you. *Bhallai ka zamana nahin raha.*'

Maybe she was right, Mona wondered now. Her outfit reeked of desperation. Who was she trying to impress? As the minutes ticked by and there was no sign of him, she began to look around, biting her lip. She must look so funny, sitting here waiting for someone who was probably never going to show up. She wondered if he was just a figment of her imagination – something her mind had conjured up during a time of great stress. It wasn't outside the realm of possibility, given how much the blackmail had been weighing on her mind. It had almost driven her to the brink of insanity, so maybe this was just a method of coping. Stranger things had happened.

But he had looked so real. She'd held his hand – the same hand that had caressed her countless times. She was convinced that it was Ali. But then, she'd been convinced of his death too. It wasn't hard to remember events from that fateful night when Ali was forced to don a suicide vest by the terrorist mastermind, Mir Rabiullah, and storm Bilal's event in Karachi, the night she thought she'd lost Arslan in the stream of blood that erupted from her. However, it wasn't Arslan she'd lost, but his father.

Ali.

Finding his humanity at the last moment, he'd fled the event, leaving everyone unharmed, and instead, waded into the Arabian Sea and blown himself up.

At least, that's what she thought he'd done. Now… now she didn't know anything at all, and maybe, if Ali managed to show up, he'd run for the hills after seeing her in the harsh glare of the sun. She slid the sunglasses down so that he wouldn't be able to see her crow's feet. If she had a collar, she'd wear it too, just to hide the veins that stood out in her neck.

Stop it, Mona!

She was so lost in her own thoughts that she didn't hear him approach.

'Hello, Mona.'

She jolted forward as if hit by a car. Even after all these years, his voice got her heart racing. He was behind her, but she couldn't bear to look at him. It would mean that she had spent years grieving someone who wasn't dead, someone who hadn't even bothered to tell her that he was alive.

The strangest cocktail of anger and elation rushed through her, winding her. However, in the end, it was the anger that won, and with that, Mona rose from the bench, not caring that her back pinged with the suddenness of her movement, and faced Ali.

There was a sharp intake of breath from both of them as they stood gazing at each other. The anger she'd felt a moment ago dissipated as the earnestness of Ali's expression struck her. It was as if no time had passed at all, and yet over a decade had. Unlike her, he wasn't wearing any sunglasses, and Mona could see that the beginnings of fine lines were starting to appear around his eyes, and his stubble had bits of grey in it. For some reason, the sight made her want to cry. She had never imagined that she'd get to see him age, but here he was, standing before her, looking more handsome than she remembered.

A grin spread across his mouth, crinkling the skin around his eyes. 'What do you think? Do I look acceptable?'

'How are you alive?'

His smile grew wider. 'Am I to understand that you're not happy to see me? I did save your life the other day, you know.'

'How did you even know where to find me?'

Ali shrugged. 'I've been watching you, but that night, I was forced to intervene.'

Mona's anger flared up again. 'You've been watching me?'

'Mona, after all these years, I just didn't know how to make contact again.'

Before she could stop herself, she pushed him. He staggered back a few steps but maintained his balance.

'I guess I deserved that,' he murmured.

'I mourned you, Ali. I mourned you for years, only to find out that it was all a lie. All those years of my life that will never come back.' Her voice broke. 'I am fifty-three years old. I've spent the best part of the past decade mourning you.' In the sunlight, her hands looked wizened and dry. She thrust them in the pockets of her jeans. 'I can't even look at you right now. I don't even know why I came here today.'

Ali took a step forward. 'I think you do.'

'Do I?'

The challenge in her voice made him hold up his hands. 'I was in hiding. As long as Mir Rabiullah lived, I couldn't show myself. Not to anyone. Not even you. I would have endangered your life. Both yours and...'

It sounded like he knew about Arslan, but she had to be sure. 'And?' she echoed.

Ali looked down. 'I just couldn't take the risk. I couldn't let him find out that we had a son together.'

The breath caught in her throat. Despite the warm weather, a chill spread through her, right to her extremities. So, he knew. Of course he did. And if he'd been watching her for years, he would have seen her with Arslan as she raised him, took him to school and did all the things a parent did for their child.

All of it from a distance.

'What has changed now?' she asked.

Ali looked up, his face sombre. 'I told you, he's dead. The threat is gone now. I am finally free.' Gesturing towards the bench next to them, he added, 'Shall we sit?' Before she could answer, he reached out to take her hand. 'Don't be angry with me, Mona. I don't think I can bear it.'

An electric current shot through her at his touch, and she immediately withdrew her hand. 'I – I can't,' she muttered. 'Please don't.'

'Then sit, please. I promise I won't touch you without your permission.'

Mona gingerly sat down next to him, taking care to cross her legs so that her thighs wouldn't spread all over the bench. Even now, she couldn't help but look her best for him, and the thought mortified her.

They sat in silence for a long time, gazing at the Royal Fort in front of them.

After what felt like aeons, Ali said, 'Did you know why the gates of the Royal Fort are so tall?' When she didn't reply, he continued, 'It's because the kings used to ride in on elephants. And those Mughal kings knew how to love. Just take the Taj Mahal as an example.'

Mona all but scoffed. Anyone who lived in Lahore and had visited the Walled City knew why the gates of the fort were so tall. And the story of the Taj Mahal was as old as time. 'I don't know where you're going with this,' she said finally.

'Just that those kings riding elephants may have faded into history, but their love remains, etched in these buildings.'

'I don't remember you being so philosophical.'

Ali laughed. 'I never was very philosophical, but I guess time changes us.' He turned to her. 'Am I to be deprived of the opportunity to see your beautiful eyes?'

Mona blushed. The bastard still knew what to say to get her to melt. She took the sunglasses off. 'I don't want you to see how much I've aged.'

'You look the same. If anything, you're even more beautiful now, Mona.'

Mona smiled, ignoring the way her heart leapt at his praise. 'Best get your eyes checked, then, Ali. How old are you now?'

'I'll be turning forty next year.'

'I was forty-one when we – you know – met for the first time.'

She could see his hand inching towards hers. Their eyes met, and he smiled. 'May I?'

Mona's immediate thought was of refusing him, but then she looked around the deserted lawn, and something in her shifted. She nodded before she could change her mind. 'You may.'

Her hand fit into his just like it always had. A sense of security she hadn't even realised she had missed returned to her and she let out a sigh. When he squeezed her hand, she returned the pressure.

'It's good to see you again,' she whispered. 'I am still angry with you, and I wish you had told me, but I am also glad that you're alive. Your death broke my heart.'

'But you're happy now, aren't you? With Bilal?'

All of a sudden, his hand felt like it was scalding her skin. She whipped it back, wiping it on her scarf as if it was dirty. 'Yes,' she said after she had composed herself. 'I am very happy with Bilal. He has changed. He is a much better man.'

If Ali had noticed her wiping her hand, he didn't show it. Instead, he asked, 'And how is our son?'

She glanced at him. 'He is Bilal's son, Ali. He was brought up as his son, and he will always be his son. You weren't there, and as such, you have no right to call him your own. Bilal loves Arslan, and he loves him back. More than anything. Even more than me.' Watching the expression on his face, Mona softened. 'I just mean that he hasn't known any other life.'

Ali slouched, his head hanging down as he rested his elbows on his knees. 'Of course he's *his* son. He's taken everything from me. I hope he's happy.'

'He didn't take anything from you. You threw it all away.'

He shrugged. 'Maybe you're right. That's life, I guess.'

Mona reached out to pat his hand, surprising even herself with the gesture. 'He's growing up to be a handsome young man. You'd be proud of him. He's got your mother's eyes.'

Ali's face brightened up, making him look like the young boy he used to be once. 'Can I see him? Just once?'

Mona took her hand back. 'I don't know about that. I haven't told Arslan anything, and I want his life to remain the way it is.' But as she said the words, she knew it would be cruel to deprive a father from seeing his son. Changing tack, she added, 'Having said that, I will figure out a way to make it happen as long as you promise not to approach him or talk to him. I don't want word of this reaching Bilal.'

Ali nodded once. 'I promise.'

They spent some more time discussing Arslan's facial features and how much he had grown when Mona noticed that their shadows were expanding. How long had she been sitting here with Ali? Her phone answered the question for her. It was almost three in the afternoon, and she had a dozen missed calls and countless messages. With a pang, she realised that she didn't want to go. At this moment, she wanted to reach out and hold Ali. She wanted him to enclose her in his arms, just for a second.

She initiated none of these things and, instead, rose to leave.

Ali did the same. 'When will I see you again?'

'Soon,' she lied. She had no idea when there would be a next time. Mona wasn't even sure she wanted to. Seeing him today had started the process of awakening things in her, things she didn't think she had full control over.

No, that was all in the past, and that's where it had to remain. What on earth was the matter with her? Hadn't she learnt her lesson? Alive or dead, Ali was bad for her. She had a loving husband waiting for her at home, and here she was, spending time with a man who had almost destroyed her life by faking his own death.

'Why didn't you die, though?' she asked. 'When you blew yourself up.'

Ali laughed. 'Funny story, actually. Like most things in Pakistan, the bloody jacket was faulty. I pressed the button several times, but nothing happened. It wasn't until I'd ditched it in the water and retreated that the bomb went off.' His eyes assumed a faraway look. 'Sometimes, I wish I had died, because that way I wouldn't have had to spend all these years running from Mir Rabiullah.'

As they watched each other, waiting to say goodbye, Ali took a step towards her, their shadows merging.

'Meeting you has made me realise what I have been missing. It's brought back all those times we spent together. Do you remember, Mona?'

Of course she remembered. She had been thinking of little else for the past few days. Instead, she asked, 'Are you married, Ali?'

The skin around his eyes crinkled again as he gave her an enigmatic smile. 'What do you think?'

Mona shrugged. 'How am I to know? For all I know, you could have seven children.'

'Seven? Come now, isn't that a bit much?'

'How would I know? You were always pretty energetic when it came to those things.' She was trying to play along, but her heart was pounding.

His smile grew lopsided. 'Energetic in what regard, may I ask?'

Mona huffed, to which he laughed, but once he'd quietened, his face grew serious, his eyes boring into hers.

'To answer your question, no, I am not married, and I am not seeing anyone.' He didn't even blink as he continued, 'For me, there was only ever you, Mona. There has never been anyone else since, nor will there ever be.'

His statement unleashed something in her. She knew that if she didn't leave right now, she'd regret it afterwards, so she turned around and fled, not daring to look back. People looked at her strangely as she rushed down the path leading to the parking area. Pulling out the scarf she'd brought, she covered her head and held the edge of it against her mouth. The combination of sunglasses and scarf obscured her face completely. By the time she reached her car, she was breathless. His words still swirled in her head, and for a long time afterwards, she sat in the car gazing, unseeing, wondering what had just happened as the people around her milled about the fort.

—

A few days later, she sat with Meera as they went through the upcoming launch of a high-end boutique hotel, where everyone from Lahore's high society to local and international celebrities was invited. It was boring work drawing up invitation lists and reaching out to people for confirmation, but for once, Mona was invested in it. In fact, she hadn't felt happier. Ever since her meeting with Ali, they'd been texting. Ordinary, innocuous messages, but somehow, they made her smile. There was an odd reverence to his messages that had never been there before, as if he was awestruck to be talking to her. If she was being honest with herself, she felt the same way. During her darkest days all those years ago, when her yearning for Ali was at its peak, she had contemplated suicide. The thought of dying and joining him up there had appealed to her more than being alive and with her family. In those days, she had noticed Nighat watching her, and when breakfast trays were brought up to Mona, they would be missing knives and forks. Only a single spoon would be provided. Nighat had even taken to monitoring what pills she took. Mona had never had an easy relationship with her mother-in-law, but she couldn't deny that the woman was intelligent and, behind that thorny exterior, very caring too.

'You seem awfully pleased about a task that is so dull that it's boring me to tears,' Meera remarked, her reading glasses making her eyes appear comically large.

Mona wiped the smile off her face, but within moments, it was back. Her blackmailer was gone – she hadn't heard from him since she'd paid him off – and Ali was back. Life simply couldn't be better. 'Just having fun with work. You ought to loosen up a bit more, Meera. Life is to be lived and enjoyed.'

'I say, it does feel nice to see you happy. You've been so quiet and grumpy lately that I was starting to worry.'

Mona typed away on her laptop, sending another email with a flourish. 'Life is strange, Meera. Full of surprises. But why were you worried about me?'

'Why? Am I not allowed to worry for you? You're better today, but lately, it was as if you were here, but your mind wasn't.'

'Very perceptive,' Mona murmured. She didn't give Meera enough credit for being observant. 'I guess I was going through some stuff, but it's better now. I think I might have taken care of it.' The memory of that blackmail came crawling back, but she sent it packing. There was no need to dwell on the past.

Meera raised her eyebrows. 'It wasn't just me who was worried. Others were too.'

'Like who?'

'Nothing.'

This was strange behaviour, even for Meera. 'No, tell me,' Mona said. 'What's with all this cloak-and-dagger bullshit?'

Meera took off her glasses and set them aside on the desk. 'I shouldn't have said anything at all. You've been so distracted that I was beginning to think that maybe you were having an affair. Wouldn't that be insane?'

Mona blinked. 'I am fifty—'

'—three years old,' Meera finished for her with a smile. 'I know that. You've said it countless times. But I am fifty-three too, and I have plenty of affairs. Being fifty-three doesn't mean you stop living.'

Mona laughed, but she could hear the falseness in it. 'You're made of sterner stuff, Meera. None of us can compete with you.'

'So, you aren't having an affair, then?'

'Of course not.' Mona shook her head, but a sense of unease spread through her. The thing with Ali was on the tip of her tongue, and she knew that of all the people in the world, Meera was the one person who would truly understand. She would be able to make sense of the storm of emotions inside her right now. But Mona didn't say anything. She wasn't sure of what was going on herself, so what was she supposed to tell Meera? It all felt like a dream.

'Do you think you may have another affair in you?'

God, she was like a dog with a bone. Mona watched her, aghast. 'What's got into you all of a sudden? Honestly!' But then, she surprised herself by saying, 'Do I have another torrid affair in me? Who knows, maybe… don't we all?'

There was a small smile playing on Meera's lips. 'Nice try. You *are* hiding something, though. I can't quite put my finger on it, but there's something going on in your life.' She shrugged, rising from her chair and walking towards the window that overlooked Garden Town. 'If there's ever anything, you can tell me, you know.'

Mona didn't quite understand where she was going with this. 'Meera, I—'

'I just don't want to lose my best friend again,' she whispered. 'When we weren't speaking for all those years, there was always that nagging thought in my head that my life was incomplete.' She turned around and returned to her seat, facing Mona. 'I don't ever want to feel that way again.'

It had been decades since the incident that had caused a rift between them. Although she preferred not to, she could still remember that moment clear as day, when Meera had forced her to the boys' hostel to meet a prospective boyfriend, but what had ended up happening was beyond their worst nightmares. Meera's then boyfriend, Iftikhar, had several boys waiting for them and, when they'd arrived, the door behind them had clicked shut before being locked. While Iftikhar remained unpunished for the part he had played in ruining their lives, the friendship Mona had with Meera ended. They didn't speak again for over twenty years. The memory of all those hands on her still gave her sleepless nights sometimes, but Mona had come to realise that it hadn't been Meera's fault. At that age, she couldn't have known that men could be such savages. Even though Meera had suffered at the hands of Iftikhar too, Mona hadn't been able to forgive her, not until they were both in their forties.

She looked at her friend now. They had missed out on so many years of friendship because of that incident, and she wasn't going to let anything come between them again. Not if she could help it. 'Meera, you are not going to lose me,' she murmured.

But Meera wasn't done yet. 'In many ways, a close friendship ending is worse than a relationship ending. When a relationship collapses, at least you have your best friend to turn to, but when that best friend leaves you, where do you go then?'

Mona flicked a stray tear from her cheek. 'You're making me cry now. You're my best friend, Meera, and you always will be. Nothing can ever change that.'

To her surprise, even Meera's eyes were damp. 'I know, but promise me that you'll tell me if something serious happens? If you don't want to tell me, then at least tell Bilal.'

Mona narrowed her eyes, suddenly wary. 'Why do you mention Bilal?'

'He loves you, you know. As shocking as it may sound. He really does.'

Mona was spared from responding as, at that very moment, her phone rang. The guilt she felt at hearing Bilal's name was compounded when she saw his name on the screen.

If she didn't pick up, he'd just call again and keep calling until she picked up.

'Are you going to take that?' Meera asked her.

Mona rose from where she was seated across from Meera and withdrew to her own cabin. It was much smaller than Meera's and very sparse, which was why she liked spending more time in Meera's decadent room.

Swiping her thumb across the screen, she held the phone to her ear. 'Yes, Bilal?'

'You will not believe what I'm about to tell you.'

She had expected him to complain about something, but he was so excited that he sounded breathless.

Her thoughts immediately went to her kids. 'What's happened now? Are the kids okay?'

'Everything is fine, Mona. I just wanted to tell you before you heard from your friends.' He took a deep breath. 'Fahad is back. He was released by the gang once your friend paid the money. Quite swiftly too.'

'Oh, thank God!' She had a message waiting from Alia, but she hadn't opened it yet. She would call her now. 'Thanks for letting me know. Where are you right now?'

'I think the bigger question is why you took my call. These days, you always ignore me, calling me back hours later.'

Mona lowered herself into a chair and rummaged around some papers to appear busy. 'I never avoid your calls intentionally. You know that.'

'Do I?' His tone wasn't hostile. If anything, he sounded amused. 'Sometimes, I am not so sure that you love me.'

Despite herself, Mona smiled. 'Well, I am at work right now, Bilal Sahab, but I promise to make it up to you.'

He groaned. 'When?'

'In the fullness of time.'

Without warning, they both broke into a fit of laughing.

'Love you, woman.'

After a beat, Mona replied. 'Love you too.'

As soon as she ended the call, her phone beeped. She smiled, certain that it was Bilal being silly again, but it wasn't him.

The text was from Ali.

> When can I see you again? Please meet me tomorrow.

For the first time in many years, Mona was unsure of what to do.

Chapter 15

Fakhar

Sahab ji had finally forgiven him. How could he not, since Fakhar did most of his dirty work for him? Besides, Sahab ji had bitten off more than he could chew with these high-profile kidnappings, incurring the wrath of the Punjab Police, who were now on the prowl.

It had come to a point that they had let a man go even though his wife hadn't paid the full amount.

Sahab ji was in over his head, and the thought made Fakhar's toes curl with excitement because if anything happened to him, everyone knew that Fakhar would be the most obvious choice as the person to continue the noble work.

Lately, the reverence with which he treated Sahab ji had vanished, replaced by a hatred he'd only ever felt for his father. The intensity of it shocked him. The way Sahab ji had tortured him reminded him of his life as a boy, constantly being bullied and beaten by Abba Jaan.

After his mother succumbed to her injuries, Fakhar was truly alone. With nobody to look after things at home and nobody to warm his bed at night, Abba Jaan took out all of his frustration and anger on him. He began using the leather whip, mildly at first, but then the frequency quickly increased just to see how much Fakhar could endure. The irony wasn't lost on him that the same whip he'd let his own mother die for was now torturing him.

However, it wasn't the whip that eventually caused him to snap. When it was obvious that the whip wasn't going to kill him, the abuse took a new turn. Soon, Fakhar's nights turned sour too, as every other night, he would get a visit from Abba Jaan… a different kind of visit. The pain took on a new turn, one that literally took his breath away.

Thinking about it still took his breath away.

Sahab ji had made him revisit that pain, and for that, Fakhar would make him pay, if that was the last thing he did.

That pain had caused him to drive a knife into Abba Jaan's belly – one hundred times, to be precise – and he was going to do the same to Sahab ji.

Chapter 16

Mona

It began with a brief exchange of messages, but soon they were talking every day, mostly over texts, but sometimes over the phone as well. It was the strangest thing; she'd wake up in the morning, and whatever anxiety she'd be feeling would vanish as soon as she remembered that Ali was alive. And not just alive, he was in contact with her. She'd be unable to start her day unless his text arrived asking her how she was doing. And it would arrive, at seven fifteen in the morning. Like clockwork. Her eyes would snap open of their own accord five minutes before the text, and they would then spend the next few minutes texting about everything and nothing as Bilal slept on, oblivious.

It was like getting a new lease of life, to have someone care and worry for her without expecting anything in return. Although Bilal cared for her too, he always expected reciprocation, and he could get very unkind if he didn't get it. It shocked her how easily Ali had inveigled his way back into her life, as if he'd never left. There were still moments when it hit her that he'd hidden his existence from her for over a decade, but then his earnest face would come to her mind, and she'd relent. Briefly.

> Do you ever feel like you could love with abandon again?

Mona sat up on the bed as she read this latest text from Ali. It was late afternoon, and Bilal was still at work. Throwing caution to the wind, she typed a reply.

> Loving with abandon at fifty-three isn't something I've considered. For starters, my knees wouldn't allow me to kneel and propose to someone.

> It's the man that usually proposes, and you don't look a day over forty. We're basically the same age.

His reply made her smile.

> That's very kind of you to say, but I think my ship has sailed. Even if I wanted to love with abandon again, I'm married.

> Mona, you've always been a beautiful woman, and that hasn't changed. I could eat you up if you'd allow me.

Her eyes widened, her sluggish heart beginning to race. She dropped the phone on the bed as if scalded. So far, their messages had been platonic. Ali had made no reference to how things had been between them in the past... until now. And why wouldn't he? What exactly did she hope to achieve by texting with a former lover? For some reason, she had believed that all the time that had elapsed would act as a natural barrier and dissuade Ali from making any overtures, but then she thought back to what Meera had always said: 'When you really love someone, it's forever.'

Ali's message was proof of that.

Mona let out a loud 'hmph'. What did Meera know of love? She fell in love every month.

A sense of guilt assailed her as she looked at the framed photo of her and Bilal on the wall. What on earth was she thinking? In fact, she didn't understand what Ali was playing at. What gave him the right to return to her life like this and then make such offhand comments? How dare he?

When she didn't reply to his text for fifteen minutes, her screen lit up with his name as she knew it would. She let it go to voicemail, but then he called her again.

Casting off the duvet from her burning body, she lowered the thermostat on the air conditioner and swiped the phone to the right.

'Sorry, I was in the bathroom,' she lied.

There was silence for a moment, before he said, 'No, you weren't. I can still tell when you're lying.'

Of course he could. It was foolish of her to even consider lying to him. He'd always managed to see right through her.

'How are you today?' she asked, trying to deflect attention.

There was a smile in his voice as he said, 'I'd be better if you agreed to meet me today.'

Mona closed her eyes and allowed her head to sink into the soft pillows, letting the cool air from the air conditioner wash over her. 'Lahore is a small place, Ali. And we did see each other the other day.'

'That was weeks ago, and I'm not sure if you've checked on the internet, but Lahore now has a population of fifteen million people.'

'There are eyes everywhere.'

'What are you scared of, Mona? It's not like we're doing anything wrong. What's so bad about two old friends meeting?'

Her eyes snapped open. 'For starters, we have a difficult history together. And, if you haven't noticed, I have a husband.'

Ali scoffed. 'You had a husband twelve years ago as well.'

'That was a different time, Ali. I was a different person.'

'Meet me, please? I'm desperate. Meeting you once was not enough.'

'What do you even see in me, Ali? I'm a plain middle-aged woman. What's there to be gained by meeting me?'

There was a pause before he whispered, 'Everything.'

—

A few days later, she purposely chose a time when other parents wouldn't be around and invited Ali to come and see Arslan. It was all probably one big mistake, but she could think of no other way that wouldn't invite trouble. This way, Ali could just peek at him without Arslan knowing anything. She had a quick-witted son, and he was of an age where he would question the strange man who kind of looked like him.

However, to get to Arslan, they had to pass the main administration building. Mona looked up for strength as she waited outside the school gates for Ali.

One thing at a time, she thought.

She didn't have to wait long before Ali arrived in a nondescript white Toyota Corolla. He was wearing a black shalwar kameez with his hair gelled back. Coupled with aviator sunglasses and a light beard, it looked like he had made a conscious effort to appear irresistible, and when he gave her a lopsided grin, she knew her hunch was right.

He was trying to woo her with his looks. However, sadly for him, she wasn't that shallow any more. It would take much more than looks for her to forgive him, but even so, she didn't quite understand the feelings coursing through her. On the one hand, she couldn't deny that he did look enticing, but on the other, the thought of it made her feel guilty to the bone.

Was this what being middle-aged was like, that you worry about everything?

'Hey,' he said, leaning in to kiss her on the cheek, his lips lingering as the kiss lengthened, growing more and more wet.

With a jolt, Mona pushed him away and looked in every direction to check if someone had seen. At this time of the day, the road was deserted. The security guard behind the gate was watching through the bars, though, a greedy expression on his face.

It turned Mona's stomach. 'What did you do that for?' she said, rubbing away the damp from her cheek. 'The security guard saw. What if he tells someone?'

Ali shrugged. 'So? We'll just say you're my wife.'

'Bilal also comes here, Ali,' Mona muttered, astonished at his recklessness. 'What's got into you, honestly? I do have a life here.'

'You and theatrics go hand in hand.'

She stopped mid-step. 'What did you just say?'

He squeezed her upper arm briefly before letting go. 'Just this. Theatrics. Now, can we go and see our son or are you going to scold me some more for that little peck on your cheek?'

It wasn't a peck, but Mona didn't press the point. She gave him a sideways glance as they resumed walking, trying to assess whether she was, indeed, prone to theatrics or if it was Ali who had changed. The answer wasn't immediately apparent to her.

After witnessing the kiss, the guard didn't even bother stopping them, letting them through immediately. At least for him, they were husband and wife. Even so, public displays of affection weren't exactly encouraged in Pakistan, and she'd seen people take up arms for less.

Reckless, she thought again. *Reckless and arrogant.*

He almost reminded her of Bilal as he used to be, not as he was now. There was a time when she would have given anything to spend more time with Ali – hell, she had even been ready to elope with him. But right now, at this very moment, she found herself craving her husband's company. He was difficult, yes, but he was also home.

Ali was smirking. 'Did I tell you how ravishing you look?'

Mona tried not to roll her eyes. 'I literally wore the first thing I could get my hands on.'

'Doesn't look like it.'

He was right. She had spent hours deciding what to wear, and then, feeling guilty about it, she'd gone with her least favourite outfit from the lot. 'Please don't talk to Arslan when you see him,' she murmured. 'I don't want him to get confused.'

'I know you're trying to change the subject, but fine. I won't speak to him' – he thrust his hand in the pocket of his kameez – 'even though he is my son.'

A son you abandoned, she thought, but bit her tongue from saying aloud.

Taking a wet wipe out of her handbag, she surreptitiously cleaned the remnants of Ali from her cheek. The school was small but had teachers from all over the world, and nothing attracted Pakistani parents more than white people teaching their kids. That's what Bilal had wanted for Arslan as well... to give him the 'best' start in the world. Mona didn't quite agree, but she'd learned to choose her battles.

She waved at one of the new school administrators as they passed and led the way to a small courtyard beyond which the classrooms were situated. Beside her, Ali was starting to sweat, wiping his brow repeatedly with his handkerchief. It gave Mona some satisfaction to see that even someone like him had feelings. She almost wanted to make this moment last longer, just to see his discomfort.

'There,' she whispered, pointing past the metal bars and towards the playground. 'You can see Arslan sitting on that bench eating a sandwich.'

Although she didn't want to take her eyes off her baby, she had to see Ali's reaction, so she looked at him instead.

What she saw shocked her.

There was genuine emotion on his face, and although he'd rubbed at his eyes several times, he couldn't stop the tears from falling. Their eyes met. 'He looks just like me and a little like Hussain.'

It hit her then – the emotion. She couldn't stop the tears from falling from her eyes either. 'He does look like you,' she whispered.

'I miss my brother. I think about him every single day.'

She didn't say anything because it didn't seem like he wanted a reply.

Ali's gaze was drawn back to Arslan. 'It's like I'm looking at a younger version of myself.' He reached for her hand, and she let him. 'We created him together, Mona. Our son.'

Our son. The word hit her harder than she'd expected. *Our* son.

Without asking for her permission, he pulled her into a hug and wept into her shoulder. 'I love him already. I want to meet him.'

'Ali,' she began. 'I told you.'

He nodded, his face still buried somewhere between her chest and shoulder. 'I know... I know. But he is my son. Eventually, we'll have to tell him.'

His words were like cold water thrown at her face, washing away the feeling of well-being. Looking at her boy finishing his sandwich, she wondered if she'd exposed him to a lifetime of trauma.

But this was Ali. The Ali she had loved so fiercely for so long. Surely, he would never do anything that would cause her grief. And if he truly cared for Arslan as much as he said he did, he wouldn't do that to him either.

Chapter 17

Bilal

By the time they reached Alia's place, rows of cars had already lined the side of the road. Beside him, Mona was busy on her mobile. Throughout the journey from Gulberg to Cantt, she had been texting, occasionally breaking into fits of laughter. When he'd asked who she was chatting with, she'd just given him a strange look and muttered, 'A friend.'

Bilal didn't dare press her further. These days, even the smallest thing could set her off. She could run hot or cold in a matter of seconds, so tonight he hadn't bothered pushing her, preferring instead to enjoy the party that Alia had thrown for the return of her husband. Given that Fahad had been kidnapped for his obscene wealth in the first place, it was ironic that he was displaying the same wealth again with so little regard. Almost like he had a death wish.

He'd barely killed the engine before Mona was out of the car and rushing towards the garden where most of the people were assembled. For several minutes, he remained seated in the car, his hands on the steering wheel. Nobody had told him that marriages remained rocky even when you were in your sixties. He'd assumed that things between them had settled, but there it was again, something bubbling under the surface, and he had no idea how to get to the bottom of it.

He wasn't quite sure he wanted to. Sometimes, ignorance was bliss. With a deep sigh, he rubbed his chest, which had been throbbing all evening and got out of the car. A valet rushed to take the car keys from him, and Bilal let him. Over the years, he'd grown less attached to material things. Cars didn't matter to him as much as they used to; relationships did.

He'd put on his Armani blazer today, the one Mona liked the most, but either she hadn't noticed or pretended not to. Thrusting his hands in his pockets, he made his way towards the source of the noise, only to see Fahad uncorking a bottle of champagne while the people around him cheered.

Bilal closed his eyes briefly in second-hand embarrassment for Fahad, before opening them and looking around to see if there were any familiar faces. He'd accompanied Mona because he thought she'd need his company, but she was nowhere to be found... probably in the middle of the crowd cheering Fahad on. If he'd thought his day couldn't get worse, he was in for a shock as someone thumped him on the back before throwing their arms around him. From the way the abdomen pressed against his back, Bilal immediately knew who it was.

'How are you, Faheem?'

Stepping around him so that they were facing each other, Faheem grinned, his mouth smelling of barbecued kebabs. 'Bilal, my friend. Long time no see.' Bits of the kebab still clung to his teeth, but Faheem didn't seem to care. 'Where have you been all this time? Are you punishing your friend for being frisky with you, huh?'

Bilal stared at him, deadpan. 'Faheem, you couldn't be frisky with me if you tried.'

Faheem winked at him. 'But I do try.' Before Bilal could move away, Faheem clapped him on the back again. 'Just joking, my dear man. Lighten up, will you?' Extending an arm in the direction of someone in uniform, he said, 'Meet Mr Sohail Butt, the senior superintendent of police. He's the one responsible for keeping us all safe here in Lahore.'

To his credit, SSP Sohail took the joke in his stride. 'Not doing a good job of it at the moment, I'm afraid.' Curling up the edges of his moustache, he gave an embarrassed laugh. 'We won't deny that this gang has been giving us a hard time lately, but we got Fahad back for you, didn't we?'

'That's because his wife paid the ransom,' Bilal muttered. He shook hands with Sohail Butt and after the necessary introductions were made, he asked, 'I'm sorry, did you say gang? I thought there were several gangs that were operating in Lahore.'

SSP Sohail looked around before shaking his head. 'Just one. We've been tracking them. The problem is that they don't operate out of Punjab, and we've had some difficulty coordinating things with our neighbouring province. It would appear that they're based somewhere in the lawless lands of western Pakistan and only come to the bigger cities when they need to kidnap someone.'

'They tried to take my wife a few weeks ago,' Bilal said. 'I think we met during the investigation.'

Sohail nodded, his various chins jiggling as he bit into a chicken skewer. 'Unfortunately, we didn't take them very seriously initially since they weren't terrorists.' He used his fingers to air quote the word, causing a chicken piece to slide off the skewer. 'Oops. Anyway, they weren't terrorists, so we didn't think much about it and that allowed them to gain strength.'

SSP Sohail was beginning to annoy him. It sounded like he was more interested in excuses than actual results. Bilal wanted to find Mona or someone else who wouldn't be so boring. 'So what's the plan, then? You're going to allow them to keep all the rich people hostage until they're billionaires?'

Faheem held up his hands. 'Now, now, Bilal, don't you let that old anger of yours get the better of you. Don't forget you're talking to the SSP of Lahore here.'

'Some SSP,' Bilal muttered.

Upon finishing the chicken, Sohail dropped the stick to the ground. 'Well, we do know that there's one big mastermind behind the entire operation, and he's known as Sahab ji.'

'Wow,' Bilal said under his breath. 'Everyone knows that name by now, but sure, knowing it makes everything super helpful.'

'We also know,' Sohail continued, ignoring the comment, 'that you're on their list, Bilal.'

Bilal picked up a drink from a passing waiter and downed it in one go. 'Am I? Well, that's very touching. I've been on these lists for decades. I couldn't give a toss about Sahab ji or any of his minions. If they come for me, they'll all get killed.'

'Lahore will soon be safe again for everyone,' Sohail Butt said, nodding as if convincing himself. 'Sahab ji's reign of terror is coming to an end soon.'

'In your dreams, mate,' Bilal said in an undertone.

He could have gone on grilling SSP Sohail, but at that moment, he caught sight of someone he had no interest in greeting.

'What's she doing here?' he whispered to Faheem, jerking his head towards the entrance.

Faheem licked his lips. 'The beautiful Nageena. She's hot property, Bilal. What do you expect? Of course, she'll be everywhere.'

Bilal didn't tell him that Nageena kept calling him, and he kept ignoring those calls. He had no wish to take things further with her, even if she looked stunning in that emerald-green dress.

Before he could look away, their eyes met, and a grin spread across Nageena's face. She made a beeline straight for him, but Bilal hid behind SSP Sohail, looking around for a larger group of men to get lost in. Faheem watched it all with a knowing smile on his face, before proceeding to kiss Nageena noisily on the cheek when she approached him.

'Lahore really is changing,' SSP Sohail murmured, his eyes travelling over Nageena's body. 'Our high society truly is a whole new world altogether. Just look at that woman. What a perfect specimen. You wouldn't have seen the likes of her out and about thirty years ago.'

'Perhaps we all ought to objectify women a bit less and focus a bit more on making the city a safer place,' Bilal said, his voice devoid of any warmth. 'Wouldn't that be amazing?'

It was probably foolish to antagonise a senior police officer like this, but Bilal couldn't help but enjoy seeing Sohail redden. Before he could embarrass him further, a commotion broke out. Several of the ladies gasped and rushed towards the entrance. Mona stood in the middle of the lawn with her hands clapped against her mouth. Bilal followed her gaze and soon found the source of all the noise.

Mona's erstwhile friend, Kulsoom, had arrived. Catching Mona's eye, he walked up to her and, taking her hand, they both made their way to Kulsoom. From the corner of his eye, he could see Nageena watching him, but he pointedly turned away. Let her see how happy he was with his wife. Perhaps, now, she would finally leave him alone.

'I can't believe it,' Mona said. 'It's her. After all this time.'

Kulsoom wasn't dressed to impress. As a matter of fact, she only wore a simple cotton outfit, but she had at least put some make-up on and blow-dried her hair. 'I came as soon as I heard,' Kulsoom exclaimed, throwing her arms around Alia. 'Oh, my poor, poor friend. How you must have suffered.'

Alia looked like a rabbit caught in a snare. 'Kulsoom, what are you doing here? Who told you?'

'What do you mean? It's all over the news.' Kulsoom embraced both Shabeena and Mona, but as soon as Mona broke the embrace, she took her husband's hand again. Her hand was shaking.

'It's okay,' he told her. 'This is what you wanted, right? To see your friend again. And now she is here.'

Mona bit her lip. 'But so is Humaira. Oh, Bilal, I can't bear it. She's going to lose it.'

'What's she got to do with anything?'

Mona glanced at him then, her eyes red with unshed tears. 'She rules Lahori society, and she's always said that she despises Kulsoom for what she did.'

He raised an eyebrow. 'What exactly did she do?'

As if on cue, a heavily built man in a fitted shirt came in. From the way he walked, taking small steps towards Kulsoom, Bilal could tell that he was uncomfortable. He avoided looking at anyone and instead pulled at Kulsoom's dupatta. 'Let's go now, Kulsoom. You've met your friends. Let's leave. We are not welcome here.'

Alia too was looking around, as if afraid of being seen by someone. 'Yes, Kulsoom, go. We will meet again soon now that you're back in Lahore.'

Kulsoom, however, had never been the brightest bulb. Even Bilal knew that. 'Oh, I came straight from Abbottabad when I heard,' she cried. 'My dear friend, you must have gone through so much. Muzaffar here begged me not to return to Lahore, but I had to. For you, I had to.'

People were starting to gather around now, and some of them even had their phones out, taking photos of Kulsoom. Nageena seemed to be making a video, and given how she kept whispering in Faheem's ear, they seemed to be enjoying the spectacle.

'Look at her, bold as brass, as if running away with her gym instructor was the best thing she did in her life,' someone said.

'What did she do with her kids? Eat them? Look at the size of her.'

'I don't want to be caught dead in her presence. She is tainting this entire party, the slut.'

Bilal felt sorry for Kulsoom because he was sure that if the whispers were reaching his ears, they were reaching hers too. She obviously had her heart in the right place, but she'd grossly misjudged Lahori society. If she was expecting kindness and acceptance, she wouldn't find it here. And Muzaffar knew that. From the way his eyes darted in every direction, Bilal knew that he was anticipating an attack at any moment.

Kulsoom's eyes shone with tears, but she was determined. 'I don't care what anyone says. I came the moment I heard.'

Mona took a step forward, but before she could say anything, there was a cry from behind them.

'How dare you! How dare you muddy this party with your presence!'

There were a few gasps from the crowd, but mostly, people wore self-satisfied smiles, as if this was exactly what they had wanted to say themselves. At least, it was what they were all thinking. Humaira strode forward, the tail of her figure-hugging silk dress swirling behind her. She looked like a vision out of a Bollywood movie, and Bilal would have chuckled had the situation not been so tense.

'We do not wish to see you here,' Humaira continued. 'Lahore shuns you, Kulsoom, after what you did.'

Kulsoom blinked, still unaware of the danger she was in. 'What did I do?'

Humaira pointed a finger at her. 'You ran away with your gym instructor while you were still married. You abandoned your kids. You left your husband for dead. You did exactly what a woman of loose morals would do, Kulsoom. You shamed all of Lahore. Do you want me to go on?' By the end of her monologue, Humaira was panting.

Kulsoom still wore a puzzled look on her face. 'I didn't know Lahore's honour was bound to what I did or didn't do.'

'Don't try to be cute. You dare bring that filthy boyfriend of yours into polite society. He's probably never been beyond the grubby lanes of old Lahore, and here he is now, standing in Cantt. Oh, the shame! Next, you'll be expecting us to fraternise with the beggars.'

Muzaffar's mouth was slightly open as he watched the proceedings in horror.

'He's my husband now,' Kulsoom said defiantly.

'Then you are a lost cause,' Humaira boomed. 'People climb up the social ladder, but you've chosen to climb down. You have brought about your own death in society.'

Someone in the crowd chuckled. 'I say, this catfight is better than anything you'll see on TV.' Of course, it was Faheem who would say something like that.

Humaira jerked her head in Faheem's direction. 'See? This is how you become a laughing stock. I say you get out of this place this instant and take that gutter rat with you. You are not welcome in Lahore.'

In a rare display of strength, Kulsoom squared her shoulders. 'You speak an awful lot about Lahore as if you own the city. Nobody in Lahore intervened when I was abused by my ex-husband. Nobody batted an eyelid when he used his belt on me. Almost used his pistol on me.'

'Oh, Kulsoom,' Mona cried, covering her mouth with a hand. 'Why didn't you ever tell us?'

'Because you never asked, Mona. You three always thought I was a simpleton and treated me as such. Did it never occur to you that maybe I acted the way I did to distract myself from the abuse that I always knew was awaiting me at home?'

'I'm sorry, Kulsoom. I had no idea.'

Bilal closed his eyes, squeezing Mona's hand. He had used his belt on her once, and that incident still gave him nightmares. Standing here in the midst of seemingly respectable people, pretending to be respectable himself, he felt very small. How could he have raised his hand against his wife? How did he even dare?

'We've all been beaten by our husbands,' Humaira exclaimed. 'I can bet that every single woman present here has suffered abuse of some kind, be it from her husband or in-laws. You don't see them cheating. We wear our scars with pride.'

'Talk about yourself, Humaira. No man has ever dared to raise a hand against me.'

For once, Meera's arrival was timely. In an all-black ensemble, she looked ready to spit fire.

'So, are we all ganging up on one woman? Have we really sunk that low?' She surveyed the scene around her, distaste etched on her features. 'There is nothing that gives husbands licence to beat their wives and get away with it. Nothing! And are you seriously standing here and glorifying abuse? I know you have connections, Humaira, and yada yada, but I honestly think that a stint in the loony bin is just what you need.'

'You bitch,' Humaira whispered. 'You'll pay for this.'

Quietly, Mona withdrew her hand from Bilal's and marched forward to stand next to Meera. 'I agree with Meera. I will not allow Kulsoom to be insulted when all she did was come here out of concern for her friend. In fact, I will go so far as to say that you are not welcome in Lahori society any more, Humaira. We are done with you.'

Relief washed over Kulsoom's face. 'Oh, thank you, Mona.' She looked expectantly at Alia and Shabeena, but both of them avoided her eyes, looking at their feet instead.

Despicable, Bilal thought.

Humaira looked like she would explode. 'Oh really? You're shunning me? I have been very patient with you, Mona. I have supported you and that whore standing next to you in the hopes that ultimately you'll give up your friendship with her and join the crowd you truly belong to.'

Meera threw her head back and laughed. 'Do you think I care what a green little girl like you says about me, Humaira? You can dress up all you want, but you still look like you just came from burning the crop stubble in the fields.'

Mona took a step in Humaira's direction. 'Listen, Humaira, nobody needs to fight here. Let's just calm down.'

It was Humaira's turn to laugh. 'Calm down after this insult? You must be joking. You know what, Mona? I thought I'd keep quiet about this, but given the side you've taken today, you're forcing my hand.'

The way Mona's hands were shaking, Bilal could tell she was shocked. Her face had drained of colour. She took a step back. 'I think I've had quite enough now. I would like to go home.'

But Humaira was just getting started. She spread her legs and crossed her arms across her chest. 'Go? So soon? What happened, Mona? Cat got your tongue? Don't you want to know all I have to say about you?'

'Stop bluffing,' Meera said. 'There's nothing to know about Mona.'

Mona's gaze met Bilal's. He saw the panic in her eyes. He wondered what she was so afraid of, and that's when it hit him. Had Mona been foolish enough to tell Humaira about Arslan? The pain in the left side of his chest sharpened. All of a sudden, he felt breathless. There were too many people here. If this secret got out, he didn't know what he'd do. Nobody could know.

'Humaira, I have no wish to fight you,' Mona said, her voice barely more than a whisper, but the silence was so deafening that everyone could hear her. 'I'm leaving.'

Bilal closed his eyes, waiting for the fatal blow. Any moment now, Humaira would change his world forever. He took a deep breath, trying to calm his breathing. Even if the truth about Arslan got out, he was still his son. There was no doubt about it. Whatever happened, they would get over it.

However, what Humaira said pulled the ground from beneath his feet.

'Won't you tell your husband why you were meeting with a man in a secluded garden near the Royal Fort a few weeks ago?'

There was a collective gasp from the crowd as Bilal opened his eyes and looked around. This was not what he had expected. Even Faheem stood with his mouth open. Beside him, Nageena's face wore a look of triumph. Bilal's breathing quickened, beads of sweat running down his back. This wasn't about Arslan at all; this was some new secret. Was this the reason Mona had been so distracted? Who was this mystery man?

Mona's face went through all the shades of the rainbow before going pale. 'Humaira, you don't know what you're talking about,' she finally said.

Humaira smiled, exposing her teeth. 'Don't I? I was actually in the Walled City with some of Hamid's white friends who were visiting from London, or I would never have seen you so nicely ensconced with your mystery man. And in the pleasure gardens of the Royal Fort, no less.' Stepping closer to Mona so that only the people in the inner circle could hear them, she added, 'I told you not to cross me, Mona. It always has devastating ramifications.'

'How dare you try to malign me, Humaira?' Mona whispered. 'After all I have done for you.'

Humaira screeched with laughter again. It was a most unpleasant sound. 'You didn't do anything for me, you fool. This city bows to the rich, and I happen to be loaded. You may have introduced me to your silly kitty parties, but I put in the real work. I worked hard to be the queen bee that I am today, and I only need to say the word and Lahori society will tear you to pieces.'

'You're a monster,' Kulsoom said, hands on her face.

Mona's gaze met Bilal's again, and he saw something… a flash of panic before she rearranged her features to a neutral expression. Whatever Mona's secret may be, he wasn't about to let someone like Humaira have a go at her. He took a deep breath and moved towards Mona, but a small shake of the head from Meera stopped him in his tracks. She glanced at him, then, and shook her head again. And with that, she faced Humaira.

'Before you hurl accusations on respectable women, you ought to confirm the facts. Mona was there on my request. She was meeting with a client.'

Humaira arched an eyebrow. 'Strange place to have a meeting, don't you think?'

'That's our business where we have meetings. And, if you don't mind, I think we're done here.' She took Mona's hand. 'Come, Mona.'

It was now or never. If he didn't support his wife now, he would never be able to live with himself, so he strode forward and threw his arm across her shoulders. 'Thank you, Meera. Let me take my wife back home.'

Mona's bottom lip trembled. 'Bilal, I—'

He squeezed her shoulder. 'We'll talk later. I am with you, Mona. Every step of the way. Always.'

She burst into tears, burying her face in his jacket. 'These accusations will follow me forever.'

'No, they won't,' he whispered. 'I won't let them.'

'Well, I'm not staying here a moment longer,' Meera cried. 'However, before I leave, there's something I need to do.' She quietly walked up to Humaira and pulled at the bag hanging from her shoulder. Looking around at the crowd, she said, 'I will have you all know that she buys all her designer stuff from the back alleys of Bangkok, not London or New York, as she'd like to tell you.'

Humaira snatched the bag away, her eyes widening. 'Liar! I got this from Sloane Street. This is authentic Chanel.'

Meera laughed. 'I saw you, idiot. I was in Bangkok too, in the same shop where I saw you haggling over the price of this knock-off Chanel bag. I never said anything until now because I don't believe in pulling down women, but you deserve it.' She reached for Humaira's hand, which she batted away. 'Also, I happen to know that your diamonds are all actually zircons. Your husband has been losing money for months. He's made you sell all your diamonds.' She nodded. 'Yes, the jewellers you visit now have been getting my patronage for decades, and they talk. You might pretend to be the queen bee, but you are rotten to the core. Both morally and financially.'

Loud gasps followed this announcement, and Bilal was glad to see that some of the colour had returned to Mona's cheeks.

Meera turned away from Humaira just before she attempted to reach for Meera's hair. However, with her hand swiping through empty air, Humaira lost her balance and stumbled, falling to the ground on her knees. She shrieked as one of her heels broke, causing the place to erupt with laughter, Faheem and Nageena laughing the loudest of all.

'Yes, and that's what happens when you wear knock-off Amina Muaddi heels,' Meera said as a parting blow, her voice acerbic. Even SSP Sohail let out a guffaw. Bilal wondered what he was making of this high-society drama, although perhaps he saw these things every day.

'Bravo!' Kulsoom cried as Meera walked past her. 'This is what you call a true friend.'

Turning to Alia and Shabeena, who still stood with their heads bowed, Meera continued, 'It is during times like this that one gets the true measure of a friend. You have been Mona and Kulsoom's friends for decades, and yet, when the time came, you stood there with your heads in the sand.' She spat on the ground in front of her. 'Shame on both of you. I hope you're never forgiven for this.'

Before any of them could say anything, she turned on her heel and left, leaving a whimpering Humaira on the floor.

If he'd expected to get any answers from Mona in the car, he was sadly mistaken because she spent most of the journey crying, and when he attempted to discuss what had happened, she just said, 'I don't want to talk about it, Bilal. Please, just get me home.'

'Meera lied for you, didn't she?' he asked again, his hands shaking. He gripped the steering wheel tighter. 'You weren't meeting a client at the Royal Fort.'

'Bilal, I don't want to talk about it right now.'

He slammed his fist against the wheel, causing the car to judder to the right. 'Then what the hell do you want to talk about, Mona? I supported you back there, knowing full well that it wasn't a fucking client you were meeting in secret. The least you owe me is an explanation.'

Mona roughly wiped the tears from her cheeks. 'So, this is the limit of your trust, then? I meet someone, and you just presume that I'm having an affair.'

Bilal swerved to avoid hitting a car. Damn, he was going way too fast. 'I did not say anything about an affair. I just want to know what's going on with you. You haven't been yourself for ages. I thought we had worked our way through these issues.'

Mona pulled at her hair before bunching it in a ponytail. 'It's not that I don't want to tell you, Bilal. There is just so much to unpack here that I don't even know where to begin. Can you give me some time, please? I need some time.'

'You're beginning to scare me now.'

The fact that she didn't reply scared him even more.

'Is someone blackmailing you?'

Her head whipped in his direction so fast that he was afraid she'd sprained her neck. 'What makes you say that?'

Bilal took his foot off the accelerator and parked on the side of the road. Behind them, their security van stopped too, the guards leaping out of the vehicle, fingers on triggers as they looked around, alert to any threat that might come their way.

Without any sudden movements, Bilal took Mona's hand in his and squeezed it gently. 'Are you being blackmailed, Mona?'

She wouldn't meet his eye. 'I – I don't want to worry you. I know you've got health issues.'

Don't lose your temper, he thought to himself. He closed his eyes briefly. 'This suspense that you're keeping me in is harming me much more than anything else could. So tell me, what is going on?'

Mona's eyes swivelled around as if she was contemplating how much to tell him. 'It began a few months ago. Text messages from unknown numbers at first, but then they started calling me.'

Bilal tried not to let his shock show. 'Months?' he echoed. 'This has been going on for months?'

Mona glanced up at him for only a second before lowering her gaze again. Her hand in his was clammy. 'Don't worry, I paid them off.'

Bilal released her hand from his grip, his head hitting the window behind him. 'You did what, Mona? Do you have any idea what you've done? Why didn't you tell me?'

'I didn't want to worry you,' she whispered.

It took every ounce of patience in him not to lash out. He had to remind himself that his wife had been thinking about his health because if he didn't, his rage could take over completely. He took a deep, measured breath. 'How much did you pay?'

Before she could reply, he held up a hand.

'Actually, don't tell me. I don't want to know right now. I need to process this, but did you not know that you cannot give in to blackmailers? That's how they work, by keeping on asking for more.'

'They haven't asked for more, Bilal. I told you I took care of it.'

'Then what was the meeting at the Royal Fort about?'

She shook her head. 'I told you, give me some time. I'll tell you everything.'

Bilal started the car again, revving the engine so that the guards outside rushed into the van too. As he eased the car back on the main road, he looked sideways at his wife. 'You're not making any sense at all.'

With her head down, she looked very small.

'What were they blackmailing you about, anyway?'

She didn't reply for a few moments, but when he pressed her again, she finally said, 'Arslan. They were threatening to reveal where he really comes from.'

All the anger and frustration fled his system then, replaced by pure, unadulterated fear.

Arslan. His little boy, Arslan. Of course! What else would anyone be blackmailing her about?

'He's my son, Mona. End of.'

He attempted to keep his voice level, but even he could detect the wobble. If word about Arslan got out, the boy would never be able to live it down. It would destroy him and their entire family. Bilal had a sudden, frightening thought of what Qudsia would say if she found out.

By the time they arrived home, a small part of him could understand why Mona had paid off the blackmailer. It made sense, but the bigger question was why there was a blackmailer in the first place. Only a select few people knew what had happened between Mona and Ali, and Bilal didn't think any of them could have blabbed.

So, where had this blackmailer come from?

As Mona washed up in the bathroom, Bilal collapsed in bed, fully dressed, his mind ablaze with thoughts of the blackmailer and the person Mona had been meeting secretly. He gazed at the ceiling, his eyes settling on the black mark in the corner. He'd asked the maids to take care of it so many times, but it was as if they didn't hear him.

'The house is falling into a state of disrepair, Bilal,' Qudsia had said the other day. 'This is what happens when the lady of the house is absent. The servants grow lax and the entire household caves in on itself.'

Things weren't as dire as Qudsia said, but it was true that the servants had grown lax, and the blame for that was on both of them, not just Mona. Bilal had been so preoccupied with his health issues and trying to find a new plot of land for development that he'd neglected his home. And so had Mona.

Lost in his thoughts, he almost didn't notice Mona's screen lighting up with a new text message. The split second it took him to decide whether or not to read the message was all it took for the notification to vanish, leaving the screen blank again.

He didn't know her passcode, and he'd never had any reason to find out. He'd trusted Mona blindly, but picking up her phone now and turning it in circles between his fingers, he wondered if he'd been lax with his own wife too.

Before he could set the phone aside, it lit up again with a new message from an unsaved number.

> I need to see you again. There's so much to talk about.

Bilal froze for a few moments before dropping the phone on the bed. A cry escaped his mouth that he smothered hastily. *Please God*, he thought. *Don't let it be an affair.*

With the water still running in the bathroom, he turned on his side and quietly wept into his pillow, letting all his tears soak into the pillowcase. He bunched up the duvet in one fist and thrust the other against his mouth, groaning. The message had vanished before he could take a good look at the number, but it wasn't rocket science to figure out what was going on.

His wife was in over her head.

If this was what he thought it was, he could tell now that he wouldn't survive it. Not for a second time. It was too much. He massaged his chest where his heart beat erratically, and just for a moment, a flash of pain tore through his chest. The intensity of it made him gasp. The pain extended all the way to the fingertips of his left hand, and just as he was about to cry out for Mona, it stopped. His breathing was ragged, but his mind felt clearer, and when the door to the bathroom clicked open, he felt well enough to lift his head.

Mona didn't meet his eye as she turned off the lights and slid into bed with him.

'While you were in the bathroom, lots of text messages arrived for you.'

Her breath caught, and the room was briefly illuminated by the blue glow from her phone. 'Did you read them?'

'Of course not,' he lied, letting his head rest on the pillow again. 'Why would I? But who is texting you at this time of the night?'

She didn't even hesitate as she said, 'Meera. It's just Meera.'

'I see.' His heart was breaking, both literally and figuratively, and there was nothing he could do about it. He couldn't even cry now that Mona was lying next to him. Besides, men didn't cry. Wasn't that what he'd been taught by his father? His mother had always dismissed it as nonsense.

'Don't listen to your father,' she used to say. 'He's from Dera Ismail Khan and doesn't know the difference between a horse and a man. Men do cry and should cry. There is no shame in it, and if that bumpkin tells you otherwise, then I will deal with him.'

Of course, Nighat had always been popular for her hyperbole and held no sway with her husband at all. If anything, Bilal's father exerted a great deal of influence over them, and it was probably because of him that Bilal had turned out so toxic.

He allowed a few more tears to slide down the side of his face and onto the pillow, and once he was sure that Mona was asleep and breathing deeply, he picked up his own phone and scrolled through his missed calls.

Fifty-two missed calls.

All from a single number.

He had to hand it to her for sheer perseverance.

Before he could talk himself out of it, he opened WhatsApp and typed:

> Sorry for not taking your calls or saying hello at the event. I was busy. Do you finally want to meet?

The reply came almost instantly.

> YES! I've been waiting for you to message me, sir. I've never waited so much for someone in my life.

Despite himself, he smiled.

> I find that hard to believe. A woman of your calibre... what could you possibly want with someone like me?

> There's only one way to find out.

The smile spread wider across his face.

> And what's that?

This time, she didn't reply. In fact, several minutes passed as Bilal waited, his thumb poised over the keypad. It had been over a decade since he'd exchanged so many messages with a woman who wasn't Mona or someone in his family.

> Let's meet in a hotel and get to know each other.

He'd forgotten the thrill that accompanied it, how it felt to reach for the forbidden fruit that had been denied to one for so long. He also knew that he was only acting out because of what his wife was doing to him. Still, he kept texting...

> And what does meeting in a hotel entail?

This time, her reply was instant.

> Come and find out tomorrow. Book us a room at the new Gulberg Boutique Hotel and we'll find out.

An emotion he hadn't felt in a long time assailed him as he typed 'Done' and put his head down to sleep. He was almost on the brink of falling asleep when he realised what it was.

It was guilt, the kind that only came from cheating.

Chapter 18

Mona

For once, she woke up before the alarm could go off. Every part of her body screamed in protest as she sat up. All the stress from last night was finally catching up with her. She massaged her calves to get the blood pumping through them and then rose from the bed.

Today was going to be another challenging day. Although Bilal had taken the news of the blackmailer remarkably well, she knew he'd never be able get over Ali's reappearance. He would never trust her again, that was for sure, and she did not want that sort of existence any more. She would have to lie to him about the meeting in the Royal Fort. It was imperative that Bilal never find out that Ali was alive.

Ali... that was another challenge she had to tackle. Last night, after she was certain Bilal had put his phone down and gone to sleep, she'd texted him again, reluctantly agreeing to meet him today. Even though Bilal's eyes would be on her, she hadn't been able to refuse Ali. He had never been as demanding as he was last night, and Mona knew that the fault was solely hers.

She had encouraged this behaviour by meeting with him repeatedly. She'd encouraged him to fall in love with her again. But the big question that she kept asking herself remained unanswered: did she love him too?

She looked back at Bilal's sleeping form, his face slightly open as he snored. Sleeping straight had smoothed out the lines on his face, making him look twenty years younger. He resembled the man she had first fallen in love with all those years ago as a newly married bride, the day she'd stepped into this house and stumbled, but only for a second, because Bilal had been there to catch her. Their years together flashed before her eyes, their three kids, the countless memories, both good and bad, but lately, mostly good.

As she watched him, Bilal stopped snoring. He never did that. His snoring was the one thing she could always depend on. In the hum of the air conditioner, she couldn't hear him breathing. She couldn't even see the rise and fall of his chest. Mona rubbed her eyes and looked again.

Bilal wasn't breathing.

All the tiredness and pain left her as adrenaline shot through her body, but as soon as she knelt next to him, it was obvious that he *was* alive and breathing. He was just fast asleep, not stirring even when she touched his hand. It was warm, and Mona sent up a silent prayer of thanks. A life without Bilal was unfathomable. She couldn't envisage a life where Bilal didn't check up on her six times a day, only to end up arguing with her five out of those six times. Her husband, who was living proof of the fact that people could change, and change spectacularly at that. No, life without Bilal wouldn't be worth living, and that was why she couldn't be with Ali.

It didn't matter if she'd once had feelings for him, feelings intense enough for her to consider leaving Bilal. It didn't matter that he was back in her life and keen to take things forward. What mattered was that he had disappeared when she had needed him the most, when their child needed him the most. He'd let her cry for him for years, never bothering to send her a mere message to say that he was alive. She didn't care that a part of her still loved him – would always love him – because she had come to realise that he wasn't permanent. Bilal was. It was Bilal who had stayed, who had stuck with her when she was at her lowest. It had always been Bilal for her.

She would let Ali down gently. If he loved her enough, he would understand.

Quietly, she opened the door to the bedroom and proceeded towards the guest room to get ready. By the time Bilal woke up, she'd be long gone.

In the years since Ali had disappeared, she'd never ventured into Iqbal Town. She had no reason to. But as she approached the address he'd texted, a sense of déjà vu struck her. She'd never been to his house before, and yet, somehow, it felt like she had. It was the strangest feeling, like going to the place of one's childhood. Her fingers on the steering wheel were clammy as memories of their time together flashed in her mind unbidden... the way he would touch her when he thought nobody was looking, the way she would lean into him for warmth and security. Was going to his place even wise? What if one thing led to another? She shook her head. No, that would never happen. She may be nervous, and there may have been chemistry between them once, but it was all over. Ali was no longer a part of her life.

Just like earlier, she had taken a Toyota Corolla instead of her Beemer, so that nobody would give her a second glance, and as far as she was concerned, nobody had. Lahore had warmed up considerably, and unless people had business, nobody really ventured outside in the heat. If there was one good thing to come from it, it was that people like Humaira remained cooped up inside their air-conditioned living rooms. She'd heard nothing about Humaira, except that she was licking her wounds. She'd be back to rain hell on everyone, but Mona found that she didn't care. She just steadily drove through the traffic, only pausing outside the University of the Punjab for a few moments, watching students in bright clothes as they laughed their way out of the gates. Nostalgia clawed at her, as did the realisation of how much time had passed, but she swallowed the lump in her throat and pressed on.

Ali's family home was much smaller than hers, squeezed into a row of houses of similar size. Mona parked a few houses before Ali's just to be safe and stepped out, and almost instantly, the pollen in the air choked her. With the advent of summer, Lahore was blooming. She held her dupatta to her nose and walked up to the house.

The façade told her that the house hadn't been in use for a long time. It was derelict and neglected, and she was surprised that Ali was living there. A nest of electric and telephone wires hung on the poles, some dangling dangerously close to the ground. Seeing the state of the place made her wonder if Ali had enough money… she'd never thought to ask. Well, if he needed some money to get started, Mona was more than happy to contribute. That was the one thing she did have control over, and she would like nothing more than to be able to help Ali in some way.

The rusted gate creaked when she pushed it open, and before she could knock on the front door, it opened. Ali smiled at her. 'You're here!'

He was freshly showered, smelling of Old Spice shampoo and deodorant. The scent took her back to the past, but she stood her ground. None of that. He'd even made an effort to trim his beard so that the contours of his face were more visible. He still hadn't lost that chiselled jawline, but there were a few dimples on his cheeks when he smiled that hadn't been there before.

He took her hand, guiding her inside. 'Come, come. Let's sit in the living room.'

As they made their way from the tiny reception to the equally tiny living room, Mona thought she could hear chatter from upstairs.

'Who's upstairs?' she asked, suddenly nervous.

Ali shrugged. 'Just some friends bunking with me. Don't worry, they're harmless.'

Mona drew herself up. 'You've got people in here? I categorically asked to meet you alone. You know what, I'm leaving.'

He didn't let go of her hand. 'Hey, relax. Why are you so strung up? I told you, they're harmless. They don't know you're here, and they won't come down without my permission.' She must have looked unconvinced because Ali grinned. 'If it makes you feel better, we can talk in my bedroom.'

'Somehow, the bedroom sounds even worse,' Mona murmured, shaking her head. 'Ali, I needed to discuss some things with you, and I just hope that you'll understand where I'm coming from.'

She was keen to get this over with and return home where Bilal would be waiting for her. The mere thought of him sitting at the breakfast table now, chatting with Qudsia, brought an inexplicable yearning in her to get in the car and join them there.

'Okay, sit here.' Ali indicated a sofa that had seen better days, the teal having faded to a dusty grey. 'Sorry, I haven't had the chance to redecorate since I've been back. I don't usually stay here.'

'But where have you been? Where do you live?' Mona asked, lowering herself onto the sofa. 'Whenever I ask you, you just give me a roundabout answer.'

Instead of taking the sofa, Ali knelt in front of her and proceeded to sit cross-legged.

'Ali, what are you—'

'Shh, Mona, let us just talk for a bit.' He took her hands in his own. 'I'm tired of meeting you like a thief in the night. I'm tired of seeing you waste your life with that bastard husband of yours who doesn't even know your true worth. And I'm sick of seeing him raise my son.'

She took a sharp intake of breath. 'Arslan *is* Bilal's son, Ali. You cannot take that away from him or from Arslan. You know what Pakistan is like. Our society would never forgive it.'

He scooted forward so that their feet were touching. He was close enough to rest his head on her knees. 'But, I have the means to raise him now. I have the means to provide for both of you. All you need to do is come away with me.'

'Come away with you?' she echoed. Her palms were starting to sweat, so she withdrew them. 'You do realise that I have a life here, right? I can't up and leave at a moment's notice.'

'That didn't seem to stop you the last time.'

Mona exhaled, leaning back. 'Things have changed.'

'So, you don't love me any more. Is that it?'

'Love is such a complicated word. It's not as simple as being in love with someone or not being in love. There are many aspects to it.'

Ali smiled, but it was a sad smile. 'But that's the beauty of love, Mona. It *is* simple. Like, for example, I know that I love you. Always have, always will. You were my first and only love.' His eyes assumed a faraway look. 'You taught me love.'

Mona bunched up some of the dupatta in her fist. This was proving to be far more difficult that she had thought. It had been foolish of her to come here. They should have met in a more neutral place, where she could get the upper hand. Watching his face right now made her want to throw her arms around him, but she held back. Ali deserved a proper life with someone who could love him unequivocally. Someone who wasn't in love with her husband. She needed to free Ali.

'Look, Ali—' she began softly, but he cut her off.

'Why do I get the sense that you're getting ready to break my heart? Don't do it, Mona. I don't know what you're thinking right now, but remember that we belong together. We created a child. We are meant to be together.'

'I belong with Bilal,' she whispered. 'Deep inside your heart, you know it too.' She reached out and cupped his face in her hand. 'You have no idea how happy I am that you're still alive, but try as I might, I just don't feel the same way about you any more. What we shared was truly pure, and I will cherish it till the day I die, but the woman you see sitting in front of you now is not the same Mona.' She wiped a tear that rolled down his cheek. 'You will love again, Ali.' He shook his head, but Mona squeezed his cheek, making him meet her gaze. 'You will. Believe me.'

Before Ali could reply, there was an almighty crash upstairs, followed by shouting.

They both stood up together.

'What on earth is going on upstairs?' she asked.

Ali backed away towards the staircase, not taking his eyes off her. 'Stay here, Mona. Just don't go. I'll be back. This isn't over.'

It was over as far as she was concerned, but she still sat down again. It felt like a huge burden had been lifted from her shoulders. She could finally breathe. There was nothing stopping her from going back to her life now.

Back to Bilal.

With nothing to do in the living room, she rose to take a look around the bedrooms. She wanted to see where Ali slept. For a house so neglected, it was a surprise that the door didn't creak. Inside, there was just a single bulb illuminating what was a small room. There was a small double bed, neatly made with a bedspread that matched with the curtains. It made her smile. No matter how filthy the rest of the house might be, Ali's bedroom was spotless. Every surface shone. As she stepped inside, the sound of her footsteps was absorbed by the carpet. There was a small writing desk with a lamp in one corner, and, in the other, there was an oval-shaped thing that had a piece of cloth thrown over it. Except for these things, the rest of the room was empty.

She was drawn to the oval-shaped thing. It only took a few steps for her to reach it, and once she did, it was easy enough to pull at the cloth and let it slide. Mona tilted her head, examining what was in front of her. It was certainly not something she was expecting.

In a wrought-iron cage rested the most beautiful bird she'd ever seen. It had red, blue, and white plumes, and, right now, it was asleep. Mona stood there, gazing at the peaceful creature, wishing her own life could be like that.

'Penny for your thoughts?' Ali murmured in her ear, making her jump several feet away from him.

'God, Ali, don't do that to me. I'm not as young as I used to be. Do you want my heart to stop?' She stood, clutching her chest, realising with a pang that this was exactly how Bilal sometimes stood. She wished he would take his health seriously.

'I think you use your age as a defence mechanism,' Ali said, advancing on her slowly. 'It helps you banish feelings you don't want to acknowledge. Feelings like love.'

'I don't know how else to tell you—'

'You need to be loved, Mona,' Ali said, interrupting her. Within seconds, he had closed the gap between them, holding on to her shoulders. 'And deep down, you know that only I can give you that love. Not Bilal. Not anyone.'

She narrowed her eyes at Ali. 'What was going on upstairs?'

'Don't change the subject,' he whispered, his lips grazing her forehead. 'This is our moment.'

'Ali, please,'

'Shh, Mona.'

She was about to push against his chest when she saw a shadow darken the doorway. A young man in his twenties with electric-green eyes and beautiful blond hair stood there.

She yelped, taking hold of Ali's arm. 'Who is that?'

'You are needed upstairs,' the young man said with a smile that didn't quite reach his eyes.

As Ali turned to look at the man, Mona let go of him and backed herself against the wall. Every instinct in her told her to run away. This man in front of her was pure evil. There was something about his eyes that made her want to flee. They were dead. 'Ali, who is this?'

The man smiled, revealing perfect white teeth. 'Won't you tell the lady?'

'I am busy,' Ali hissed, his lips curling in disgust. 'How many times must I tell you not to disturb me when I am busy?'

'The boy has woken up. The sedation you gave him has worn off.'

Mona tried to quell the rising panic in her. Who were they talking about?

She turned to Ali. 'What is he talking about? What boy?'

The man in the doorway laughed. 'Why, Bibi, your son, of course.'

'Shut up, Fakhar!' Ali shouted, making Mona flinch.

'Arslan?' she whispered, hand on heart. 'My son? What do you mean?'

'Well, we picked him,' Fakhar said as if it was the most normal thing in the world.

Ali turned around. 'Fakhar, I swear to God…'

In the doorway, Fakhar was laughing. 'What's wrong with having a bit of fun with the lady?'

Mona felt like her heart had stopped. 'You picked up my son?'

The man's eyes gleamed. 'Not me. The others did it.' He nodded at Ali. 'He doesn't trust me enough any more with sensitive missions.'

'Where is my son? What have you done to him?'

'Why don't you ask Sahab ji? He will tell you.'

She wasn't listening. Her mind was running a mile a minute. Nothing made sense. She made to leave the room, but Ali pulled her back, throwing an arm across her chest so she couldn't move. She could hardly breathe. 'Fakhar, get the hell out of here!' he shouted.

Mona was rooted to the spot. There was little else she could do, but in the midst of the worry for Arslan, something else occurred to her. There was something about that name that rang a bell.

Sahab ji.

As Fakhar backed away out of sight, Ali's grip on her loosened.

And then, it came to her. Her entire body shook as she looked at the man she had once loved, the man who had turned out worse than she could ever have imagined. 'You are Sahab ji?'

—

Her body felt frozen... useless. Her gaze flitted around the room, attempting to focus on anything but the face in front of her. She couldn't bear to look at him. Her eyes landed, instead, on the bird that had awakened in the commotion and now gave a loud squawk.

She blinked. She had heard that exact sound before, but her mind refused to accept it.

Blood rushed in her ears, her breathing quickening. The migraine to end all migraines threatened to hit, but she blinked several times. No, she was sure there was a perfectly good reason for this. There were probably thousands of people in Lahore who kept these sorts of birds and thousands who were called Sahab ji. But such a rare parrot? This wasn't a common parakeet, but something very exotic.

As she watched the bird with her hand over her mouth, she became aware of the sound of Ali's breathing. It was the same measured breathing that she'd come to hate. She couldn't believe she'd never made that connection before. How could she? He was supposed to be dead.

The parrot squawked again, only serving to confirm what she already knew. This was where she'd been blackmailed from, and the person who had done it was standing right in front of her.

'Mona, listen to me.'

'Let Arslan go,' she whispered. 'Ali, please. Whatever sick game you're playing, leave him out of it. He's just a child.'

'He's my son too, and I assure you he's quite safe. I would never harm him. What do you think I am, an animal?'

She attempted to look at his face without flinching, but failed. A strange fog seemed to have filled her head, not allowing her to think clearly. She was struggling to understand why Ali would do something like that – how could he have become so diabolical? To kidnap a child, his own child?

If it was money he wanted, he could have just asked, but something told her that this wasn't about money. That wasn't what Sahab ji was famous for. With Sahab ji, it was about both money and humiliation. He liked to dehumanise his victims, as if he had a personal vendetta against them. Did he really hate her so much – hate Bilal so much – that this was what he'd become?

Ever since she'd seen him in front of that deserted park in the dead of the night where he'd saved her, something about him hadn't sat right with her. There were holes in his story that she'd ignored at first, but thinking about them now, she wondered why she had even agreed to come here today.

Just for a moment, she felt afraid for her life, but then she dismissed that thought. This was Ali. No matter how bad he might be, he would never hurt her.

But isn't that what he does, a voice said to her. *He specialises in it. He made your life hell for weeks and weeks with the blackmail, never relenting. He's been kidnapping people for months – years!*

Looking up at his face, those arresting eyes that had charmed her all those years ago, she refused to believe that he could harm anyone like that. 'Take me to my son.'

Ali scratched his head. 'In a moment. I want to clear the air first.'

'Sahab ji,' she said.

His smile faltered as he took in her expression. 'You know that name.'

'It was you,' she said. 'All this time, I have wondered who could possibly have known about Arslan. For a time, I even thought that my friend Meera might have let it slip, but it was you. You would make a pariah out of your own son?'

To his credit, his face remained impassive. 'I still don't know what you're talking about, but I feel you spend too much time with that slutty friend of yours. There isn't a man left in Lahore she hasn't had her way with.'

'You kidnap and torture people, Ali! Do you really get to take the moral high ground here?'

It took everything in her not to slap him across the face. Who was this person? This wasn't the innocent young man she had fallen in love with all those years ago, who was ready to lay down his life for her. No, his eyes were different now. They had hardened like his face. This man had seen things, done things that had forever changed him.

For the second time, she feared for her life, and once again she pushed the thought away. Fear would only make it easier for him to sway her, although if he was thinking he could convince her to elope with him, he was sadly mistaken. There was just the door out of which she could escape, but right now, Ali was blocking her path. In fact, he was so close to her that she could even smell his cologne, his mint-fresh breath. It made her stomach churn.

She took a deep breath. 'Drop the act, Ali. You spent months threatening me with messages and calls. I know what you did, but what I don't understand is why you did it. Why blackmail me like that? Why turn my life into utter misery?'

The smile was almost gone now, but the expression that replaced it was even more terrifying. It was vacant. 'I admit everyone knows the name Sahab ji by now, but how did you figure out it was me behind the blackmail?'

It was the way he spoke, so matter-of-fact, that made her gasp. Of course, it was him. The fog in her head finally cleared and she saw him for who he really was. This wasn't her Ali any more. This was a stranger in his body, a stranger she wanted nothing to do with. She tried her best not to cry out, but she couldn't help herself. She wept into her hands, not caring how loud she was. 'I don't even know who you are any more.'

Far from comforting her, he pulled her hands from her face. 'Tell me, how did you find out? I want to know.'

With all the strength she could muster, she slapped him across the face. The sound of it rang out in the empty room. 'You want to know how? Whenever you called me from this room, I could hear you breathe, and I could also hear that fucking bird of yours. That's how.'

'That fucking parrot,' Ali muttered, holding a hand to his cheek. 'I should have killed it. It was a gift from Mir Rabiullah.'

'Given what you've become, you should have stayed with him, then,' Mona all but spat. 'Why come back here?'

'Because he is dead, Mona. And because you needed to be taught a lesson.'

She stared at him, aghast. 'What?'

He pulled at his hair. 'Shit. I should not have said that.'

'Ali, what on earth…'

He sat on the edge of the bed, head in his hands. 'It was not supposed to be this way. I didn't want you finding out about the blackmail or anything else. Now that I've done it, I'm not incredibly proud of it. I am not proud of a lot of things. Besides, I would never have told your secret to anyone. It was just a game.'

She wanted to slap him again, but she clenched her fists and held them down by force. 'Is that your defence? That you're not proud of it? That it was all a game?'

He looked up. 'Yeah, what else do you want me to say? It's not like you didn't deserve it, the way you were so *in love* with Bilal. It was sickening.'

She couldn't bear it. She raised her hand again to hit him, but this time, he leapt up and held her arm. 'Careful, Mona. Even my patience has its limits.' He pulled her closer, their lips almost touching. 'You don't want to make an enemy out of me. I am being courteous with you only because I love you. Otherwise, I am known more for my cruelty nowadays.'

She pulled her arm away. 'I'm leaving, and I am going to take Arslan with me. How dare you use him for your sick games!'

She made to stride out of the room, but Ali's next words made her stop in her tracks.

'You cannot leave. I won't allow it.'

'Can't I?' she breathed. 'Watch me.'

Before she could move, he'd caught her by the arm and forced her on the bed. 'Sit down.'

Chapter 19

Bilal

It all felt foreign to him, being in bed with someone who wasn't his wife. The cold air from the air conditioner made the hair on the back of his neck stand up, and he shivered. It had been so long since he'd done this that he'd just forgotten how it felt to be in another woman's embrace. Nageena was unbuttoning his shirt, one button at a time, trying to make the moment last, but Bilal wanted to be anywhere but here. It had been a huge error of judgment to agree to this.

Mistaking his shivering for desire, Nageena smiled. 'Excited, aren't we?'

She was wearing a silk magenta nightgown, but her face was fully made-up and judging by her neat hair, it was obvious that she'd just been to the hair salon.

Why does this woman want me so much?

From what he knew, Nageena went out with some of the richest men in Pakistan, so it couldn't be that she was solely after his money. And he knew for a fact that it wasn't his looks either. He had been fairly handsome back in his day, but now there were bags under his eyes, and, in the wrong light, he looked like he could be in his late sixties or, God forbid, early seventies.

He had a paunch forming, and in the mornings, if he was stupid enough to look at a mirror before showering, he usually did a double take, unable to believe that this was who he had become. People told him all the time that he looked good. Hell, Faheem had been lusting after him for as long as he could remember, but Bilal didn't feel it. Deep in his bones, he knew he was getting older… old, actually. He was growing old, and he wanted to spend his remaining years with his wife of three decades, not holed up in some hotel with a woman who did the same thing to dozens of men that she was now doing to him.

Having successfully unbuttoned his shirt, Nageena drew her arms around his bare torso and squeezed. 'This feels nice,' she murmured. 'To finally see what all the fuss was about.' Looking up at him, she raised herself on tiptoes and attempted to kiss him.

Bilal pulled himself free and took a step back. 'Sorry,' he said. 'I haven't brushed my teeth yet.'

Nageena closed the distance between them. 'I don't care. I want you. So bad.'

'I haven't showered either,' he said, desperate to get away. God damn it, what had possessed him to do this?

Her face grew thoughtful. 'Maybe we could take a shower together?'

Relief flooded him. He could make his escape while she was in the shower. 'You go and get the hot water started, and I'll join you in a bit. Just need to make a call.'

Nageena took his hand, pulling him to the bathroom. 'Bilal Sahab, this is a five-star hotel. There's no waiting for the hot water to start. And besides, no work while we're having fun.'

He attempted to smile back. 'Okay, just let me make that money transfer to your account. It would be awkward to do this without paying you.'

Her smile grew wider. 'A man with scruples. Well, this will be an interesting shower.' She made a show of dropping his hand. 'There, I've let you go. I'll get the shower started' – she stepped out of her nightgown – 'and you can just join me there.'

It was a sign of how things had changed for him that even the sight of a perfectly shaped woman like Nageena did nothing for him. He was glad he was still wearing his pants because he didn't want her to see how little effect she was having on him.

He gestured towards the bathroom. 'I'll only be a minute. You go ahead.'

However, before she could step away, her phone rang. Tiptoeing towards her phone in just her underwear, she checked the screen. Her face changed, and she held up a finger, signalling him to be silent. 'Yes?' she said as soon as she picked up. 'Yes, of course. You really don't have to worry. We've been through this, haven't we? For the last time, yes!' She almost shouted the last word and then threw her phone on the bed before turning back to Bilal. 'Clingy clients, you know. Always asking for more.'

Bilal raised an eyebrow. 'It sounded more than a clingy client. You've gone deathly pale.'

Nageena fanned her face with her hand. 'I'm naturally pale, Bilal Sahab. You better get used to it.' Before heading to the bathroom, she winked at him. 'A minute is all you get. Remember that.'

Bilal sighed as soon as the bathroom door closed and the sound of the shower started. This would keep her busy for a few minutes. He made the money transfer –

she deserved that much – and quickly rooted around for his things. He'd send Nageena a message once he was on his way back home. He knew she'd destroy his reputation with Faheem, and he in turn would spread the gossip to others, but Bilal found that he didn't care at all. All he cared about was being back home with his family.

With Mona.

He found his boots underneath the bed, so after buttoning up his shirt, he sat down on the bed to put them on. He'd barely picked up one of the boots when Nageena's phone pinged. He didn't pay any attention. Probably the same client.

It pinged again. And then again.

That was one persistent client. Curious now, he checked if the bathroom door was still closed – it was – and tapped on the phone to illuminate the screen. To his utter surprise, the phone was unlocked. While he was marvelling at Nageena's stupidity, the phone pinged again.

Bilal almost laughed. Someone like Nageena ought to know better. She carried the dirty secrets of Lahore's elite in that phone and yet didn't have the decency to keep it locked. Out of curiosity, he swiped down to check who was messaging her. Maybe he knew the guy.

However, the name he saw made his entire body go rigid. It was a name that had always been on his mind. He shook his head. This was bullshit. There were probably hundreds of people with the same name in Lahore. But then the urgency with which Nageena had wooed him came to him, coupled with how she had blanched when she'd received the call just now. He opened the conversation.

His eyes widened with the shock of what he was reading.

> **Ali**
> Make sure you show him a good time or else the deal is off.

> **Nageena**
> When have I ever not fulfilled my end of the bargain? Men go weak at the sight of me.

> **Ali**
> Not as weak as you think. You've been wooing him for months and nothing. He can't be that in love with Mona.

> **Nageena**
> Patience is a virtue.

So, he was still alive? It all began to make sense now, the way Mona had been so distracted and snappy, how she had ignored him on more occasions than he could count. He wondered if she was in love with the bastard again. Who was Bilal fooling? Of course she was in love with him again. But, as Bilal scrolled down, the messages became more alarming.

> **Ali**
> I want that bastard on camera. Make sure you get a good angle. I've given you three cameras for the task.

> **Nageena**
> All deployed successfully. Bilal's sexual adventures will be viral by tonight.

> **Ali**
> I don't care about that. All I care about is that Mona should see it.

> **Nageena**
> Your wish is my command, Sahab ji.

Sahab ji? The name froze the blood in his veins. Everyone knew that name, but never in association with Ali. Ignoring the bile rising in his throat, he scrolled down, and as he read the final few messages that had just arrived, everything became crystal clear.

> **Ali**
> Where's the bloody video? Send it to me now. I need to show it to her.

> **Ali**
> I need you to keep him occupied. He should not be able to pick up his phone. Hide it.

> **Ali**
> Why aren't you replying? If you're busy with him, remember to keep him occupied. He cannot find out his wife is with me until we've left this place.

> **Ali**
> ?????

> **Ali**
> I swear to God, if you are unsuccessful, I'll have my men pick you up, Nageena. You'll wish you were never born.

His hand that held the phone started shaking, causing him to drop it, the phone disappearing somewhere underneath the bed. Sahab ji… The penny finally dropped, but it made him all the more terrified. If Ali was Sahab ji, then Mona was in grave trouble. Did she even know how much danger she was in?

And Arslan? Did Ali know about him too? The thought chilled him to the bone. He had to call the school and check.

> **Ali**
> He cannot find out his wife is with me.

The words rang in his head like sirens. Ali and Mona were together while he'd been duped into spending a night with Nageena just so there would be proof of his infidelity.

He must be way more stupid than he looked. Ali had probably been planning this for months. He held his face in his hands, trying and failing to stop himself from shaking.

He took another moment to feel sorry for himself but then forced himself to be pragmatic. No matter what had happened in the past, right now, Mona was in danger, and he had to save her. Ali sounded like a deranged psychopath. What on earth had happened to him that he'd turned out like this?

He was so preoccupied with thinking up possible ways to rescue Mona that he didn't even notice the bathroom door open.

It wasn't until Nageena hugged him from behind, pressing her soaking-wet body to his, that he came to his senses. In a swift motion, he turned around and grabbed her by the throat.

Nageena yelped, immediately trying to kick him in the stomach, but he was too fast for her. He had the advantage of height and strength, and within moments, he had her pinioned.

'I know your secret,' he hissed at her. 'I read those messages. I know that bastard is still alive and that you've been helping him. You need to keep a more watchful eye on your phone.'

Nageena's face went from red to puce as she tried to breathe, beating her fists against his chest, but Bilal's grip was too strong. Before she could turn blue, he reduced the pressure on her neck, allowing her to draw in a few precious breaths.

'I could just as easily choke you again, Nageena.'

She shook her head, tears running down her eyes. Seeing her like that, something in him melted, and he loosened his grip further. He wasn't a murderer.

'I will release you if you co-operate,' he said. 'Will you?'

She glanced at him, relief on her face, and blinked.

The first thing she said when he released her was, 'You don't want to mess with him, Bilal. He is dangerous.'

Bilal let out a savage laugh. 'Oh, please. I've known this man for many years. He's a fucking coward.'

Nageena sat against the headboard, massaging her neck. 'He's the mastermind behind the kidnappings. They call him Sahab ji now. I only call him Ali because I knew of him from when he modelled.'

'I have heard of Sahab ji.'

'Then you know exactly what we're dealing with.'

'There's no we in this, Nageena.' Bilal averted his eyes. 'All I know is that he's got my wife, and no matter what comes my way, I will save her.'

'He'll kill you. It would be so easy for him.'

'Where is she?' he asked Nageena. 'Where is he keeping my wife?'

'I don't know,' Nageena replied quickly – too quickly.

Bilal advanced on her again. 'You know.'

Nageena looked at him with pleading eyes. 'Please don't ask me. I don't know what he'll do when he finds out I've been unsuccessful, but if I tell you his location, he will surely kill me. He has this guy that works for him…' She shivered. 'Fakhar. He is the devil. I've never seen someone as evil as him. I only know where he is because I'm supposed to go there for my payment. Sahab ji doesn't believe in online payments.'

Bilal rose from the bed. 'I don't care. They don't know who they're messing with.' With his knees, he climbed on the bed again. 'Tell me now, Nageena. Do the right thing because if you don't, what Ali does to you will be the least of your worries.' His voice broke as he added, 'Please?'

Nageena reached forward for her scarf and covered herself with it. For a long time, she was silent, her eyes glazing over, but then something clicked, and her expression cleared, as if she'd made up her mind. 'Fine... fine. This constant stress is no way to live, anyway. I regret ever getting involved with him in the first place. I will tell you. I'm done with Ali and his games.'

Chapter 20

Ali

In a way, he was glad that everything was out in the open. He was tired of hiding behind this mask of kindness. It was a long time since he'd needed to put it on, but then he would do anything for Mona. She probably thought he was lying about loving her, but if there was one thing he was sure of in his life, it was his love for her. A lot had changed over the years – he had changed – but there was one thing that had kept him going... Mona. A lot of women had been made available to him – hundreds, perhaps – but he had never touched a single one of them. Not even for fun. *Never for fun*. No woman deserved that.

Mona was the only one he wanted.

However, he hadn't been entirely truthful to her when he'd said that he was running from Mir Rabiullah. Over the years, lying had become so easy for him that he no longer felt any remorse for it. The truth was that Mir Rabiullah had spent the final years of his life training Ali, systematically wiping out every emotion in him.

'A human robot is what I want you to become,' he told him, bunching his white beard in one hand. 'You're my little experiment, Ali. I want to see how far I can go with you, how much more it would take to make sure you cease being human.'

And so, it began... Ali's stint at Mir's camp. The horrors and torture he witnessed put him off conventional violence forever, leading him to question whether there was another way to reign supreme. Not everything had to be about blood, gore and killing innocent people.

'You're such a hypocrite,' one of Mir's men said to him when he voiced his thoughts aloud. 'You live off violence here, and you have the audacity to question the hand that feeds you. You dare question Mir Sahab? Terror is the only language these people understand.'

Ali begged to differ, but he remained silent.

As much as Mir Rabiullah tried to poison him, the one thing he wasn't able to take away from Ali was his anger. That was the one emotion he held on to as he trained under him, seeing him kidnap people, starve them, mutilate and humiliate them, only to murder them in cold blood. He saw him send out young boys he'd brainwashed to their deaths. Mir Rabiullah changed him irrevocably, but he couldn't change the fact that he'd ordered the death of Ali's family, and for that, Ali never forgave him.

So he waited. He waited until the time was right, until he was influential enough to topple him. When the former leader, Abuzar, was killed in combat, leadership finally fell to Mir Rabiullah, and with his ineptitude and the government's ruthless crackdown, their once formidable group just became a random training outpost in the middle of nowhere.

Old and forgetful, Mir Rabiullah grew sluggish, so when Ali suggested they head out for a walk, he gave him a toothless smile.

'Of course, my dear boy. Let's go. I would trust you with my life. I've trained you, after all.'

His rheumy eyes gazed at him with such love and admiration that Ali wondered if the man had genuinely come to care for him, and for a moment, he faltered. That train of thought only lasted for a second, though, because he knew that people like Mir Rabiullah didn't change. No, Rabiullah deserved a fate worse than death. While earlier he would have been surrounded by security men, when Ali took him out to walk, there were none that day. While Rabiullah's influence had waned, Ali's had only grown.

Ali made the old man walk until he was ready to collapse. When he asked for water, Ali refused him. When he staggered, Ali dragged him all the way to the pack of rabid dogs he'd been feeding and training. That was probably the only time Mir Rabiullah got wary. Ali's betrayal crystallised in his eyes, his mouth forming a silent O. That was when Ali smiled in triumph. Watching him being stripped to pieces wasn't a lot of fun, but his begging and pleading certainly was.

Ali returned to their headquarters alone and announced the death of Mir Rabiullah. Nobody batted an eyelid. Everyone had been ready for the real leader to assume control. Gone were the days when terrorism brought in money. Over the years, Ali had seen Mir Rabiullah's coffers dry up as the Pakistani government turned on the heat against them. Ali met with rival groups, did his research and basically everything that Mir had never done, only to come to the conclusion that the money was in kidnappings.

Of the rich and famous.

And it was on the dying embers of Mir Rabiullah's empire that he built his own.

'Ali!'

It was the stricken look on Mona's face that brought him back to the present.

'Hey,' he murmured. 'It's okay. You're safe here. Soon, we'll be on our way out of Punjab to live life on our own terms with our son.'

Mona was rocking herself on the bed. 'Why did you do all of this? Why ruin my life like this?'

He laughed. 'You rich people are all the same, aren't you? You only think about yourselves with no concern for others. Conceited. The blackmail wasn't even serious, Mona. I mean, come on. It was just a game to make you realise that life wasn't a bed of roses. Grow up!'

'Do you think I don't know that? Since when has my life been a bed of roses?'

Ali shook his head. She didn't appreciate the privileged life she had been living while he had been going stir-crazy in some backwater with Mir Rabiullah, plucking out bits of chicken from Mir's rotting teeth. 'Instead of mourning for me, you were out there falling in love with your husband again.'

She looked at him like he was mad. 'But I did mourn you. For years, Ali.'

'But you didn't lose your mother and brother, did you? Mine were killed. I spent years suffering only to come and find you happy with that bastard, raising our son with him. How dare you, Mona! If you had a shred of dignity in you, you'd have dumped your abusive husband years ago.'

She shot up from the bed. 'You don't know *anything* about my husband. You don't know anything about my life. I suggest you hand over Arslan to me now and let us go before I get Bilal and the police involved.' Just as quickly, her face softened. 'Ali, please. For the sake of what we had? I am happy that you're alive, and I don't want your life to come to any further harm, so if you let us go, I won't let this escalate. I won't even tell anyone that you're Sahab ji.'

From the doorway, Fakhar laughed, a cold, heartless sound. 'Do you think Sahab ji cares about the police? He's been playing with them for years. He bribes most of them. He's been picking up people from under their noses all along.' He marched in, his green eyes blazing. 'If you had any sense in you, you'd be proud to be standing at Sahab ji's side. Most of us would kill for the honour.'

'Fakhar, relax,' Ali said. 'Go and check if everything is in order.'

God, the boy was an absolute nutcase. He'd have to figure out what to do with him once he'd sorted this out. Maybe he'd kill he was too dangerous to be set free.

Fakhar lowered his head in deference. 'If you say so, Sahab ji.'

As soon as Fakhar left, Mona strode forward and gripped Ali by the arms. 'Look at me, Ali.'

He craned his neck away from her. 'No.'

With her hand, she tilted his face towards her. 'I know you're in there somewhere. This cruel, inconsiderate man is not you. The Ali I know is thoughtful and kind, generous and loving. The Ali I know would never allow his loved ones to suffer like this.'

Her brown irises drew him in, and he felt something threatening to break – the dam of emotions he'd kept securely walled for so many years. If he let that dam break, chaos would ensue. At this moment, he needed his mind to be clear and listening to Mona was only serving to distract him from his purpose. 'The Ali you're talking about is long dead. He died that night on Karachi's beach.'

Mona closed her eyes, releasing him from her grip. 'Then that's the Ali I've been mourning.'

'We can be happy, Mona. I know it. True love never really dies. It might change, but it doesn't go away, and what we have is true love. We have a child together.'

She crossed her arms over her chest. 'If I wanted to leave this place with Arslan right now, would you let us go?'

'No,' he replied. 'I wouldn't. Both of you are coming with me.'

'Then, this isn't true love.'

Ali checked his phone. There was still nothing from that bitch, Nageena. He knew that the moment he showed Mona proof of Bilal's infidelity, she would willingly leave with him. The last thing he wanted to do was drag the woman he loved by force. He phoned Nageena again, but it simply went to voicemail.

Shit.

Chapter 21

Bilal

The Beemer screeched as its tyres tried to gain traction against the polished tiles in front of the hotel's main entrance, but Bilal was relentless. There was no time to lose.

In the rear-view mirror, he caught his driver rushing towards him, teacup in hand, but there was no time for that either. Every single minute was crucial.

He banged his fist against the steering wheel and cursed aloud. He should have had Mona followed today instead of this petty revenge he had planned with Nageena to get back at her. To add to his troubles, Mona had taken out the car without a tracker. All these years, and he still let his anger govern him. And now there was a distinct possibility that Mona could be taken away from him forever.

Pulling out his phone, he quickly dialled the number for Arslan's school, but what he heard on the other end of the line almost caused him to black out.

'What do you mean Arslan left with his father?' he shouted. 'I am his father. How could you let him go away with a stranger? Where is he?'

'I'm new here,' the administrator replied. 'I just started a couple of weeks ago, and this man had visited the school previously with your wife. So, I just assumed that he was the father.'

'I don't pay you millions of rupees in fees to presume.' Bilal couldn't stop shouting. 'You are an incompetent fuck.' He also couldn't believe that Mona had introduced that bastard to their son.

'And...' The administrator hesitated.

'And *what*?'

'Arslan resembled the man, so once again, I just assumed—'

'Fuck off!'

He threw the phone aside, only to pick it up again and dial the police. Five precious minutes later, they agreed to send out a unit to the address he gave them.

'Send your entire force,' Bilal shouted. His spit flew everywhere, but he was past caring. 'This is the kidnapping gang that has been keeping Lahore hostage. Send everyone you can spare.'

'You need to relax first, sir,' the police officer said drily. 'We're doing what we can.'

'Are you not listening to me? Get me on the line with SSP Sohail Butt.'

'He's out of town.'

'Get me his senior, then!'

The police officer tutted. 'If we were to disturb the seniors on the whims of every common citizen, then this would be a zoo, not a police station.' Before Bilal could interrupt, he continued, 'There's a unit en route now, so try to relax.'

The line went dead.

'Unbelievable,' he muttered, too spent to shout now. 'Just bloody unbelievable.'

Racing down Canal Road, holding the steering wheel in one hand and the phone in the other, Bilal wracked his brain for contacts. It had been quite a while since he'd had any interaction with the police, as he'd mostly relied on his own private guards. Plus, he'd pissed off SSP Sohail Butt at Fahad's party. It took everything in him not to bang his head against the steering wheel.

Quickly, he dropped a text to Meera, hoping she would be able to use any influence she had with the police, but then, all of a sudden, Faheem came to his mind. As he made a sharp turn, causing the car behind him to honk loudly, he prayed for Faheem to pick up the phone.

Only he could save them all now.

Chapter 22

Ali

When Ali heard raised voices outside, he knew that Nageena hadn't been successful. In fact, she'd just led the devil to his door. All those months of planning had come to nothing. He had really hoped that he wouldn't have to kill any more people, but it seemed like he had no choice.

He had expected Mona to fall in his arms and for them to have their happily ever after, but after what had happened between them and now Nageena's failure, that looked like a distant possibility. In retrospect, he shouldn't have resorted to blackmail, but what could he have done when he came to Lahore only to find her living an enviable life with Bilal, everything else forgotten?

He had waited for weeks to see if she would visit his fake grave, but she never did. He had watched her closely, and there wasn't a single time when Mona had seemed unhappy or as if she had missed him.

His mother used to say that time healed all wounds and that no matter how much you loved someone, with time, the grief started to fade.

But there were some wounds that never healed. If someone had taken Mona from him and killed her, he would never have rested. He would have destroyed the world and himself with it.

But Mona… she had betrayed him. She'd shown him just how shallow her love was, and he refused to believe that Bilal was her forever. Believing that would be the end of him, and he'd rather end her before that happened.

Over the noise outside, Mona's eyes met his. 'Who's there?' she asked, trying to rush out, but Ali grabbed her again. 'Ouch! Let go of me.' She tried to pull away. 'Ali, you're hurting me.'

He relented with a smile. 'Might as well take this outside.'

She gave him a look dripping with heartbreak and disappointment, but Ali steeled himself. That's how he had survived the last twelve years, and not even Mona could change that aspect of his personality now.

'Where is she?' said a man's voice outside, and Ali closed his eyes. This was a man he despised more than anyone else in the world, except for Mir Rabiullah, probably.

He followed Mona out of the bedroom to face his nemesis.

'Bilal,' Mona cried, the love and emotion in her voice cutting through Ali like a knife. He staggered as if physically wounded and blinked back the tears that came. This was not the time to show weakness.

There was once a time when she had called out to Ali like that, and if everything went according to plan, she would again. Ali was sure of it. So, without a care in the world, he approached Bilal, sizing him up. 'You've aged since we last met.'

Chapter 23

Bilal

The wretched creature looked even more handsome than he remembered. But it wasn't his beauty that scared him. What scared him were his eyes. They were dead, all warmth in them gone. This man was a criminal, and right now, he had both his wife and son captive while Bilal had nothing. Not even a gun to defend himself. He'd driven straight to this place without thinking, without planning, and now it seemed like he would die in a similar fashion because, at present, a single file of men with guns was coming down the stairs. In the small living area, everything got crowded quickly.

He could see Mona with her hands clasped together, tears in her eyes, but there was no sign of Arslan.

'Where's my son?' he asked.

Mona made to rush over to him, but one look from Ali and she stopped in her tracks.

Ali turned to him, his brow furrowed. 'Last I checked, I had fathered him. He is not your son.'

The familiar rage reared its head in Bilal, but he pushed it down. Age may not have taught him much, but it had taught him to choose his battles wisely. 'He is as much my son as Farhan is.'

Ali laughed. 'Bullshit! How do you figure that?'

The men around him laughed too, but Bilal wasn't cowed. He drew himself to his full height. 'Were you there when he caught pneumonia after birth and needed to be cared for?'

'Save it, Bilal,' Ali snarled.

Bilal, however, took a step forward. 'Were you present through all the late-night feedings? Did you attend all the school events? Did you kiss all his scrapes and scratches away? Did you wipe the tears from his face and hug him?' He was rambling, but he found that he couldn't stop. 'Did you hold his hand while he went to sleep? Did you…' His voice finally broke, and he shook his head. 'Did you love him more than anyone in the world?'

From across the living room, Mona sobbed. 'You still have the chance to do the right thing.'

'The right thing is for you and Arslan to come away with me,' Ali snarled.

'You can't take someone's wife away like that, Ali,' Bilal said. 'Even you ought to know that.'

Ali grinned at him. 'I took her away from you once, so I am sure I can do it again.'

'No, you can't,' Mona whispered. 'I don't love you, Ali. I want nothing to do with you. You need to let this go. You need to let us go back to our lives.'

'And where should I go then?' For the first time, Bilal detected alarm in his voice. 'How am I supposed to live?'

The phone in Bilal's hand vibrated, and from the corner of his eye, he read the message from Faheem:

> We're almost there.

He took a deep breath. Help was at hand, but first he had to secure his family. There was no telling what Ali might do. 'If you really love them as you say, then do the right thing, man. Let them be happy. Deep down, you know they'll never be happy living in a backwater with you.' He took another step forward. 'And most of all, you will not want Arslan to grow up a hardened criminal. I know you, Ali. More than you give me credit for. I know you wouldn't want the same fate to befall you—your son.'

Something flickered in Ali's eyes, his mouth curling downwards like he was about to cry.

Before he could say more, Mona touched Ali's arm. 'After your mother and brother, I think I know you the most, and you are no villain. You are a man who has loved and been loved. You survived the very extremes of life, and despite the kidnappings, I know you're not a murderer. You never were.' She turned him so that they were facing each other. 'For the sake of the love we once shared, won't you do the right thing?'

Her words burned through him, but Bilal stood his ground. Nothing was more important than their lives, not even his dignity.

Ali's cheeks were damp, and he nodded at one of his men. He, in turn, waved at someone behind him, and as the line of men parted, Fakhar walked through, holding Arslan by his hand. Bilal's heart fell as he saw the terror in his poor boy's eyes. There was a wet patch on his trousers where he seemed to have wet himself.

Bilal clenched his hands into fists. He was going to make each of these bastards pay for terrorising his child. Arslan looked up as if aware of Bilal's eyes on him and his expression brightened. 'Dad?'

Ali's face, however, immediately grew stormy. Bilal thought he was angry with Arslan for saying the word 'Dad', but he seemed to be addressing Fakhar. 'Who gave you permission to touch the boy?' he demanded. 'How dare you run your dirty hands on him? Muzammil,' he said to someone in the line of men, 'take Arslan from Fakhar and bring him to me.'

Fakhar's hand tightened on Arslan's wrist. 'No. Sahab ji, you don't know these people. This boy is our bargaining chip.' He pointed at both Bilal and Mona. 'Look at their faces. They are desperate to get their hands on the boy. You hand him over and you're done.'

'Fakhar!' Ali's voice was loud and sharp, like a whiplash. 'Do as you're told.'

There was a pause before Fakhar jutted out his chin and said, 'No, I don't think I will. You've gone soft, Sahab ji. You're lusting after this woman while your organisation suffers. You're willing to risk everything for her. That is not the kind of leader I can get behind.'

And it was then that the distant sound of sirens filled the air.

Ali's face whipped in Bilal's direction. 'You bastard. You gave us away? I will kill you.'

He launched himself on Bilal, taking him entirely by surprise. Bilal barely had time to lift his arms to protect himself before Ali crashed into him, sending them both rolling on the ground. The impact knocked the wind out of him. It had been many years since he'd engaged in any physical combat, and even then, nothing quite like this. Ali was over twenty years younger and there wasn't an ounce of fat on him.

Bilal wheezed as the first punch landed in his abdomen. The second hit him in the neck, making him see stars. At this rate, Ali would kill him.

He could hear Mona screaming in the background, but Bilal was too caught up trying to breathe. With as much strength as he could muster, he raised his leg and brought his knee hard against Ali's groin.

Ali squealed but didn't let go.

'Let go,' Bilal panted. 'You're strangling me.'

Ali's eyes were rimmed with red. He looked like he hadn't slept for months. 'I will kill you,' he whispered. 'I will kill you for taking her from me.'

'Sahab ji, the police are coming,' Fakhar shouted.

Ali, however, was still trying to kill Bilal. On top of him now, he wrapped his hands around his throat. Bilal sputtered, punching Ali's torso, but it was pointless. Mona was kneeling next to him now, attempting to uncurl Ali's fingers from his throat.

'He's going purple,' she screamed. 'Do you mean to kill him? Let him go.'

Ali's face was red with the effort of keeping Bilal down.

'Sahab ji, the police are coming,' Fakhar repeated, but once again, he was ignored. From the corner of his eye, he could see Ali's men beginning to panic as some paced around the room restlessly, while others fled. Fakhar remained, holding on to Arslan.

'Leave my father alone,' Arslan shouted.

Bilal wished things could have been different, that he could have done more to save his family, but his world was going dark now.

'If you won't listen, Sahab ji, then I will kill the boy.'

That did it. In an instant, Ali's hands were off him, and Bilal sputtered and breathed. His heart was racing and didn't seem to want to slow down. But he'd heard Fakhar too, and despite the discomfort he was in, he lifted himself up on his elbows.

Ali advanced on Fakhar. 'Give me the gun, Fakhar.'

Fakhar was crying. 'You promised you would take care of me, Sahab ji. You let this woman and child come in the way of your work. Our work.'

'Ali, stop him,' Mona cried. 'Don't let him hurt my child.'

Ali lifted a hand, beckoning Fakhar to him. 'Come to me now, Fakhar, and leave the boy. Listen to your Sahab ji and all will be well.'

'Look at what you've done!' Fakhar screamed. 'Your men are fleeing. The shack you keep us holed in is a disgrace.' His expression hardened. 'Let them all leave. I will stand my ground. I will not surrender to the police like this. I will make sure I wipe out the people who caused this first.' He pointed the gun in Ali's direction. 'Maybe I ought to kill you too, Sahab ji. You broke my heart. You let useless human emotions like love govern your behaviour. You're an insult to the memory of Mir Rabiullah.'

'Fakhar, I should have killed you when I had the chance.'

Fakhar bared his teeth. 'But you're no killer, Sahab ji. You never had the appetite for it, whereas I... I was born to kill.'

Ali was still advancing on Fakhar. 'You were always a heartless bastard, and your time has come to an end.'

Fakhar's bottom lip quivered, and saliva dripped down his mouth. 'We will see about that, Sahab ji. I will kill you, but not before I've had some fun with your beautiful boy.'

'Fakhar, don't you dare!' Ali shouted.

Fakhar's expression grew dreamy. 'You have no idea how succulent a scared little lamb is. How tender and juicy.'

There was an almighty crash as Ali leapt at Fakhar, slamming him against a china closet, followed by two loud shots as both Fakhar and Ali collapsed on the ground.

Many things happened in quick succession after that. The police rammed their way through the door, Faheem following close behind them. A few seconds later, Meera arrived, her face as white as a ghost.

However, it was the fourth thing that Bilal hadn't thought would happen so soon.

His heart stopped, and the world around him went dark as he collapsed on the ground once again.

Chapter 24

Mona

'I heart you,' Bilal had said to her a few years ago.

Mona had laughed into her hand. 'Wherever did you hear that from?'

'What?' Bilal laughed with her. 'Aimen told me that this is what young people say when they're expressing their love for each other.'

'So?'

Bilal raised an eyebrow, throwing an arm around her shoulders. 'Well, young love is supposed to be potent and deep.'

'As deep as ours?' she asked, leaning into him.

Bilal laughed again, his chest rumbling with the sound of it. 'Perhaps not, because my love for you is endless, like the ocean.'

'The ocean isn't endless, Bilal,' Mona had replied. 'It's finite like everything else.'

'Not the ocean of my love.'

She'd always heard that a person's life flashed in front of their eyes before they died, and although she wasn't dying, somehow this scene played in her head as she watched Bilal fall.

Oh God, please let him be alive.

Some instinct led her to Arslan first. She enclosed him in her arms, holding him tight. 'I am so sorry, baby,' she whispered in his hair. 'For everything. Are you okay?'

He nodded, shaken but unharmed.

His eyes were drawn to the man who lay in front of them.

His father. Her husband. Their whole world.

Everything had happened so fast that she didn't even have any time to react. One moment, Ali was trying to strangle Bilal, and the next, they had both fallen. All of a sudden, her legs gave way, pain shooting up her knees as she hit the ground herself. She didn't have the strength to go to Bilal. What if he was dead?

Police officers were still milling about, but it looked like someone had called the ambulance because there were paramedics in the room now too. Before they could get to Bilal, Mona's eyes met Meera's, and without exchanging a single word, Meera nodded.

She knelt down in front of Bilal and held two fingers to his neck.

Mona whimpered, clutching Arslan tighter to her. Beside her, Ali lay motionless too – dead probably – but she found that she didn't have the headspace to deal with that. Maybe she never would.

'What is it, Meera?' she wheezed. 'Is he alive?' Her voice broke. 'Please tell me he's alive.'

Meera had her eyes closed, but as soon as she opened them, Mona knew. Meera didn't even have to say anything. As the paramedics pushed her aside and hauled Bilal on a stretcher, Mona wailed. Releasing Arslan from her grip, she crawled on all fours towards her husband, the man she'd spent over thirty years with. He couldn't be dead. She wouldn't let him.

'Do something! Perform CPR on him,' she screamed, trying to reach him, but they'd already taken him away. She never even got a chance to say goodbye. 'Bilal,' she whispered, her tears falling on the floor. 'Please, don't leave me.'

Meera enveloped her in an embrace, and Mona screamed into her friend's shoulder.

'I can't continue without him. I don't want to. Kill me too.'

'Courage, my friend,' Meera whispered. 'Courage for your child. Don't let him see you like this.'

When they carried Ali away, she was surprised to discover that she didn't feel anything. 'Is he dead too?' she asked quietly.

'Yes,' Meera murmured. 'Too much blood, and he wasn't moving.'

Mona closed her eyes, wishing that he could have died sooner so that at least Bilal could live.

It seemed that the ocean of Bilal's love was finite after all.

Chapter 25

Mona

Dubai, United Arab Emirates – One Year Later

They both sat watching the sun set behind the Atlantis hotel, bathing everything in orange one last time before going under. Beside her, Meera reached for her hand and squeezed it.

'Another mimosa?'

Mona smiled. 'You know I don't drink any more.'

Meera was leaning against a recliner with her sunglasses on. 'I was asking whether I should have another one.'

'You've already had about five. I honestly don't know how you maintain your figure with all this drinking. Look at you in this swimsuit.'

Meera flashed her a smile. 'I work hard for it, and Dr Carlos up in Los Angeles has helped loads too, God bless him.'

Mona looked down at her own chiffon kaftan and the glass of Diet Coke she held in one hand. She would never have thought that she'd give up drinking and would never feel the inclination for it again. Drinking was one of the things that had turned her away from Bilal, and she deeply regretted that now.

She regretted all the opportunities where they could have been happy, but weren't. Somehow, resentment had always got in the way, and it had taken her decades to realise that Bilal had always been the one for her. Ali had merely been a blip and a nasty one at that. She sighed. It wasn't as if she could turn back time.

'Instagram is awash with photos of Humaira's husband getting arrested for fraud,' Meera said with some satisfaction. 'Oh, the shame of it. I hope she takes Shabeena and Alia down with her.' She held up the phone for Mona. 'Look at her, dressed in knock-off Dior as if the people in jail will care.'

Mona took one glance and looked away. 'I don't feel happy about it.'

'You're such a softie,' Meera said. 'That woman was like a terrorist for our society. Thank God her tyranny is finally at an end.'

'Just like Ali's,' Mona murmured.

'What was that?' Meera was back to scrolling down her phone screen.

'I mean that it still shocks me that Ali did all that stuff,' Mona continued. 'I loved that man once. To think that I could love someone so heartless, so depraved.'

Meera batted a hand in her direction. 'Will you please let that go? It's been a year already. The man was deranged, and that person he trained with didn't help matters. Ali was insecure and vulnerable to start with, and it all only worsened from there.'

'Still,' Mona said, running her finger over the rim of the glass, 'there is something called humanity. He didn't have any left by the end.'

'In his own weird way, he did love you, so there was *some* humanity in him.'

Mona tutted. 'If that is what he thought love was, then I truly feel sorry for him.'

'And so you should. Some people in this world are meant to be pitied.'

'At least Lahore is much safer now,' she mused, desperately trying to find something good in all that had happened. 'And thank God, the police took that horrible Fakhar in custody. I hope he rots in jail.'

Meera sat up straighter, finally looking at her. 'Didn't you know? Fakhar slit his wrists in prison. He's dead as a doornail. Good riddance, I say, because rumour had it that he would have succeeded Ali.' Shrugging, she took a sip of her drink. 'The police have closed up Ali's shop. They've finally managed to round up every single one of those bastards who escaped. To think Ali and his men had all that money and still lived like cave rats, hidden from the world.'

Mona sighed again. She wanted to change the topic. This would just take her mind to a darker place and open up things that were now kept locked. 'So, what's the latest on you and Zarrar?'

Meera cackled, downing the remainder of her drink and tossing the glass in the sand. 'I dumped his ass. Even I have my limits.' Turning to Mona, she winked. 'Who knows, maybe I'll find someone here in Dubai's sultry sunsets.'

'Don't you always?'

There was a question on Meera's lips, but before she could ask, their food arrived – a delicious seafood platter that smelled divine. Mona's stomach rumbled.

To her surprise, even Meera sat up. 'Honestly, when the food smells this good, it is a crime to let it get cold. Let's dig in.'

They were just about to reach for the prawns when a shadow darkened the platter. 'Starting without me?'

Mona looked up and smiled. 'I was going to keep some aside for you first.'

'I know.' Bilal leaned down and kissed her on the lips, eliciting catcalls from Meera.

For once, Mona didn't chastise him. She realised that she didn't care what anyone thought any more. An angry red scar ran down his chest – evidence of his heart bypass – but otherwise, Bilal looked just the way he always had. If anything, he looked healthier than ever.

Last year, after his heart stopped and they'd all thought he was dead, one paramedic had decided to persist in the ambulance, doing everything he could to revive him. And to their utter surprise, Bilal's heart had started again just in the nick of time. There had been no brain damage, and as soon as he was able to, he was taken in for surgery.

Over the next few months, as he'd recovered, they had only grown closer. And now, he stood in front of her, sun-kissed and dripping in salt water.

Mona knew she'd be leading him back to the hotel room after dinner. 'Dubai suits you,' she said, giving him the shy smile that made him go crazy.

It did the trick because Bilal didn't even reach for the food. 'I think I would like to go back to the hotel room now. Will you accompany me?'

Smiling broadly now, Mona took his hand. 'Yes, I think we ought to make a start on the packing.'

Meera spat out her prawn, laughing. 'Good God, is this the excuse people are peddling these days? You guys couldn't be more obvious if you tried. Just get out of here. I'll finish the food.'

'All of it?' Mona asked, astonished.

'All of it. Now get lost.'

As they walked back, Mona rested her head on Bilal's shoulder. The weather in Dubai had turned hot, but the sea breeze helped, as did the sand, which had cooled somewhat. Mona enjoyed the sensation of sinking her feet in it, curling her toes. 'Shall we check on the kids back home first?' she asked.

Bilal shrugged. 'Arslan is with Qudsia and the others are grown-ups. Do you really want to ruin this moment?'

Mona smiled and squeezed his hand.

In the hotel lobby, as they waited for their lift to arrive, she spied a man watching her with interest. When she stared back at him, deadpan, he coloured and busied himself with his phone.

'You've still got it, missus,' Bilal whispered. 'That young man can't get enough of you.'

'I don't care about that. He was probably counting the lines on my neck.'

'Nonsense. You, my lady, are just as ravishing as you were the day I first saw you.' Bilal pulled her close to him, his hand digging into her waist. 'You know, I am so glad I slowed down. I get to spend more time with you.'

Now that his shirt was buttoned, she ran her finger down the area she knew his scar to be. 'You had to slow down, or else you would have died.'

'For a moment, I did die.'

Mona was glad that the lift arrived at that moment as she didn't want Bilal to see the tears in her eyes.

His arm was still around her waist as he leaned into her. 'I am not going anywhere. I look after my health now. I am here to stay.'

God willing, she thought. She didn't know what she would have done if she'd lost Bilal. They would have ceased to exist as a family. The day of his heart bypass, even Farhan had come running from London to spend time with Bilal. Her husband had tried to hide it, but she'd seen the rainbow of emotions on his face, one after the other, as he laid eyes on his firstborn, opening his arms wide even though the effort cost him.

Things had been trickier with Arslan. It had taken the better part of the year and countless visits to the therapist for him to learn to trust his parents again. As Farhan had hugged Bilal before he was led into surgery, Bilal's eyes kept searching for Arslan, and when he found him, he beckoned for him to join in the hug.

'As soon as I am better, we're going on that trip together. Just you and me. My son…'

Despite having remained stone-faced most of the time, Arslan had lit up at the words, and he'd dived in for the hug too, elbowing Farhan out of the way.

'Aimen's going to be seeing the fertility specialist today,' Bilal murmured as they stepped into their hotel room. 'Perhaps we ought to check on the kids after all.'

Mona knew that the moment she checked her phone, she'd see a dozen calls from Aimen, countless messages from Arslan and even the odd text from Qudsia and Farhan. Everyone from friends to work colleagues would be trying to get a moment of her time.

Everyone could wait for a bit.

Mona worried about her kids, especially Aimen, with her doctor's appointment, but she also knew that life and all its accompanying problems would never stop, and these brief moments of respite were what made everything bearable.

So, she didn't check her phone, and to drive the point home, she pulled Bilal's phone out of his pocket and dropped it in her bag too. Then, she took her husband's hand and drew him further into the room. 'Maybe later. This, right now, is our moment.'

A letter from Awais

I am so excited that Hera Books have published *In the Shadows of Love*, the sequel to my bestselling debut novel *In the Company of Strangers*. A debut novel is very close to an author's heart, so when the opportunity arose to write a sequel, I immediately jumped on board.

Due to a variety of factors, *In the Company of Strangers* has enjoyed widespread critical and commercial success. It is a novel that delves into the secret lives of Lahore's elite. On a balmy September morning in 2023, I arrived at Dishoom, London, with my agent, Annette Crossland, to have brunch with Keshini Naidoo and Iain Millar. Little did we all know that halfway through the brunch, this small idea of writing a sequel to *In the Company of Strangers* would evolve into a full-fledged plan. What happened next was that I was given a tight deadline but also the wonderful opportunity to immerse myself back in Mona's Lahore. In many ways, it was like coming home.

I have always strived to write fiction with a social issue at its heart, but I also want the world to know that Pakistan is not just about crime and terror as the Western media will often say. For many people, life in Pakistan is very similar to life in any big metropolis in the West with parties and social gatherings, lunches and kitty parties, business events and art exhibitions – in short, life goes on here just like anywhere else. I got very lucky with *In the Shadows of Love* because one doesn't often get the chance to revisit one's debut. I was able to recapture the high-powered, luxury lifestyle of Lahore's elite, but also their insecurities, fears and vulnerabilities.

In the Shadows of Love moves the story forward by twelve years with Mona Ahmed now in her fifties, as she navigates married life with Bilal, her husband of over three decades. While they may have weathered the storm of Mona's infidelity, with Bilal embracing the child born out of that secret love affair, their marriage remains far from perfect.

With Mona's heart broken with memories of her lost soulmate, she hides her pain behind becoming the perfect wife, hosting glamorous, high-profile gatherings for the rest of Lahore's high society, and keeping up appearances for fear of inviting gossip. Each day has the same slow, regular rhythm… until the first message arrives, and everything in Mona's life changes in an instant.

Set in high society Lahore, *In the Shadows of Love* offers an honest, if at times disturbing, look at marriage with all its secrets and challenges.

I always love to hear from my readers, and can be found pretty widely on social media:

Instagram: @awaiskhanauthor
Twitter (X): @AwaisKhanAuthor
Facebook: @awaiskhanauthor

I hope you enjoy reading this book, and I can't wait to hear your thoughts. Once again, my thanks to Hera Books for publishing it.
Best Wishes,
Awais Khan
Lahore, Pakistan
May 2024

Acknowledgements

Writing a book may seem like the work of one person, but it isn't really. It literally takes a village. For making *In the Shadows of Love* happen, I would like to thank:

My parents and entire family for their staunch support and infinite belief in my writing career. Support begins at home, and I am so grateful to have had that for as long as I can remember.

Keshini Naidoo, for being the best publisher anyone could ask for. From her astute observations to her jovial nature, working with her on this book has been an absolute honour. Back when we met at Dishoom in September 2023, this book was merely an idea in my head. To see it turn into a book with Keshini's support has been a joy to witness.

Annette Crossland, my agent of almost eight years now, for always being a source of support and reason. I still remember meeting her in 2017 for the first time, terrified out of my mind, but little did I know that not only would we end up in a successful professional relationship, but we would also become the best of friends.

Iain Millar, for being a staunch supporter of my work ever since I have known him and for always treating me to coffee and meals whenever I see him. It has been an absolute pleasure to work with Canelo alongside Hera on my books.

Ross Dickinson, for being a most thorough and professional copy editor, not to mention laugh out loud funny too.

Lynne Walker, for doing the best proofread I could hope for.

Hazel Orme, for being my very first editor, and the one person I know I can always rely on.

Faiqa Mansab, for being a wonderful mentor and friend over the years.

Alex Chaudhuri, for being the best launch partner I could ask for and a genuine friend and confidante. Life just wouldn't be the same without her.

Alan Gorevan, for being my first reader, trustworthy friend, all-round supporter and for constantly surprising me with his brilliant sense of humour.

Juliet Mushens, my wonderful friend whose support I greatly cherish, and whose Instagram memes I literally cannot live without!

Paula Robinson, for being a source of reason and encouragement.

Shirin Amani Azari, for being a true friend and my home away from home.

Heleen Kist, for always being honest in both her friendship and feedback.

Eve Smith, for always being so generous whenever I visit Oxford.

Saba Karim Khan, for being the reason Abu Dhabi feels like home.

Sabine Edwards, for being the PR maven extraordinaire authors are lucky to have behind them.

Paul Waters, for his boundless support and enthusiasm for my books. I may not be able to match his energy, but I do admire it.

Nadia K. Barb, my wonderful friend who constantly surprises me with her talent and generosity.

N.N. Jehangir, for inspiring me with his astonishing talent and immense focus on his craft. It is a privilege to be his mentor.

Liam Chennells, for inspiring me with his boundless enthusiasm, energy and support.

Lubna Sayed, for being my most supportive and loyal reader as well as a dear friend.

Kirstie Long, for her solid support that I greatly cherish.

Ali Arsalan Pasha, for bringing so much energy and cheer to my life.

And last but not the least, my dear readers, without whom I'd be nothing.